RED BEAM OF DAY

TOMMY CONLON
BOOK 3

DAVID MICHAEL NOLAN

Rough Edges Press

ROUGH
EDGES
PRESS

Red Beam of Day
Paperback Edition
Copyright © 2023 David Michael Nolan

Rough Edges Press
An Imprint of Wolfpack Publishing
9850 S. Maryland Parkway, Suite A-5 #323
Las Vegas, Nevada 89183

roughedgespress.com

Paperback ISBN 978-1-68549-255-7
eBook ISBN 978-1-68549-254-0

RED BEAM OF DAY

PROLOGUE

18 Hours After Purification

Two of them caught up to him. He was just about to make it to a tree line coming down off a ridge. If they hadn't been so enthusiastic, so eager to kill him there and then, they might have had him.

He was exhausted; he had lost too much blood—dripping down his hip from the wound in his side in a steady, pulsating dark stream—and the girl only seemed to be getting heavier with each step he took.

As it was, he had labored up the hill, through bracken that clung to his trouser legs and nipped at his ankles with bitter little teeth, then across some scrub at the top and down, down through more bracken, relief a mental balm as he saw the dark shelter and cover of the wood ahead. The girl was in and out of consciousness on his shoulder, as she had been for all of the hours since the last skirmish near the coast.

His legs felt rubbery at this point, and his knees were buckling regularly. He was stumbling every so often, keeping himself up through sheer force of will, his old survival instinct as powerful as it had ever been. He had to concentrate on his footing so that he would not turn an ankle. He had stopped briefly to attend to his wound, but he knew it was due more attention, knew that he could not afford the time, knew that he would most likely regret this later. The rifle clubbing against his buttock with each step felt like an encumbrance, but he had two rounds left, and they were precious out here, with the hunters at their back.

He saw the wood from the top of the hill, and made for it, thinking of its shade, its water, the opportunities to ambush, trap, and hide that it presented. It stretched off into the distance. The village was that way. He wished he had memorized a map instead of relying on vague impressions, but he was confident of this one thing: the village was that way. The island wasn't that big. It couldn't be too far.

Through the bracken he stumbled and swayed, the girl moaning on his shoulder, and when he was perhaps thirty meters from the tree line, a bullet spat through the bracken five feet to his right.

He heard the echoing crack of the rifle a fraction of a second after.

Already he was dropping, lowering her beside him and half dragging her behind a rocky outcrop, his eyes and head flicking around rapidly to see if he could spot the marksman.

And he did. Two of them, on the ridge he had just crossed, easy to spot framed against the sky.

He couldn't recognize them from this distance, only to say that one was down on a knee, the other, standing behind him, might as well have had his hands on his hips.

Another shot cracked, and this bullet was no nearer the mark, springing bracken up in its wake, exploding a bird into the air.

He rolled, moving the rifle off his shoulder and into a firing position, and propped himself up for a quick look. There they were, fixed in position. They possessed the type of complacency that only a significant, unassailable advantage gives you. In their case, the high ground.

He dropped down again.

The girl's eyes were still closed, and she looked peaceful now, lying on her back, her arms artfully framing her head. He breathed. Slowly, inhaling through his mouth, exhaling through his nose. He felt weary. He didn't know when this hunt would be over, or how much longer he could run.

He rolled sideways, sighted in an instant—the world narrowing suddenly into a tiny fixed point of extreme focus, all else falling away—and fired one shot.

The standing man went down, backwards. The noise of the gunshot was thunderous in the stillness.

Conlon rolled back behind the rock. Movement caught his eye from the direction of the trees. He looked up. Two men were approaching, coming silently across the ground from out of the wood. Both of them were pointing rifles at him. Both of them wore the Centurion sash high on their right arms. He vaguely recognized the one on the right. That one was nodding, a smile spreading like oil on the surface of water across his face.

They had flanked him. That meant that they had caught up with him some time ago and enjoyed enough time that they were able to get around in front of him and the girl. Then the two behind had betrayed their presence deliberately in order to distract him so that these two could get close enough to take him.

Ordinarily none of this would have worked. He would have thought of it, anticipated, taken action to ensure it didn't work. But he was too exhausted, too distracted by carrying her, too desperate to see any of it. And it had worked. Now they were calmly closing in on him, not even worried that he presented any threat. Despite the fact that they would have seen what happened back on Avalon.

The rifle was still in his grip. One round remaining. He looked back over the rock. One man from the pair on the ridge was descending, the other sat on the grass, cradling his arm. The other two still approaching.

Conlon put his head down and closed his eyes. Listen. Listen to their feet moving against the tough gorse, the way it scratches. The one coming down the hill, moving with all the grace of a cow in a slurry pit, the scramble and clatter of his feet and behind on the earth.

One of them spoke when he was perhaps twenty feet from Conlon and the girl, a Birmingham accent, an ex-Tommy, like most of the others: "Is he dead? Are you dead, mate?"

Conlon didn't respond. He waited, listening. Allowing them to get closer. And then Conlon moved.

He shot the smiling one as he came up. The bullet took him in the sternum and he staggered with his hand on his chest, then sagged to one knee. Conlon was advancing on the second Centurion and swung the rifle, in almost the same movement, as if it was a hurl. It arced through the air and smashed into his throat. Conlon changed his grip and battered the butt into the man's agonized face. He was already going down, strangled sounds hissing from between his teeth.

Conlon had already turned and was moving towards the one coming off the ridge. This one had begun his descent with a secure sense of triumph; he and his friends had tricked their prey, they had trapped him, and they were about to gut him. That had changed when he saw Conlon dispatch the other two. His face was confused now and he raised his revolver and fired a series of shots. But he was still moving downhill, with big, juddering steps and leaps, and his shots were all wild, bullets flying off in every direction.

Conlon went around the rock and closed the distance between them in a few steps. He swept the gun away and planted a right cross into the man's nose. He went down heavily, and Conlon pinned his hand to the ground, prized the gun from his grip and shot him in the head.

Conlon went back around the rock and finished off the other two, both of whom were writhing in the grass, like maimed game. Then he moved up the ridge. He could hear the man up there as he climbed, already crying and begging for mercy. He began to scream for help before Conlon had reached him.

Conlon checked the pistol. He had one bullet left.

The man was stuttering and sobbing. Conlon sat beside him and waited for him to calm down and be quiet. Finally, confused, the young man looked at him.

"You're not going to kill me?"

Conlon said, "You were going to kill me. You were going to take her back to one of your ridiculous rituals.

When the rest of your Centurions get here you'll tell them which way we've gone and exactly what condition we're in. Give me one reason why I should let you live. One good reason."

"Because I'm a human being, like you, and—"

Conlon shot him in the side of the head.

He went through his pockets, took his rifle and ammunition, then took the ammunition from the other bodies, too. One of them had a bag containing some bread and cheese, and a canteen of water. This he hung over his shoulder.

The sun was beginning to slide down in the sky, and he had hoped to be in the village before dark. He crouched beside the girl, and with a great huff of effort, he pulled her onto his shoulders. Then he faced the woods and began to walk once more.

1

10 Days Before Purification

IT SAID SOMETHING ABOUT THE PEOPLE LOOKING TO HIRE him that they had him collected from his flat in a motorcar. There was a driver—a shuffling, bowing young man who Conlon supposed had learned to drive in the British Army.

Conlon had learned to drive there, too, but he had abandoned uniforms forever when he left the service. This young man had swapped his for another; altogether more fancy, with shining brass buttons and a smart leather peak on his cap.

"Mr. Conlon, sir?" was what the driver said when Conlon answered the door, his accent thick with the bog. Conlon nodded.

"I'm to take you out to meet Mr. Naessens."

"Right so. Give me a moment please."

Conlon went back upstairs, found his cap and jacket, and rejoined the young driver. He was waiting, with his back to the door, watching Smithfield life, his hands clasped together behind him. He wore black leather driving gloves.

Conlon slammed the door and said, "Alright then?"

The driver walked him around the corner, and tried to open the back door for him.

Conlon shook his head. "I'll sit in the front."

An awkward instant then, with the driver plainly unsure of what he should do.

Conlon made it easier for him, opening the passenger door himself and climbing up and onto the seat. A beige leather interior here, probably costing more than all of his possessions, he supposed. He watched the driver make his way round the front of the vehicle and climb in himself, with a nod at Conlon.

When they were moving, out onto the quays and then running alongside the river, the late September sun low and warm through the windshield, Conlon said, loud to be heard over the belching engine: "Do you have to keep the cap on when you're driving?"

"Mr. Naessens prefers me to, sir."

"Ah, you can drop the sir, as well. Where did you serve?"

"With the 6th Connaught Rangers." An edge of pride there, at least.

"You at Guillemont?"

"I was. Were you?"

"I was out of it by then, and back here."

"Who were you with?"

"I joined up in London. And moved around a fair amount."

"The Somme?"

"The Somme. Turkey. Italy."

The driver looked at him then, as they waited at a

crossroads. His eyes evaluating now, searching for something in Conlon.

"You wondering what your Mr. Naessens wants to do with me?"

The driver chuckled and moved the car forward.

"I'm wondering that myself," Conlon mused.

They were silent for a while, and then the driver surprised him. "Are you a contractor? A workman or something?"

"No. Does he hire many workmen?"

"Ah, they're always working on the house. Bits of it need fixing up. Electricity hooked up. New machines. I don't know what's going on half the time."

"What does Mr. Naessens do?"

The driver shrugged. "English money. Family money. He doesn't do much except go to London."

Conlon was glad the man had softened.

"Is he a good boss?"

"The pay is decent. I enjoy the car. His wife used to be nice to me."

"Used to be?"

"She's changed recently. Different personality, almost. Her and him and the daughter had been fighting like cats and dogs for months."

"How old's the daughter?"

"She's at college. Awful clever, her mother says. She moved out a while ago and I haven't seen her."

"Is that why her mother has changed?"

He nodded, but his, "Probably," was clipped. He feared he'd said too much.

But Conlon was already thinking: the daughter was why he had been summoned.

He let the driver have his silence the rest of the way.

They left the city behind and headed west, out towards Kildare, through areas Conlon barely knew at all. The countryside was still green and verdant, trees swinging in the breeze under the sun, the occasional motorcar passing them on the bumpy, uneven roads, the odd bicycle; but mainly carts drawn by sorrowful-looking horses.

Small towns gave way to smaller villages.

They had passed that space where the city and its outskirts became the countryside and Conlon had been unaware of it. Dublin was growing, slowly, suburbs steadily rising up beyond the center, but out here the rotten haze of the city felt distant and vaguely unreal.

The people looked different, dressed differently. He knew they would consider themselves as a breed apart from Dubs. The pace was slower, quieter. And yet, in a motorcar or even on a bike, you could be at the Phoenix Park in twenty minutes. Conlon, who had fought and seen countries across the continent, felt himself wondering at how small the world increasingly seemed.

They eventually turned off and through a wide, high posted gate and up a tree lined drive that ran perhaps a half a mile back from the road.

"How many acres are the grounds?" Conlon asked the driver.

"Sixty-two, I'm told. Mr. Naessens likes to take his English friends hunting."

"There are deer, I'd say?"

"There are. And rabbits and hare and foxes. They love killing animals for some reason, Miss Naessens says."

Conlon chuckled and the driver grinned at having made him laugh.

"That the daughter?"

Concentrating on the road here, he nodded.

The drive curved around into a graveled crescent and the car shuddered to a halt near the front door. The gravel sounded a wave crashing on shore as it shifted around the tires. The driver looked at Conlon.

"I'll be running you home. Martin will take you to Mr. Naessens."

"Martin?"

Conlon followed the driver's gaze to the steps up to the house. A man stood near the top; short and middle-aged, with carefully oiled, shining black hair and the dapper, precise clothing of a butler.

He climbed out of the motorcar.

"Mr. Conlon?" Martin said. "If you'll follow me, please, sir."

He had one of those old Dublin accents that were starting to disappear—it sounded posh to Conlon, yet unmistakably of his city. It was being replaced with something else. His own generation was less likely to speak this way, even those from the affluent Southside suburbs who would have inherited it. Their accents sounded airier to him, whereas this was nasal and urban, but without the sharp edges and dropped sounds of his own way of speaking, which would instantly mark him out to any Dubliner as being a native of the inner city.

Martin was just as much a Dubliner as he was, just from a different part of the city, and of a different time.

Their eyes met for an instant, the butler nodded and turned up the steps. Conlon took in the building as he followed. It was an archetypal big house, the door a prim mouth at the top of the granite steps, large windows flanking it at intervals all the way to the end of the building on each side. There would be basement rooms and probably an attic in addition to the two floors he could see as they came into the reception room; a grand hallway, with a sweeping staircase leading up to the bedrooms, he assumed. A piano played somewhere.

The walls were a deep green, all of the furniture chosen to set off the color; deep natural shades of brown and wood. Electric lamps in the corners, illuminating huge portraits hanging on the main wall-spaces.

A house designed to impress and intimidate.

The butler walked smoothly through the reception and turned into another huge room—a library or study of some kind, with an entire wall of books on shelves, seemingly arranged by spine color, a nest of small armchairs and settees occupying most of the rest of the space and a large desk by the windows, three chairs facing it.

The butler stopped before the desk, nodded to the man sitting behind it, half turned and intoned, "Mr. Conlon, sir."

The man behind the desk stood, and walked around it to greet Conlon.

"Edmund Naessens, Mr. Conlon. A pleasure to meet you."

"Mr. Naessens."

Despite himself, despite having lived in England and spent years fighting in her armies alongside her sons from Plaistow and Hull and Plymouth and Walsall, despite knowing better, still Conlon had an image of an Englishman in his head: slight, chinless, thin-lipped, pale-faced. This better described many Irishmen he knew and yet he had somehow expected Naessens to look like this, based upon the driver's description and tone.

But Naessens was not remotely like this.

He was a big man, an inch at least above six feet tall, bearish shoulders and a bulk about him that suggested great strength. He took Conlon's hand in one great paw and shook it firmly. He wore a dark moustache and was dressed casually, without a tie, his shirt sleeves rolled up, his tweed jacket laid upon the desk.

"Would you like a drink, Mr. Conlon? Brandy, scotch?"

"No thank you, sir, not when I'm working."

"Quite right, quite right," he said. His accent betrayed some English, certainly, though it was plainly that of an Irishman.

"Sit down, please, Mr. Conlon."

Conlon made himself comfortable, and watched Naessens pace a little, then dismiss the butler with a hand gesture and a nod. Then he, too, sat down, rubbed his face with both hands and looked steadily at Conlon.

"So, you come very highly recommended."

Conlon nodded, already impatient. "Mr. Naessens, tell me why I'm here."

Naessens laughed in surprise. "Alright. My daughter. My daughter has disappeared."

"And the police haven't been able to help?"

"We'd prefer not to involve the police at this point. I'm something of a public figure. Some of the details could be embarrassing."

Conlon nodded and took out his notebook and pencil. "What's her name and age?"

"Her name is Philomena. It was her nineteenth birthday two days ago."

"Do you have a picture of her?"

Naessens pushed one across the desk towards Conlon. A dark haired, dark-eyed girl, with a wildness in her face despite her smile, posed with Naessens and a beautiful, severe-looking woman.

"And this would be Mrs. Naessens?"

"It would. She's...having a difficult time coming to terms with Philomena's disappearance."

"Of course. I'll need to speak to her. And your staff. The butler. Do you have a cook, maids, a gardener?"

"We do."

"I'll need to talk to all of them."

Naessens nodded. "Yes, yes."

"Do you think she ran away? Is that likely?"

"What do you mean? Are you asking if she was abducted?"

"Is that possible?"

"In this country at this time, Mr. Conlon, I think we both know that anything is possible. Abductions? Certainly."

"I'll be more specific. Do you think Philomena was abducted?"

"No, I don't. But I'm not sure she was *not*, either."

"Right. When was Philomena last seen?"

"Here?"

"Your driver told me she moved out and was living elsewhere."

"No, no, I'm afraid he misspoke. She lives here. She has been spending a great deal of her time out. Gallivanting, I suppose you might call it."

"I see. So, when did you last see her?"

"I'm not absolutely certain of the day. Here, you mean?"

Conlon shrugged. "Anywhere. But yes—when did you last see her? Roughly."

"It would be...almost three weeks ago now. Nineteen days."

"In the house?"

"Yes. We had a disagreement."

"Concerning?"

"Some of her friends. Some of her views. She wasn't shy about sharing them, at a gathering we had. Friends, some business partners and their wives."

"I'll need the names of these friends, too."

"My friends?"

"Well—yes. But I meant Philomena's."

"I don't know them. I don't know any of them."

"Will her mother?"

"No. No. Some of her old friends might—her school friends. They're more our—I can give you their names."

"You may need to let them know I will be asking around."

"Why would I need to do that?"

"Sometimes the kind of people we're discussing aren't accustomed to being approached by the likes of me. If you don't mind me saying. Sir."

Naessens' eyes focused on him for a moment. He nodded, wordlessly.

"What was it about her new friends that you objected to?"

"They were—she began to hold extremist views. She was studying drama. Wanted to be an actress, of all things. So her friends were...bohemian, I suppose you'd say. She spent a lot of time in radical circles. At parties, in cafés around Sackville Street. Spouting Marxist nonsense, befriending Fenians, suffragettes." He shook his head.

"But I could understand that. She's young. Youth is the time for innocent idealism. It melts away with experience of the realities of the world. But she became religious."

"Which church?"

"No church. A group of—of—a cult. They follow some self-proclaimed Holy Man."

"What are they called?"

"I don't know. They must have taken her. She was very secretive these last few months. She stopped attending her lectures. She stole money from us. And now she's gone."

He looked devastated from recounting it, emptied out, bereft.

Conlon was quiet, making notes. "You've no idea where?"

"None. None. She was a stranger to me. When we spoke, she fairly spat venom. I was a personification of all that she despised in the world."

"I'm sorry to hear that."

"I just want her back home. And to be assured of her safety."

"Of course."

He snapped himself out of it. "I suspect that you would like to speak to my wife."

He pushed a lever by the door and somewhere off in the house Conlon heard a bell jingle.

"Martin will take you to her. She is expecting you. If there is anything else I can do?"

"I'll need those names."

"Of course. I'll have it for you. Numbers and addresses. Before you leave."

Martin was in the doorway.

"Take Mr. Conlon to see Lady Naessens, Martin."

Lady Naessens? Conlon thought.

Naessens was up and rounding the desk once more. He shook Conlon's hand.

"I just want her back, Mr. Conlon. No expense spared. Whatever it takes. I have full confidence in your abilities."

"I'll do my best, Mr. Naessens."

The big man nodded, and Conlon turned to follow Martin from the room.

"Martin. Could I use the lavatory before I see Mrs. Naessens?"

"Of course, sir. This way." Martin swerved across the main hallway and Conlon followed.

"If you don't mind me asking: the missing girl. What was she like?"

Martin had stopped outside a door, which he indicated with a hand. He now raised an eyebrow at Conlon. "I like her. She's a clever girl. She thinks for herself. She is kind to the servants here. The lavatory, sir."

Conlon nodded thanks and entered.

When he was finished, Martin was waiting. He had a way of looking at you without any eye contact, which Conlon supposed must be essential for a domestic servant.

"I'll need to ask you some questions, too, Martin."

"Yes, sir. After you've spoken to Lady Naessens, we can, if that's alright."

"That'll be grand."

Martin led him off again, through the rooms, each filled with ornaments and paintings, furniture that looked too delicate for use.

There was a sort of sunroom at the back of the house, with a wall composed almost entirely of windows, and another wall of surging, voraciously over-spilling plants giving the feeling of a hothouse in the Botanical Gardens. One end had been cleared and a large table sat there, where Conlon supposed people such as these might take breakfast on a fine morning.

Walking through this room he could see a figure through the glass, sitting on a metal chair by a metal table on a veranda of sorts, with a view of a heavily landscaped garden. She was clad entirely in white so that he had to squint when he looked directly at her, the sun dazzling off her body. She was wearing a huge sun hat so that her face was obscured to him, and reading a book while a glass of wine sparkled in the light she reflected in a little halo around her.

When they came around in front of her, she shaded her eyes with a delicate hand. Conlon could see that the nails were bitten down.

Her face was the face of the woman in the photograph Naessens had shown him. She was younger than her husband, with sharp eyes and eyebrows, a small, pointed noise and a small mouth, which seemed pressed tightly closed, the two curt lines on either side of it suggesting that she rarely smiled.

"Ma'am. This is Mr. Conlon," Martin said. "The gentleman Lord Naessens has employed to locate Miss Naessens."

"Thank you, Martin." She looked at Conlon, and

gave what he supposed was her attempt at a smile, a grim, puppet-like flexing of her face.

"Mr. Conlon. Please, sit."

He did as she asked, feeling her eyes upon him.

"Would you like an iced tea? It is dreadfully hot today."

"No, thank you."

She gestured at Martin—a sort of shrug Conlon barely registered—and the butler retreated.

He had to squint to make her out in the sun and against the glare of her clothing.

"So, you are a detective? Like Sherlock Holmes?"

"No, not quite. I don't really follow clues or solve murders."

"And the police? Do you work with them?"

"Not if I can avoid it. I find people."

"Do so many people go missing? Like Philomena?"

"You'd be surprised, Mrs. Naessens."

"I expect so. How can I help you, Mr. Conlon?"

"Philomena. Tell me about her."

"Tell you? What do you want to know?"

"Your husband didn't tell me much. What is she like? What does she like?"

"How will that help you, may I ask?"

"It can be invaluable to have a sense of the person I'm looking for."

"But I presume you mean when they have taken themselves off somehow. Philomena has been abducted."

"What makes you say that?"

"She wouldn't leave like that. Without saying good-bye, leaving all of her possessions, all of her clothes, her life. Philomena wouldn't do that."

"Your husband suggested that she'd changed a lot recently. Could that be an explanation for it?"

She raised an eyebrow. Theatrically, he thought. "She has always wanted to be an actress. Since she was a little girl. My husband didn't pay much attention to her when she was growing up. She made some new friends, and some of them had interesting ideas. But she didn't change. She was still my Philomena."

"He mentioned a cult."

She shook her head. "She never told me about that. Some of her friends were religious, I think, but not Christians. For the most part they seemed to be bohemians with Fenian sympathies. But isn't the whole country rife with sympathizers these days, Mr. Conlon? Since they shot those rebels?"

"I think the country is changing."

"For the better?"

"Well...that would depend on your opinion of how good it is at the moment."

She smiled, a sincerer smile than the one that had greeted him. "I believe some of Philomena's new friends might have exposed her to a life she had never even suspected existed before. Not just actors and poetry and politics. She sat in cafés and public houses with people from the same circles she had grown up in. People from the same few schools and families, I would imagine. I'm not blinkered enough to believe that there is not an entirely different Dublin beyond our world, Mr. Conlon. And some of her friends were determined to improve that Dublin. Not Fenians. Socialists. They wanted to help the poor. To go into the slums and give them food and medicine."

"And God?"

"Yes. Their God, whoever he may be."

"People in those 'slums' already have their God. They need him more than people from outside will ever understand."

"I'm sure you know more than I do about it."

"But your daughter. Do you know any of her new friends? Their names? Anything?"

"No. Her schoolfriends may. She has been more private since she began at university. We saw less of her."

"Your husband suspects that she ran off. Because they no longer got along."

"She's strong enough to cope with not getting along with her father. And has a love of drama devoted enough to take some pleasure in it, I assure you. No. She has been abducted. A mother knows, Mr. Conlon."

Conlon nodded. "I'll need to have a look at her room."

"We haven't been very helpful, have we?"

"It's not strange for parents to be a bit unfamiliar with a child's life, once they reach University."

"But perhaps if we knew more...this might not have happened."

"You can't say that. Nobody knows what perhaps could have been. Life is strange and people are unpredictable."

"Are they? How do you do your job then, Mr. Conlon? I would imagine you depend on people being extremely predictable...?"

"I depend on asking questions and poking my nose into people's business. That usually does the trick."

"So in this case, who do you ask?"

"There's always somebody who knows something

useful. They might not even know what that is. Somebody will have seen her somewhere, or heard her say something, and that'll lead me to somebody else who will know where she went, and that'll take me to where she is."

"And then?"

"And then I go and see if she wants to come back."

"And what if she does not?"

"She's an adult. I can tell you where she is, but I'm no kidnapper."

"My husband might not see matters in this light."

Conlon shrugged.

"And if I'm correct. If somebody has taken her, against her will?" she said, evenly.

"Well then...I'll take steps to take her back."

"Steps?"

He nodded.

"Were you a soldier, Mr. Conlon?"

"I was."

"You fought in the Great War?"

He nodded again.

She mirrored his nod.

There was a moment of silence then. Conlon knew this moment well. It often followed the realization that he was a veteran of the War. People wanted to say something, but they had no idea what to say. What was proper? Was he scarred? Had he suffered from what they were all reading about in the papers now—something they were calling shell shock? Was he loyal to the King? So instead they were silent, trying to decide what was fitting, and the silence dragged on.

Conlon let it.

Eventually, she seemed to decide to dismiss the

entire idea, and her face changed. She was instantly business-like.

"Is there anything else I can help you with, Mr. Conlon?"

"I don't think so."

"Very good. Please, please, think nothing of contacting us if you anything occurs to you, or if there is anything you need, any help we can offer you. If you go back through those doors and push the lever by the window, Martin will see to you."

He stood. "Thank you."

"Thank you, Mr. Cònlon. I do hope you're successful. I miss her dreadfully."

"I'll do my best."

———

HE HAD Martin lead him to Philomena's room, at the front of the house with huge windows and a view of the drive in and the trees which lined it, bright and still in the sun. It was quiet; at the end of the landing, if felt tucked away from the rest of the house, from the rooms where Conlon had just spoken to her parents. The walls were painted a shroud like cream yellow. One picture on a wall; dancers twirling in a blur of paint. To his eye it felt like a hotel room; impersonal and lacking in any sign that an actual human being had grown up there. It was tasteful, but cold.

Martin lingered in the door while he poked around.

"Martin. Was this her room as a child?"

"Yes sir. Although Lady Naessens had it redecorated eighteen months past."

"Did she keep a diary that you know of?"

"Not that I was ever privy to, sir."

He opened drawers and checked underneath, pulled the few books—Rousseau, some Shakespeare, Swift, Robinson Crusoe, Wuthering Heights—off the shelf and looked through them for notes or papers. She had a large closet, and the smell when he opened it was a wash of the feminine into the room: perfume and soap and skin creams. Conlon thought of Theresa with a pang.

It was the only part of the room where he got some sense of Philomena as a human being.

He pushed through some of her clothes—dresses in lush, expensive fabrics. Shoes sat neatly on a shelf; scarves snaked around one another off a series of hooks on the inside of the door. Pictures that looked as if they had been painted by a child were stuck to a wall, low down.

He opened a hatbox and it contained, disappointingly, a hat.

He spoke to Martin as he worked. "So you said you liked her."

"I like her, sir, yes."

"Just between us, then. Do you think she's run away? Her mother thinks she's been taken."

He said this with his back to the butler. Martin's pause was lengthy.

"She wasn't always very happy here. But she knew her own mind. So either could be true, I suppose is what I'm saying, sir."

Conlon turned to look at him. "Could you imagine her leaving?"

"Oh yes, sir."

"But you don't necessarily believe that she did?"

"Exactly right, sir. She was too used to her luxuries, I'd say, sir."

Conlon nodded.

"Did you know any of her new friends?"

"She never introduced any here, sir. But she did mention some names. An Alan and a Viv."

"Alan and Viv."

"Yes sir. She only began to mention those names over the last few months, I would say."

"Mention them how? In what sort of way?"

"She might say she'd had dinner with them. Or that she had been to the theatre with Viv. They seemed to be very fast pals, sir."

Conlon took this in.

He went to the bed, forced his fingers down the side, past the sheets, drawn tight by a zealous, expert maid, and lifted the mattress. Underneath, flattened to the springs, was an envelope.

Inside were a handful of love letters—all from different men—and a photograph. It captured Philomena, her hair down, a cigarette between her fingers and a glass of wine before her, sat smiling at a table beside a young man. Handsome, with dark hair, sharp cheekbones and piercing, dark eyes, he looked directly into the camera while she was looking at someone unseen.

Conlon held the photo for Martin to study. "Do you know who this is, Martin?"

"No, I don't, sir. I've never seen him before. Maybe that's this Alan, sir?"

"Maybe it is."

He looked around a little more, and from Martin's answers, determined that none of the other household staff knew Philomena well enough to be worth interviewing at this point. They were something he could come back to, if he got desperate enough at a later stage.

He had enough.

Martin escorted him back downstairs, asked him to wait in the hall, and disappeared for a moment. When he reappeared, he carried a large envelope. Conlon opened it, noting the presence of the photograph Naessens had shown him, and quickly perused the list of names, addresses and telephone numbers. He wondered if Naessens himself had compiled the list and decided that he must have a secretary or assistant for such tasks. Still, the paper was crisp and felt expensive, the handwriting so fluid and fancy it was almost difficult to decode.

"Martin. Mr. Naessens said that the last time Philomena was here, they had an argument. At some sort of party."

"Yes sir. There was quite a large dinner."

"Can you point out the names of any young people who might have been there on this list?"

Martin squinted at the list when Conlon handed it to him. Then, with hands as quick as those of a stage magician, he had drawn a pencil from inside his jacket and ringed two names on the list. He nodded at Conlon, who thanked him and then followed him out to the car and the waiting driver, who was polishing the bonnet as they came down the steps from the front door.

He raised his eyebrows in acknowledgement of Conlon, who thanked Martin again and was already in the passenger seat when the driver climbed in.

About halfway back into the city, when the silence had become habitual and comfortable, Conlon asked him, "Miss Naessens. Philomena. Do you have to drive her much?"

"Not for a few weeks now."

"But before that, did you?"

"Sometimes aye."

"Where would she go?"

The driver looked at him for a second, then back at the road.

Conlon explained. "I'm sure you and all the servants know. She's missing. They've asked me to find her. So you can help me. Where would you usually drop her off?"

"Around the General Post Office. There's a few cafés around there she was fond of. And at her College. The Abbey Theatre as well."

"Did you ever see or meet any of her friends?"

"No. She'd have me drop her off somewhere a bit of a walk away. She was private like that."

"Did she talk to you?"

"A bit."

"Where do you think she is?"

"Run off with a fella, I think. She always had fellas chasing her."

"Do you know any of them?"

"No, no. She was even more private about that than everything else."

Conlon nodded and watched the road, trying not to think of Theresa, and inevitably, of Orla.

After another minute or two, when they were riding beside the Liffey once more, the young driver asked, "Should I drop you home again?"

"No, thank you. If it's no trouble, could you drop me at the GPO?"

20 Hours After Purification

HE JUST ABOUT MADE IT THROUGH THE WOOD.

He could feel his strength ebbing further and knew he would have to rest soon or else he was liable to collapse. The day was sliding into evening now, the sun low, and he decided to sit and rest when they reached a large pool at the bottom of the slope on the other side of the wood. He laid Philomena down, as gently as his shuddering muscles would allow, and slumped against a tree.

He had chosen to stop just inside the tree line with a view across the pool and the natural bowl that cupped it. Birds hung overhead against a cloudless evening sky. Taking some of the bread and cheese from the bag, he divided it into rough quarters and ate one portion, washing it down with water from the canteen. The metallic taste reminded him of the War. So many things reminded him of the War. He had to stop himself from drinking more, the exertions of the past twenty-four hours catching up with him.

He knew if he slept, when he woke and rose the aches and pains would be intolerable, and yet he knew he needed to sleep. His eyes hurt and he felt that weightless feeling, almost on the edge of faintness, which was a familiar sign of exhaustion.

These decisions—the life and death decisions, where he had to weigh which risk was most acceptable and decide which outcome he felt best able to handle— these decisions also reminded him of the War.

First he had to see to his wound. He rolled up his shirt. It was sodden with blood on one side, its grey soaked a rich burgundy. But already stiff, the blood drying, which was a good sign. It meant he was no longer bleeding. The wound was perhaps two inches long. The blade had missed any vital organs but the amount of blood he had lost suggested that the cut had been deep. Still, he had been lucky. He was lucky that way, he always had been. But then the Major had told him many times that you made your own luck, that the blade didn't nick a lung or his liver because of the way he had twisted away from the thrust at just the last instant, that it was all down to the decisions he made, to his skills, to his instincts.

He poked at it gingerly. The pain was bearable now.

He ripped the sleeve completely off the shirt on the other arm then, using his teeth, tore a long strip of that, then another and awkwardly; cursing his fumbling, weakened fingers, knotted them together. Then he wound that around his midriff, having first pressed a triple-folded handkerchief in place over the caked wound. He pulled the long strip of shirt tight, winced at the pressure on the wound, and tied the ends together. Then he rolled the shirt down again and collapsed back.

He thought they had a few hours at least. The Centurions would be thrown by what he had done to the men back at the ridge, and by the fights on the island and at the shore. Enough of them were ex-military with the knowledge to know that he was something more than that. They would be hesitant going into the wood. They would see him in every shadow, hear him in every rustle. If they were sensible, they would wait until first light to move.

He could rest for a few hours, he thought, as long as he and the girl were up and moving as soon as he awoke.

He turned his head to look at her. She slept on her side, her face untroubled and peaceful. He was regarding her, and then he was asleep, too.

3

10 Days Before Purification

THERE WERE A FEW BARS AND CAFÉS AROUND SACKVILLE
Street where a certain brand of young student gathered.
Some of them hosted meetings of various Republican
groups and sold Fenian papers; a couple were just
cheap and atmospheric, a fact that appealed to all
students, even those from affluent backgrounds like
Philomena Naessens; and the owner was not averse to
keeping packages behind the bar, no questions asked, as
long as you were willing to pay a small fee.

Conlon started there.

It was a large pub, with snugs and dark little corners
aplenty. You could be sat in the back, near the stairs to
the function room or the doors to the filthy toilets, and
nobody would know you were there unless they went
looking for you. The landlord was a cheapskate, and he
kept the lighting as sparse as possible, meaning that in
the spaces at the rear, the only light came from a few

flickering oil lamps, which regularly went dark, and the murky skylight near the middle of the room.

The landlord also watered down his wine and sold toasted sandwiches filled with week old ham and beef. The toast and margarine it was slathered in before it was grilled somehow made it excusable, and students and the city's many poor were happy of the low prices, so the place always seemed to be busy.

Conlon had approached it down a busy street. The shopping streets off Sackville Street were the busiest in Dublin, the place where the various tiers of society mingled most freely. The cobbles didn't cover the whole street here but the dry weather had turned the mud pale and flaky, so that crossing the street wouldn't ruin shoes as it did in winter. Street urchins roamed in packs, eyes alert, some with rags on their feet, many with dirty faces and scabbed knees. Conlon had been one of those children once, before his ability to hurt people with his hands had changed his life and sent him into a boxing gym and the ring. That seemed centuries ago now.

Alongside the street children there were working men. Dockers passing through on their way across town to the East and North Wall, carrying their lunch in knapsacks or bundles, wearing caps and rough jackets, boots rather than the shiny shoes favored by the clerks and business workers they passed on these same streets.

Those men wore different hats: derbies and bowlers, homburgs and fedoras, the odd top hat and boater. Men from the middle classes wore hats to identify themselves as successful, as belonging in the shops and restaurants they frequented. Their suits were tailored or from better department stores. Their shoes shone with the polish Conlon remembered from the army. They carried newspapers and smoked pipes, wore waistcoats, worked in offices across the city center.

The women echoed the men. There were not as many society women here as he would have seen on Grafton Street, but still the occasional expensive fabric was visible on a Christmas tree of a dress, a hat like something from a painting, all feathers and glittering textiles. And women who worked—in sober, darker dresses and skirts; modest hats. All moving around the beggars, the street girls on their way to and from the Monto, only a quarter mile away from the GPO, the British Army men, the delivery boys and drivers, a city bursting with life and variety.

And beyond all that, on the street—a funeral cortege. They had passed one in the automobile out to the Naessens house, too, he recalled. How many did he see each day now? A long stream of mourners, dressed in black, heads down.

The Spanish flu continued to take a toll on the country, and scattered through every crowd would be a handful of people wearing masks over their faces, eyes hunted and watchful among so many potential virus-carriers. By then thousands had died. Dublin, a city accustomed to plagues, to the poor dying ceaselessly in their filth, had never seen anything quite like this.

The city felt tense to Conlon at the moment; as if it was holding its breath, waiting for the next thing. The next murder, the next raid, the next disease. They all knew something was coming. Violence, most likely. It was just a question of when, and how bad it would be. Since he had returned from the War and slipped once more into the flow of Dublin life, he had adjusted to it. A constant drip of violence, of rumors. People he knew and had known were involved. It had allowed some of his own activities to slip by, almost unnoticed. Just more violence in a city and a country becoming all too accustomed to them.

But at the moment the tension felt acute. People drank and made merry as if they might never get a chance to do so again. It was exhausting. He remembered the feeling as he slipped into the pub, swapping the relentless din of the city and its people, always on the way somewhere, for the low murmur of a pub in the late afternoon.

The barman knew him, as many in the city center did.

"Tommy. What can I get you?"

"Pint please, Frankie."

Conlon sat on a stool in the center of the bar, and threw a casual look around as he did so.

"How's your boy doing? John, isn't it?"

"John yeah. He's not too bad at the minute, Tommy, thanks be to God. Consumption can be fierce bad for spells and then grand for a while. Up and down, you know?"

Conlon nodded.

"You not got the lassy with you today?" Frankie asked.

Conlon thought for a minute—he and Theresa had seen Frankie with his wife and children in the Phoenix Park about six weeks previously. Conlon and Frankie had nodded and waved.

"Ah, we broke it off," Conlon said.

"Aw, I'm sorry to hear that, Tommy."

"It's for the best."

Frankie nodded. "Often the way."

He moved away up the bar to serve a couple of old men, yelled an order for beef sandwiches into the kitchen hatch, then returned to Conlon.

"So...would you be here on the job, then, Tommy?"

Conlon marked it instantly—Frankie was one of those people who thought that his work was glamorous and craved involvement. He wanted to help, he wanted to be part of it, it was all a big adventure in his imagination.

Conlon said, "I would, as... it happens. You get a lot of students in here, don't you?"

"If you'd've been in here an hour ago you'd've seen how it is. The place is black with them."

Conlon had already extracted the envelope from his inside pocket, and now he slipped out the photographs. He slid the picture of Philomena and the young man around and looked at Frankie. "Do you recognize her?"

"Both of them, they do come in, sure. Not every day, like. But regular enough."

"You seen them recently?"

"He's been in, alright. I haven't seen her though, no, now that I think of it. A few weeks, I'd say."

"Do they have a crowd they hang around with?"

"Oh aye. Big load of them. Theatrical types, I'd say. But there's a few groups that sort of mix with each other. They spend more time in Maisies I think, some of them. They're not short of a few bob."

Conlon nodded.

Frankie said, "Who are you looking for, Tommy? That's what you do, isn't it? Find people?"

"Yeah. She's disappeared. Her parents want me to find her."

Frankie nodded sagely. "I'd go to Maisies. Her mates are sure to be there, some of them."

"Thanks Frankie, I'll do that. Are any of them called Viv, or Roger, do you know?"

"Viv is like the boss woman. Like the Hen, the rest of them all bow and scrape to her, sure. I don't know any Roger but sure there're a load of lads who come around and don't stay in the picture."

"Is Viv likely to be at Maisies, too?"

"I'd say so. She's a bit older than the rest of them. I think she's an actress, from the sound of it."

Conlon finished his pint, said goodbye and made his way to Maisies, only about fifty meters away, but more of a café then a pub. Nice food, high windows, pleasant décor—it styled itself as a Viennese-style experience for Dublin's pretentious middle classes. Of course drama students would adore it.

The smell of coffee was strong even from outside, which in a city of tea drinkers was a badge of some sort of distinction. Conlon loved the smell but hated the taste, and he took a small table near the window and ordered a mug of tea and a pastry from the smiling, busy waitress. He took his cap off and scanned the room.

And there they were. A big, loud group in the corner; all exaggerated laughter and put-on funny voices, braying posh accents clamoring to be heard over each other.

He took off his jacket and pulled the Jack London novel he was reading from the pocket. When the waitress had returned with his tea, he sat half turned in his chair, the novel open in his hands and held up so that he could scrutinize the group. He tried to focus on them, to listen to what they were saying, noting names, trying to work out relationships and status before he moved in on anybody. He ate his pastry, poured and drank his tea, ordered another, together with a crumpet and scrambled eggs, and when he was finished, he used the lavatory, and filled in some blanks.

Viv wasn't there at first, but she arrived after about an hour, fresh from college and instantly dominating the group. All eyes turned to her; all conversation ceased to hear what she might say. She had long dark hair and blue eyes and she wore a fur around her neck in dramatic fashion and moved as if she were already on stage, her steps and turns all pinpoint and overdone to the point of absurdity. He watched her, and straight away he could see why she had a hold over the group. She had a magnetism, a presence that made you want to see what she would do next, to hear what she might say.

Their conversation was mainly gossip and the usual opinion you could hear in any pub across the city— Spanish flu and the latest news, the prospect of the War ending soon ("My Uncle Gilbert is a Field Marshall or something, and he says the Gerries will surrender by Christmas"), a murder that had been attributed to the Rebels near Queenstown—mixed with the kind of thing only students of theater or literature would ever spend time debating.

First, one of the young men ranted about a playwright by the name of Synge, before he and another became embroiled in a bitter argument over whether Hamlet or Macbeth was the greater role. Viv settled this by quoting Hamlet at length, which set them all off, quoting Shakespeare in increasingly operatic tones. They then complained about one of their teachers with vehemence and supremely detailed recreations of various interactions with him, impersonating the man as a lisping pedant, overly critical of their work. Then they were back to gossip, and the goings-on at a party a few nights before.

· None of the lads really stood out. None had a big enough personality to face off with Viv, and there was no charismatic loner on the edge of the group. So Viv it would have to be.

He drifted out after a while, jotting some points on various other ideas in his notebook as he sat there and the group began to break up, leaving in ones and twos. He paid the waitress, left her a decent tip, and went outside. It had that briskness that an evening can have in late summer. Grey suddenly a vice around the day, its cold steel teeth biting. He stood across the road, his back to the café, watching its reflection in the hat shop window he faced.

Viv came out last, with two of the lads, verbally jostling for her attention. Showing off, trying to outdo one another. He recognized such behavior, even if it had never been his way. For her part, she smiled tolerantly. She was used to this.

Conlon allowed them to make a turn before he followed, then kept a ways back as they crossed the Liffey and headed South, crossing Stephens Green, where one of the young men departed. Viv and the other walked on, arm in arm.

They passed the Bleeding Horse and wound their way through Little Jerusalem. Finally, they stopped at a house on Bloomfield Avenue, with its vibrant trees shaking faintly in the summer evening against the red brick Victorian houses. Children were playing. Men sat on their steps and in their small front gardens enjoying the evening, even as that grey advanced into dusk. Conlon heard as much Yiddish as he did English here.

He bought an apple from the Jewish grocer on the corner, facing the church, so he could stand and watch them as he ate it, half-passing the time with the man. The grocer was closing up and tutted in mock annoyance at Conlon's cheek, then asked him which football team he supported. Conlon managed to keep a chat about the varying states of the city's several football grounds rolling along while watching Viv and the young man have a friendly embrace, before she went into one of the houses about halfway down.

Not as well-off as she seemed, Conlon thought.

He finished his apple, finished his chat with the Grocer, having assured him that Dalymount was the place he wanted to go, allowed Viv's young man to pass him by on the corner, and then he headed towards her house.

She answered. She had shed her fur and her hat, and she looked prettier and younger now, up close, slightly defensive to see a young man she didn't know at her door. The hall behind her was gloomy but the sun shone into the kitchen beyond that. He put on his best little boy smile, the one he had learned to use when trying to seem unthreatening to the middle classes. The one he had shown to Lady Naessens.

"Can I help you?" she said, accusingly.

"Howya. My name is Thomas Conlon. I was wondering if you'd have a minute to talk about Philomena Naessens?"

Her eyes flickered at the name, but, as an actress

should, she recovered instantly. "Philomena? What about her?"

"You're friends, I'm told."

"Yes, yes, we—know each other. Sorry, who did you say you are?"

"Thomas Conlon." He extended his hand and automatically, she shook it.

"Can I come in? It won't take very long."

She looked stricken at that, visibly unsure, all her theatrical poise melting away, and softly he said: "Listen, I'm not after anything or trying to hurt anybody. I just need some information. Just a short chat."

Their eyes met, properly for the first time. She nodded, and he saw a flash of her smile. "Of course, do come in. I'm sorry, its just—"

"Don't be sorry," he said, as she ushered him in. "It's good to be careful."

She took him into the kitchen, which was large enough for a table and three chairs by one wall. She gestured towards them and he sat, thanking her.

"I was just fixing myself some tea," she said, and saw to the kettle on the stove, then lifted some cups from a cupboard. "Would you like some?"

"Yes, please. That would be grand."

"How much milk?"

"A lot," he said. "No sugar."

She laughed. "A man after my own heart."

He looked around. Through the door the living room looked like a library—walls of books on each side that he could see. A bright world map on the wall over the table where he sat. Animals cut from wood on a shelf. A candelabra on the windowsill.

"Do you live here alone?"

"Oh no, I could never afford it. I share with some newlyweds. Mr. and Mrs. Abrahamson. They're barely here though, always at his mother's or her mother's or working at his father's laundry or out with friends. I see them over breakfast occasionally. It's like living alone, really."

She placed the tea before him and sat.

"Are you—" He hesitated, and she saw the question in his hesitation.

"A Jew? No. My surname is Logue, Mr. Conlon. Dublin born and bred, a good Catholic girl. Not far from here, in fact. But I've lived here all my life, and I grew up with Jews. So I feel very comfortable around them."

He nodded. The theatrical creature who had dominated proceedings in the café with her huge group of friends—that person was gone. He saw now that she had assumed a character, like the actress that she was. Like everybody did, to some extent, at some point in their lives, or even regularly, with certain people. He prided himself on always being true to who he was, but even he had to change depending on company. Certainly for work, but in his private life: he was not the same person with his ma that he would be with Theresa, say, or with Mossy. It was natural. Viv just did it exceptionally well.

The question was now: the girl who sat before him now, with a quiet smile in her eyes and an air of vulnerability...was that another character or was that the real Viv?

"But you don't want to know about me," she said.

"Not at this moment, no. Philomena Naessens."

"Is she in trouble?"

"Why would she be in trouble?"

Her pause then told him that she was censoring herself and controlling her responses. Which was interesting. "Why else would you be asking me about her?"

"She's missing."

Again he saw that register in her eyes.

"When did you last see her?"

She shook her head. "A month ago, maybe? Weeks."

"And how was she?"

She thought about that, too. "She's a complicated girl, Mr. Conlon. I'm not sure how exactly I should answer that."

"Alright. Did she seem upset, when you last saw her?"

"Philomena often seemed upset. One became accustomed to it."

"Why would she be upset?"

"She had a difficult family life. Her parents are wealthy and, I suppose they're powerful. Is it them that's hired you?"

He nodded.

"They were always fighting. Her and her da most."

"What do you mean by powerful?"

She shook her head. "Ah, I don't even really know. Her da...things she said about him. He knows people. He knows everybody."

"Anything else might be upsetting her?"

"She had several men courting her. That could get dramatic."

"Would you know the names of any of these men?"

"One or two, yes."

"Would one be called Alan, by any chance?"

"She never mentioned an Alan to me."

He nodded.

"She likes men who chase her, and then she'll push them away, and they'll chase after her even harder. She loves the drama of that kind of thing. Having arguments, storming out on them, all that. Like a little girl, in that way. Often older men, too. She's fickle with the men in our group. She likes them a bit rough, too, though she'd never admit it. She was always flirting with waiters and stagehands. She'd like you."

"Because I'm 'rough'? What kind of men do you like?"

"I don't have a type, Mr. Conlon. I don't believe in it."

They smiled together then, suddenly, some sort of complicity forming.

She said, "So are you a detective? A private detective? Like a Pinkerton agent?"

He chuckled. "Sort of, I suppose. I don't solve murders or anything."

"What do you do?"

"I find missing people."

"Ah. Hence...this."

"There you go."

"It must be exciting."

"It can be."

"For a rough Dublin boy...? Where are you from?"

"Stoneybatter."

"How did you end up in such a strange job?"

"I don't really know, to be honest. I went looking for a friend who went missing. And somehow it turned into a job."

"And part of that involves knocking on doors and asking terrified young women to answer questions?"

"It does. I get to meet some interesting people, let's put it that way."

"Oh, am I interesting?"

"Well, if I'm a Stoneybatter boy who's ended up working for the wealthy and powerful to find their missing children, then you'd be a Portobello girl who's ended up teaching them how to be an actress."

"Oh, I'm not a teacher. I still have too much to learn, myself."

"You're in College...?"

"I'm not a student, not really. I kept auditioning around town, and eventually one of the directors sent me to his friend who runs a drama course. I go to classes and rehearse but I won't get a degree out of it."

"But you're learning your craft."

"Well that's the idea. I couldn't afford it. I have to work two jobs to keep myself fed and under a roof. That and scabbing off my wealthy friends."

"Like Philomena?"

"Like Philomena."

"What jobs do you work?"

"I clean houses for those wealthy people three mornings a week. And I work in a pub out your way three nights, too."

"Out my way?"

"Well, near Marino. The northside is all the same to me."

He laughed and she joined him.

"I chose the Northside, far out, to be honest. It wouldn't do for one of my friends to be seeing me cooking black pudding in the kitchen of some pub. None of them would be seen dead out in Marino."

"You've no family to be supporting you? Or to live with?"

"My da died in India with the British Army. My ma died of the flu in March."

"I'm sorry for your loss."

"Thank you. I have an auntie out in the country, my ma's sister, we're very close. And I have a sister in London somewhere. She's the black sheep, she left when I was only young. And I have two brothers, gone to America. They were sending money home to my ma, and they both said they'd keep doing that, but nothing so far. I think they see me as old enough to look after myself and shouldn't I be settling down and having babies with some big honest farmer anyway at this stage."

"Shouldn't you?"

"Farmers aren't my type, Mr. Conlon."

"I thought you didn't believe in types, Miss Logue? And call me Tommy, please."

"A woman can change her mind, can't she? And if I'm calling you Tommy, I insist that you call me Viv."

"So, Viv. The plan is eventually you get an acting job, and you can give up the cleaning and the black pudding?"

"That's the plan."

"I like that plan. I hope it works."

"Plenty of people want to be actresses, is the problem."

"Plenty of people aren't as pretty as you are. That should help."

She let the compliment infect her smile and said, "I could be as pretty as Mary Pickford, but it won't matter if I can't act."

"You're prettier than Mary Pickford. And I know you can act."

"How do you know that, Tommy?"

"Didn't I watch you hold about fifteen students under your spell for two hours in Maisies earlier today? Based on the girl I'm talking to now, that was some performance."

"You were there?"

"I was."

"Watching me?"

"Watching all of you. Trying to sort out Philomena's friends in my head. You were the one who stood out."

"I can't believe I didn't notice you."

"Well I wouldn't be doing my job very well if you'd noticed me, now would I?"

"Were you in disguise? You really are a detective. A bit of a performer yourself, I think."

"No disguise. A book."

She laughed. They drank their tea and then she said, "I'll be honest. I've been worried about Philomena this last week or two. It's not like her to stay away like this."

"Might any of your friends know more?"

"Maybe. I'll ask around for you. Some of the lads might. She likes playing them off each other. It'll save you having to wear anymore fake moustaches or wear a dress, anyway, if I do the questions."

"Unless I like wearing dresses."

"You'll fit right in in my world then," she said.

"Some of the places you and your friends socialize in," he said, after a few more sips of tea, "they attract varied crowds."

"They do. There are a lot of political groups, do you mean?"

He nodded.

"They like to recruit students. Some of my friends are involved."

"Not you? No Cumann na mBan for you?"

"Oh Jesus Mary and Joseph no. I've met Markievicz though. They're desperate for people to work on the election they insist is going to happen once the War ends, she used to come around personally sometimes trying to recruit young girls."

"What's she like?"

"Charismatic, if you're an impressionable young one."

"But you're still not interested?"

"No. The revolution is going to happen without me. And I won't be missed. What about you? You were in the army, weren't you?"

"I was."

"The War?"

He nodded.

"So are you a loyal servant to the King? Or one of those bitter soldiers angry at Britain for what it did to you?" She said all this with a semi ironic air, a lightness that made it impossible to be offended.

"I'm neither. But I've had enough of following orders for one lifetime, and I won't be doing it again, for Eamonn DeValera or Lloyd George."

"But you'll do it for Lord Naessens?"

"I can say no to him without being sent to the stockade, or the Firing Squad."

"I wouldn't be too sure about that," she said, with an air of melodrama, and they both laughed.

"Was Philomena involved, at all?"

"In Politics? No, no, she's too...spoiled."

"What about her boyfriends?"

"Now that is possible. She always has lads that hang around Maisies or one of the pubs there coming up to her. I don't know who the half of them are."

"Alright. Well, it's a start."

"I'm sorry I couldn't be more useful."

"No, no, you were very helpful."

He took a last mouthful of the tea, rose and she walked with him into the hall, towards the front door.

"I'll ask around for you. About Philomena. How will I contact you? Do you have a telephone?"

"Why don't we meet?"

He looked her in the eye when he suggested this. He wanted her to know what he meant. She nodded, and for a moment, shyness came over her, eyes down, something bashful in the line of her mouth.

"In town?" she asked.

"Trinity?" he said.

"Ok. How about this time the day after tomorrow? We can drink more tea."

He checked his watch. "That'll be fine. Will it be enough time for you to find anything out?"

"I'm working tomorrow night but I'll have college tomorrow and the afternoon the next day. Don't worry. It'll be grand."

"Alright so. Thank you. For your help and the tea."

She opened the door. "Thank you for the compliments."

He gave her his best smile, the one only certain people ever got to see. "If you knew how rarely I give those, you'd be even more grateful."

He was out on the step now, and she laughed. "But you have no idea how grateful I am, Tommy."

"See you soon, Viv," he said.

"Bye, Tommy."

He turned and went down the path to the road. He was aware that she waited until he was at least twenty meters away, watching him, before she closed the door.

4

26 Hours After Purification

HE FELT A HAND SHAKING HIM. AS ALWAYS, FOR THE briefest flash, a fraction of an instant, he thought it was Orla. Always she had been with him in sleep, in dreams, lying in the crook of his sleeping mind beside him, the piece of his heart that she owned forever lost to him. He thought of her every day, every hour, and knew that she would hang over every relationship he would ever have with a woman, just the way she had hung over his relationship with Theresa. She was a constant presence.

And so in sleep she came quickly to mind, and as he was being awoken, he thought of her.

And then it was gone and the world was brightly filtering through and he was cold and aching and the girl was shaking his shoulder.

He sat up and his hand was already on the rifle, his head turning in a rapid series of twitches. But it seemed safe. He could see nobody, hear nothing out of the ordinary.

He looked at her. "Good morning," he said.

She was shivering, holding herself. "Where are we?"

"Rathlinn Island, I think."

"Not the mainland?"

"No, not yet."

"Where are they? They must be after us?"

"They're after us alright. But I had a clash with them last night that'll slow them down."

He looked around again. The light had a blueish, steely quality that suggested very early morning. She had been awoken by the dawn, he supposed. The chill and sparkle of dew on the grass supported this conclusion.

"If we start moving we can get to the town early and get a boat back to the mainland."

She said, "I don't understand why you're doing this. I don't understand anything."

"I couldn't leave you there. What they were going to do..."

"But why are you here? My father couldn't—"

"We don't have time. We need to move. Can you move?"

"Did you carry me, yesterday?"

"I did. You don't weigh much but still..."

"Who are you? How can you do these things?"

"I was a soldier. I'm good at these things."

"You can't be serious," she laughed.

"After everything that's happened to you, what would be funny about that?"

He pushed himself up. His side screamed at him and he winced. She saw that and saw the blood matted to his clothing.

"Oh my God you're hurt. Were you shot?"

"I was. That and a knife."

"The twins?"

"No, I think if it had been one of the Hastings, I'd be dead. One of the Centurions."

"Are you alright?"

"I'm alright. I've had worse."

"Did you kill him?"

"The Centurion? Yes."

"How many did you kill?"

"No more than was necessary."

"How many was necessary?"

"A few."

He worried as he said that that she would crumble, that the guilt of that would affect her. Instead, she surprised him.

"There were at least thirty-one centurions, not including the Hastings. Caesar won't leave the island. And they'll have to leave at least nine, or ten of them there to maintain...everything. Especially after what you did."

"I know. So there will probably be five or six of them, or so. Perhaps a few more. They'll be coming. We need to move."

She nodded, then looked at him, with comic impatience. "Which way, then?"

5

9 Days Before Purification

SOME OF THE NUMBERS ATTACHED TO THE NAMES ON THE list that Naessens had given him were business numbers. Banks, solicitors, the Dublin Branch of a London accounting firm, a travel agency, insurance brokers. These were the elite of the business sector of society, and he had dealt with many of them over the last year or so, in one case or another. It was a surprisingly regular occurrence, it seemed—the wealthy and successful seeking to escape the lives they perceived as gilded cages. It had often fallen to Conlon to find them and bring them back home. Or, more regularly, to find them and take the money they had brought along back home.

So he had often found himself in the drawing rooms of big houses in the coastal strips of the city, and in some of the offices lurking in imposing city center buildings, grilling supercilious Trinity men, who would otherwise not have given him a second glance. He always enjoyed shaking their complacency a little bit. But at the same time, he knew that he needed information. He needed them to want to help, or at least to feel comfortable enough for him to be able to tell if any of them were lying. So he had to find the balance. As always.

He was up early. He had moved to a flat in the northern edge of Smithfield in the aftermath of the split with Theresa, and he liked to run through Phibsboro and along the canal each morning. He did that, enjoying the freshness of the breeze, then ate some toast with his tea after he had washed. Then he was out and in town just after nine, waiting at the door of the office of a shipping company off Dame Street when a pair of young ladies arrived to open up at half past.

They carried a whiff of summer with them, with brighter dresses and lighter coats than Dublin's weather usually permitted, and they were giggly and bashful even as they dutifully treated him like a professional. He told them who he wanted to see and they had him sat down with a cup of tea in seconds, watching appreciatively as they brought the office to life.

The men arrived in dribs and drabs, smoking steadily as they moved and chatted, hanging hats and coats on the rack, surprised by Conlon's presence, until the boss rolled in at ten to ten, newspaper folded under one arm, pipe pluming smoke, confidence evident in his bearing and expression.

Conlon was in to see him within five minutes of his arrival. He shook hands but barely made eye contact, instead exuding an air of hectic, constant activity, so that Conlon knew that this interview was at great cost to his working day. In addition, he had that bumbling private school idiot bluster down pat. He kept talking; a confident rolling stream of words and inarticulate sounds escaping from his lips at all times, a ceaseless song of his own so that it seemed impertinent to interrupt him as he stuttered and paused over an "erhm" or a "wellllll" drawn out past the point of any sense, providing him the time as he was searching for just the right phrase. Within the first minute it was maddening Conlon, who interrupted him at the very first opportunity. The look he received in return made it well worth it. This was a man used to getting his own way.

He was monologuing about what a tremendous chap Naessens was, what a fine golfer, a wise judge of character, shrewd in business, when Conlon broke in. "I'm not here about Mr. Naessens. I've met the man. His daughter. Do you know her well?"

"I-I...ahhh—I wouldn't say that I know her, that is to suggest—I...ahh—I of course, of course I know the young lady, yes, yes, ahhhh, everyone in our circle knows her, but, but, but I ehrm, errr I would never claim to know her, ahhhh, intimately. We aren't ahhh what I might consider anything, urm, ehhhr, anything like friends."

"Did you see her on the night in question?"

"The night in ahhhhhhh question? Oh welll, let me think...ehrm, ahhh, at the party, and uhhh, a very fine gathering it was too ha ha, Naessens always likes to ehhhh treat his friends to the best. Fine food, I mean to say, ahhhh—"

"Philomena Naessens was there. Did you see her?"

"Yes, yes, I...ah—I believe I did, yes, of course, yes."

"Did you converse with her?"

"We ahhhh, uhm, ah we may have ahhh, exchanged pleasantries, I believe. Ah ha. Yes."

Jesus Christ, Conlon thought. How can anybody stand to speak to this man? How did he possibly get to where he is?

"Would you have any idea if she did spend any significant amount of time talking to anybody at the dinner? Or was she off by herself in a corner?"

"Jack Rich."

This was the first time he had said anything without his characteristic noises sandwiching each word, and Conlon tilted his head. The name had been one of those circled on the list Naessens had given him.

"Would they usually be friendly? Or did you notice because this was unusual?"

"Well, ahhhh Jack is a bit ehhhhrr younger—a bit of a relative ahhh newcomer to our uhm set, so to speak. Yes. Ha. He is from ahhhhh what I suppose one might ehhhm refer to as a uhmmm, a good family. And he has, he has found ehm, found himself an extremely, an exceedingly good uhm position with one of Naessens' companies. Made himself ehhhr indispensable, from what I've ahhh heard, yes."

"So he would know Philomena. Because they're closer in age?"

"Ahhh I suppose you could say that, ehhhm, but but then they're not, not that close in age. There were a few ahhh a few—I suppose I'd say ahhh a few eyebrows raised that they spent so much uhhhm, so much time chatting."

"And why is that?"

"Well hah hah hah. Jack had uhhhh Jack had his wife with him that night. Poor lassie sat ehhhh all on her own while her husband is uhhhhr laughing with a young girl ah ha. Eyebrows raised ah ha."

"In your opinion, do Philomena and her father get on well?"

"Hurrr ah well, ahhhh, it's a tricky thing ehm, having a a a daughter in the modern world, Mr. Mr. ahhhh Mr. Conlon. I have aaaah two myself."

"So is that a yes, or a no?"

"Ah hah hah. I would imagine, uhm, from ahhh what I've, I've personally witnessed ahhh, that they generally—generally ahhh get along ehhhm quite well. Obviously, I say, obviously, as in any, any ahhhhh relationship, there are ahhh rocky moments ah hah."

"Of course. And the young lady has certain political ideas."

"She does. Hah. Uhhr. Ha yes, she certainly does, at that. And she's not, she's not remotely shy about sharing her, her beliefs or her ahhhh, her opinions. Ha."

"And how does that go down with your 'set'?"

"Well, I'd suggest that ahhhh we're as tolerant, as as the next man ahhhh, uhm, but in polite company I'd I'd —we're not down the pub, you might say."

"Her mother. Do they get along?"

"Uhmmm yes, yes, from ahhh what I've seen ahhh ehhh yes, they do."

"Well. Thank you. You've been helpful."

He stood, eager to leave.

"So ahhhh you're ahhhh a detective, is it?"

"Not quite, no. I find missing people."

The man nodded. Conlon waited for something more, but he was already reaching for a sheaf of papers on his desk.

"Goodbye, then," Conlon said, and he waved, a little corkscrew with his wrist.

On his way out, one of the ladies who had helped him gave him his coat and enquired if he had gotten everything he needed.

Conlon said, "How do you stand talking to him every day?"

She grinned, hid the grin behind a hand, looked around quickly to ensure she would not be heard, and said, "Sure you get used to it. The hard part is not finishing his sentences for him."

"I'm sure. However much you get paid—it's not enough."

"Oh you can come back," she said with a laugh.

"Quickly, before I go...does a Jack Rich do much business here?"

"He does. A right charmer he is, like yourself. Bit more of the silver spoon about him though."

"Likes the ladies?"

"Well he fancies himself enough, I'd say."

"And where would I find him?"

"Let me just check that for you."

She went to her desk, flipped through a journal, and returned with an address and phone number written down for him. Below that she had written her own name, address and phone number. He smiled, thanked her and then was back out in the Dublin morning.

———

JACK RICH WORKED in the head office of an import firm on the edge of the docks. Conlon made his way through the Monto, which was always slightly eerie in the morning: the majority of its prostitutes sleeping off the night before; its brothels and inns shuttered; its streets mostly deserted bar the odd customer who had fallen into a drunken sleep once he had sated himself and now rushed shame-faced to work or back home to a suspicious wife.

A few of its pubs were already open, serving the hardcore drinkers, a handful of its ladies working already, and a couple bade him good morning as he passed, doffing his cap to them. The streets stank as they always did—the souring sweetness of beer and wine mixed with excrement, the scent of the sea moving up the Liffey only slightly taking the edge off the air.

He thought about the girl's number in his pocket. He thought about Viv. And that led to him thinking about Theresa. He wondered where she was, right at this moment, and how she was. He wanted to go and find her, to make sure she was alright. More than that, despite everything, he wanted it to be one of those few mornings they had together when he awoke and she was already up, making breakfast, and his bed still smelled of her, and for just a few moments he felt good about them, and wasn't thinking of Orla and all he had lost.

But in the end, he had ruined it. Like a coward, he had ruined it.

They had argued for hours. And when it looked like stalemate, like they would limp on, damaged but somehow still intact, she had destroyed them. She had invoked Orla. "Your precious Orla," she called her. And that was the end of it, really. He had seen her once since then, when she had dictated her terms, and that had been the end of it. The end of it.

He knew he might see her again, in the street or a shop, maybe. Dublin was a small city, really. But they would never speak again. He would never have one of those mornings again. And despite him knowing that she deserved to be happy and loved by somebody else, that awareness gave him an ache in his gut that was hard to bear.

Jack Rich was in an office on the third floor, with a fine view of the river and Wicklow sloping into the sky beyond the city. He had a secretary, an older lady, with thick glasses, who seemed to be responsible for all of the men in offices on that floor. There were a series of doors behind her and her desk sat in the middle of the floor like a sort of sentry post. If you wished to access those doors, those offices and those men, you had to pass her.

She watched Conlon sternly as he approached off the stairs, but her expression became wry, almost amused when she heard he was there to see Rich. She sent Conlon straight through to his office with a quiet chuckle. "Just knock, he won't be doing anything important."

His knock was answered by a jaunty, "Come in" and inside a young man sat behind a desk with his legs stretched out beside him, a newspaper in his grip. His face flashed confusion for an instant before he covered it with a well-practiced smile.

"I'm sorry, you have me at a disadvantage," he said, rising, and extending his hand. He wore a shirt with the sleeves rolled up, revealing pink, hairless forearms. A bright dickie bow sat under his chin. There was an industrial quantity of oil in his hair.

"Thomas Conlon," Conlon said, shaking his hand with enough venom to make an impression.

Jack Rich nodded, unable to keep the slight confusion that welled back up from seeping into his eyes. Even so, he was polite and professional. "Sit down, take a seat. Would you like a cup of tea, or another beverage?"

"I'm fine, thank you."

"Grand, grand. So, how can I help you, Mr. Conlon?"

Conlon sat, swept a look around the office, and then focused upon Rich. "Philomena Naessens. Tell me about her."

His face twisted and he performed a rapid series of blinks. "I—sorry, who are you?"

"Miss Naessens is missing. Were you aware of that? Do you know where she is?"

"No no...wait wait...she's missing?"

"She is. You were one of the last people to speak to her. Tell me about it."

"Are you a policeman?"

"Do I look like a policeman, Mr. Rich? Tell me about Miss Naessens."

"What about her? What do you want to know? Did her father send you?"

"You were speaking intimately with her just before she went missing. What was the nature of that conversation?"

"What? When? When did she go missing?"

Conlon decided to change tack, yet still keep Rich off balance. He smiled. "Listen. Her father and his friends don't understand her. Or you, from what I can see. You're young and hold with dangerous ideas. So they're suspicious of you. So give me something I can give to them."

Rich shrugged. "I don't know anything! I didn't even know she was missing!"

"But you're close?"

"No, no, I wouldn't quite say that. She's a pretty lassie. I like pretty lassies. You can understand that, can't you?"

"Of course. You're a married man, aren't you?"

"Ah now. Come now, Mr. Conlon. I-I—"

"I just want to find Miss Naessens. I don't care about your private affairs, Mr. Rich. Any help you can give me, I'd certainly appreciate it."

Rich looked around, as if for help, closed his eyes, rubbed his face, looked around again and then back at Conlon. Conlon had the impression he was hoping if he did this, Conlon might be gone when his eyes returned to him.

"I don't know where she is, I swear to it."

"That isn't very helpful. What do you know?"

"She was upset the last time we spoke."

"At her father's house?"

"Yes, after dinner, we had a long chat. She had a lot on her mind, it seemed, and nobody to talk to."

"Did she tell you why she was so upset?"

He rolled his eyes a bit and grimaced. "She was involved with some people. She hinted there was a man, somehow, and that she wanted to be with him."

"What do you mean some people?"

"A group of people."

"Political?"

He shrugged. "Perhaps, but she didn't say, to be

honest, it was more hints and myself vainly trying to read between the lines. She is a distractingly beautiful girl, even with your wife sitting a few feet away." He laughed at this, then bit off the laugh when he saw Conlon's face.

"So, she was trying to talk to you about whatever was upsetting her, and you were trying to have your way with her, with your wife in the same room."

Rich said, "Now, listen here, you can take yourself out of this office if you think you can speak to me that way."

"I'll go when I'm ready, Mr. Rich. You don't want me calling to your house now, do you?"

"I apologize. I know you have a job to do. Myself and Philomena were involved, before my marriage. When she was quite young. Her father isn't aware of this, and I'd rather he didn't become aware of it."

"I thought you were friendly."

"We are, in so far that he is my employer and a friend of my parents. But he is also...he's a man you wouldn't want to defy, Mr. Conlon."

Conlon nodded. "So she thought she could confide in you."

"Yes, she has a certain amount of trust in me."

"And you tried to—"

"No, no, I did not. No. I flirted with her, but as soon as she became upset, I listened. But she was cryptic. She talked about Centurions and Avalon. I didn't understand much of it, to be quite honest with you. Roman references; I wasn't sure what to make of it, but she seemed full of conviction. I was somewhat concerned about her state of mind, if I'm honest. Her mother has a nervous disposition, and it is understandable to consider that Philomena may have inherited that condition from her."

"Did she mention any names?"

"Not that I can recall. But I did get the impression that there was a man involved."

"What gave you that impression?"

"I couldn't tell you one thing, or anything in particular that she said. Just that I felt it to be true."

"Because you know her."

"Yes! Yes, of course."

"But she didn't give you any names or details."

"No, it wasn't that kind of conversation. She's playful, Philomena, she makes everything sound like she doesn't really mean it, if that makes sense. It can be dreadfully difficult to tell when she's being sincere. That might sound tiresome, but in reality it is very exciting, when you combine it with her beauty."

"Her parents. They have a strained relationship?"

"Oh, she and her mother are close, I would say. They present a united front in the face of Naessens, at any rate."

"She's afraid of him?"

"Philomena? Oh, she's hardly afraid of anyone. She may well be wary of what he could potentially do to her, I suppose."

"What could he do to her?"

Rich shrugged. "Well, as I've already said, he's not a man you'd want to defy. He has a tendency to get his own way. By any means he can. You've met the man?"

"I have."

"Ah but I'd say he was all charm with you, wasn't he? He has the gift of the gab, a fair amount anyway, when he needs to. But he'll use a hammer when a key won't do."

"Could she have been deliberately baiting him? Seeing people she knew he'd disapprove of?"

"That would be the kind of thing Philomena would do, alright. She likes pushing a joke as far as she can. You'd just be worried that she mightn't judge exactly how much tolerance he'd have for that."

"He's her father."

"Aye, and she knows him only as her father. She doesn't really know what he's like outside their house. What he's capable of."

"What is he capable of?"

"All I've heard are stories, and I can't be repeating stories to you now, Mr. Conlon. You'll have to find them out for yourself. You seem...capable. I'm sure people will be more than willing to confirm whether they're true, or false."

Conlon nodded. "Fair enough. One more question: would she run away from home? Does that sound like the kind of thing she might do?"

He shrugged and then rubbed his chin. "My first instinct is to say no, because she is a spoiled little rich girl, basically, and I doubt she'd know what to do if she found herself out in in the world where..."

He gestured towards Conlon, who finished his sentence. "Where I live?"

Rich nodded. "Yes. Obviously, no offence intended. But she's from a different Dublin to the one you know."

"No offence taken. And you're exactly right."

"But then I think about her, and what she is actually like underneath all that, and she's got a will of iron,

Philomena. She absolutely could do it. She absolutely could."

"What would it take to persuade her, though? It'd still be a big step."

"Well now. Someone or something incredibly persuasive, I'd say."

6

21 Hours After Purification

ALTHOUGH IT WAS TEMPTING FOR NORMAN TO COME WITH him, only Val led the hunting party after the Naessens girl and the serf who had taken her.

Val was the better tracker of the Hastings twins. It was him who had loved their incursions into no man's land and behind enemy lines in the trenches when they fought together for His Majesties Army in the Great War. It was him who pushed for a career doing what they did so well: killing. They peddled their wares as assassins for a time, and settled for employment as mercenaries when that had proven more realistic. It was him who had a nose for the hunt, a love for the chase.

And so in the immediate aftermath—the explosion, the confusion, the violence—at the Purification cere-mony, Val had rapidly dispatched a group to track them down, unsure of what he was dealing with. The island was chaos, and he needed to help settle it down, along-side his brother. They quickly made sure Caesar was

safe and had men and guns around him, and then Val
had sent a group.

He had instantly settled on Dodson as the leader.
Dodson was reliable, sensible and respected by the
men. He was a good tracker—not as good as Val, but
good enough. He had been in the War, as they all had,
but it sat alright with him. He had not been affected, not
really. He had a relaxed, quiet way, but Val trusted him.

So to come across him and his entire group dead on
a hillside was quite an unpleasant surprise.

For a moment Val stood in shock. The men with him
—six of them in total, all dedicated, if not quite up to
snuff in terms of their soldiering—stood around behind
him, watching him for a cue. How were they supposed
to feel about this? This was completely unprecedented
in their experience on the island. They were accustomed to the absolute authority of the Centurions. The
only violence on the island was the violence they
inflicted; in punishment beatings or at the purification
ceremonies.

Today they had seen a serf rip their society apart.
Through violence, through quite shattering violence.
And so they had been watching Val all the way from the
island on the boat, and again once they came ashore
and found traces of a gunfight near the beach. He had
crouched and parsed signs and found casings amid the
broken twigs and scuffed footprints. The serf had
ambushed Dodson's group here, and somehow pinned
them down.

They searched a while and found a body—one of
the Centurions Dodson had taken. Val didn't remember
his name, but the others did, and though they kept their
shock in check, still he could sense it. The man had a

bullet hole in his forehead. This serf was a soldier, he could shoot. One of them said he'd been one of the serfs they'd allowed to hunt—ranging the island with a rifle. That would explain how he had managed to arrange certain things.

The men around him were not only shocked, they were frightened. Val remained calm and acted as if it were all part of the plan. The way the officers had acted in the War, even when hell itself seemed to have opened up beneath their feet. Their disquiet ebbed and faded in the face of his equanimity, his lack of emotion or surprise. This was the job, is what his attitude and actions told them.

This though; all of the others dead—this was much worse. Dodson himself had been executed. That was all Val could work out about the scene. The other signs made no sense to him.

"How could one man do this? He must have help," one of the men whined.

Another voice: "Didn't you see him at the ceremony? He tore through three men; he was like an animal."

"I saw. I saw. He's trained. He's trained."

"Shut up," Val growled. "I need to think."

"But we need to go back for more men!"

"We need to calm down, boys. He's one man who's obviously ambushed them."

"How? From where? If he was in the trees, he was below them! It's fucking impossible!"

"Who is this bloke, Hastings? Who's that girl? Why has he taken her?"

Val shook his head, dismissing them. He walked the ground and tried to reason it out. But it made no sense. *Could I have done it?* he asked himself. *Could I have taken all these men out? If I was fighting for my life, I could.* And he had the girl with him. If he'd given her a gun...

"Right. You men, this is a warning for us, isn't it? Just because we've got the numerical advantage, that doesn't really give us any real advantage over this man. He's evidently quite clever, and he can fight, but he doesn't like to fight fair. So we have to be clever, too. And careful. He has the girl in his possession, and we have to assume she has taken his side. So...recovering her alive is no longer a priority. If we can manage to achieve that, then it will be a rare accomplishment. We can take her back for her purification. But if we cannot, and she were to catch a bullet..." He shrugged. "Well, that would also be acceptable."

He was no longer even aware that he was adopting a pose when he spoke like this. He had always disdained officers, as had Norman. But they were good soldiers. They did as they were told, and they were given the chance to kill a lot of Germans. But in private, they mocked the upper-class twits trying their best to lead men from the slums of the north and the docks of East London, like the Hastings twins. They had laughed at them with their poems, written in dug outs; with their braying laughter when among their own kind; their pencil moustaches and their rugby.

But now, when he needed to project authority, what did Val do? He impersonated a bloody officer. He even put on an accent. He used words he would never ever use at any other time. Norman had noticed, and mercilessly chided him about it. But it worked. The men—all soldiers, too, all accustomed to listening to their betters, and doing what they were told—stood straighter, did their jobs more attentively.

And he knew now he would need that. He had to stop this soldier man and the girl from getting off this island. They would be heading for the village on the far coast, to take a boat or arrange for passage. He had to either intercept them on the way or get there before they did.

The man was wounded, he thought, based on some of the testimonies from the people who were closest when he had fought his way out, and the girl would still be only semi-conscious at this stage. So he would be slowed down, despite this head start. Val could stop him. Val knew he must stop him.

And something more: he wanted blood. This man had pretended to be one of them—a common serf, for fuck's sake—and fooled them all. Val and Norman would have interviewed him, and Val's memory of that was hazy. He had thought the man was some Irish navvy, come to beg for work. He was angry at himself, but angrier at this man. And this man would die for that anger.

Val was going to kill him personally.

He set off, following the tracks into the woods. Behind him the men followed, fanning out.

7

9 Days Before Purification

HE ASKED HER IN THE QUIET FEW MOMENTS AFTER THEY had both finished, when she lay with her head upon his chest and her hand clasped softly in his, the way she liked to do, when their hearts were slowing, sweat drying, eyelids beginning to feel heavy. Pretending that they were a real couple.

She caught it instantly, and casually, without raising her head, she said, "Ah you always do this, Tommy. You can just ask me for information, you know. You don't have to ride me first. Don't do me any favors."

He laughed. She was one of the funniest people he knew, for all her many other flaws. No other woman had ever made him laugh as much as she did. She said that men were taught to be funny and that women were taught to laugh, but that she had gotten the lessons confused.

"I don't really see it that way," he said.

"No? You don't come here when you need to know

something, thinking that if we have some relations first, then I might be more inclined to cooperate with your enquiry?"

"Is that seriously what you think? I seem like I'm not enjoying myself, do I?"

"I'm aware that it's different for men."

"Not for me. I—we—"

"You give me a jagging."

He laughed. "I jag you because I want to."

"But you come here for information."

"No, I don't. But if I think of something I need to know while I'm here, am I meant to just not ask you for fear of offending you?"

"I'm not offended, Tommy. You've just given me a feeling precisely two other men have ever managed to give me in thirty-eight years, and both of them are dead, so you could ask me for anything at this point and I'd be inclined to give it to you. Just so you know."

"Molly. I come here because I enjoy your company. I enjoy our time together."

"So do I. You know that, I hope."

"I do." He thought he did, but she was a mystifyingly complex woman.

"How's Jordan taking it? Do you tell him I'm coming over?"

Jordan Devereux was Molly's husband, and the man who had first introduced Conlon to Dublin's criminal underworld, years before. He was a sort of advisor for Xavier, the boss who ran virtually the entire city in a complicated web of alliances and enmities with other gangs, the Fenians and the British Government. For years Conlon had believed in Jordan's prominence and importance, and then he had met Molly Devereux,

Jordan's wife, and the truth had been revealed. She was the advisor Xavier trusted. Jordan was her eyes and ears in the street, but Molly pulled the strings and made the decisions. She was a supreme politician and strategist and she seemed to know every secret in a city saturated in them.

But she was a woman, so in a world where the gun and violence was a necessary adjunct, it was best if most were unaware of her existence.

She and Conlon had met a few months previous, and despite the fact that she was culpable in dozens of murders, that she plotted and schemed and kept Xavier in his position of power—Xavier, the man who had ordered Conlon's death and ensured the death of the love of his life—there had been an immediate spark between them. Once his relationship with Theresa was over, he had found himself back here, and she had known what that meant as soon as she saw him. The sex they had was intense and prolonged, but today he had come mainly because he could not clear his head of Viv, the young actress from the day before, and Molly would help him do that. That, she needn't know.

"Jordan knows that when I tell him I need privacy, he's to ask no questions. We understand one another fairly well, after so many years. He has a girl in Crumlin, I believe. Maybe he's there, getting his end away."

"More likely he's in a pub, talking somebody's ear off."

She chuckled. "That is more likely."

She squeezed his hand, faintly, and he wondered at that moment what she was thinking, how this made her feel, why she liked it so much. This moment, not the sex itself. This intimacy.

"How did you end up with him?" he asked.

"Is that your question, then, Tommy? How did I meet my husband?"

"Why, do I only get to ask the one? Is there a quota now?"

She turned her head and kissed his chest, a little suck and nibble, just below his collarbone, then returned her face to its place against him.

"He was a Clerk then, Jordan. Quite dashing. All the girls wanted him. My first husband did business with his firm and we met at a dance. One of those dances rich people put on when they want to pretend they live in London. London fashions and London music. You wouldn't know we were in Ireland at all. He had a young lady on his arm, and my husband was already in poor health then, and Jordan danced with me on a few occasions that night. He was a perfect gentleman and a very good dancer. My husband said to me on the way home that he could make enquiries for me, if I was inclined."

"Enquiries?"

"He had terrible consumption. He died six weeks later. He wanted to make sure I'd be alright, after he was gone."

"Was he older than you?"

"Oh yes, very. A friend of my father's. Anyway, he did make enquiries. Jordan and I were married three months after my first husband's death. Both of my marriages have been marriages of convenience, Tommy. Business arrangements, really. My first husband left me some money, but I was still young, and needed a man beside me to navigate this city and its classes. That was Jordan."

"You didn't love him? Even then?"

"I love him as I loved my younger brother. With fondness and tenderness and condescension."

"So how did—I don't understand how that led you to where you are now?"

"Well...Jordan was my bridge to society and business. I needed that, in order to invest, to make my money work. I wanted...something. Power, maybe, influence, a way to make my voice heard. I didn't understand, then. I just wanted a purpose. I've not been blessed with the ability to bear a child, you see, Tommy, and that is all the world asks of most women. In a world run by men, for men, I knew I had something to say, and I needed to find a way to say it."

"Xavier?"

"Jordan hadn't quite understood the terms of our agreement. He only realized them after a month or so, when I rejected him. He took it terribly badly. He started to gamble, and drink, and whore. He lost quite a lot of money. My money."

"Ah. I see where this is going."

"Do you? I didn't, then. I overestimated how strong he is. A scared little boy, really."

"So you owed Xavier money."

"Some of his loan sharks, yes. You wouldn't know these gentlemen. They weren't cut out for their profession. So I found out who they worked for, and I went to see him."

"You just walked in?"

"I wore a nice dress. I can be extremely persuasive."

"Oh, I know."

"We got along famously. He saw my worth instantly, and then I proved it, over and over again."

"Through counsel?"

"Yes. Advice, strategy. I see things he doesn't, and he understands things I don't. It works very, very well, I must say. We complement one another. And the money is excellent."

"So there's your influence. On who lives and who dies?"

"Are you really one to lecture, Tommy? How many men have you killed? Fifty? A hundred?"

"I can't see most men just accepting this. Even Jordan."

"Jordan accepted he was lucky they hadn't killed him. And he likes all the drama. He likes the danger. It's like a big game to him. He knows I'll protect him. Still a scared little boy, you see."

"You must be lonely, Molly."

"Jordan and I are still companions."

"You know what I mean."

"I've had lovers. You're not the first. But men—men are reliable in that they always, always disappoint me. The only man in my life who has not is Xavier. He is exactly how he presents himself."

"I'm how I present myself," he said, stung.

"Yes, you are, so far. That's what worries me."

"Why would that worry you?"

"Because the first day we met, I thought to myself that one day you were going to kill us all and tear everything down. That's what you want, that's what you've always wanted. You want revenge, deep down, for what they did to you and who they took from you. If you don't do that, you'll be betraying yourself. And we both know it."

He didn't know what to say, so he pulled her towards his face and kissed her, long and hard. When she had returned to his chest, panting, she said, "But at the moment, you aren't even remotely disappointing, Tommy."

They were quiet then, for a while. She had never revealed so much to him before, and it made him see her in a slightly different light. Knowing her, that was partly why she had said so much, and she had a reason for that, one that he would not learn for a long time, if ever.

But then he did catch the odd flash of emotion from her. She cared for him, in some way. They had something, a connection, and he could feel that it affected her judgement around him.

As for him, he enjoyed sleeping with her. She was pretty and passionate and experienced, and being with her—even lying with her like this, now—made him feel good. Not many women ever had been able to do that. Theresa had not. It was not like Orla, of course. He had felt alone all his life, except when he had Orla at his side, and he knew that he would never find that again in this life. But he had to find something else.

She was something else, for now at least. But he knew that she was right. Always, in the back of his mind was the awareness that the man who had killed Orla—Xavier—was still living. And that someday he would kill him. He was patient, yes. He was waiting. But some day he would kill him. And her? She had been involved, too. As an advisor, had it been her advice to send those three gunmen after them?

The thought had occurred to him that she was sleeping with him out of some sort of survival instinct, that she knew how things would go once he ran out of patience, and she wanted his favor.

Her breathing was deep and even. He assumed she was asleep until she said, "So, what did you want to know? It wasn't a history of my marriage, that's for sure."

"Well I wouldn't be so sure, now Molly. Knowledge is power, I think you said to me."

"That does sound like something I'd say, alright."

They were quiet. She sighed loudly to indicate that she didn't like this game. He chuckled.

"You're trying to get on my nerves, are you?" she said.

"I am. A little bit."

"Alright so. It's always a person with you, usually a man who's involved in one of your cases. Am I right, so far?"

"You are."

"Is it a client or a culprit we'd be discussing?"

"A client."

"Ahhh that's harder. That could be anybody, Tommy."

"An Edmund Naessens? Is he anybody?"

"Would that be Lord Naessens?"

"I believe so."

"Is it the wife or the daughter you're after?"

"The daughter."

She was silent, and he knew this meant she was thinking, deciding what to tell him.

"So you know him. Does that mean he's—"

"He's a businessman. He doesn't have scruples about where or who his money comes from. That's all it means. The money comes from the wife's side, I've heard, but that's just whispers. He manages it all."

"What sort of business?"

"Well. His money is everywhere, but his company is in shipping, isn't it?"

"Smuggling."

"I'd say he's alright. Not in the life at all. But his friends are a different story. Colorful fellas."

"A bit more detail than that might actually save my life at some point, Molly."

"Well. He likes to invest. No risk for him, but huge rewards."

"What does he invest in?"

"I don't know everything. I'd say he has middlemen for that, but I do know he owns a few brothels in the Monto so he'd take some of the cut from those girls. Smuggling in guns is a given these days, but probably a lot of other things, too. There was talk of him doing business with some ex-army boys, but I only half remember the details."

"For muscle?"

"Sure what else are you old soldiers good for?"

"You seem to find a use for me."

"I've always been creative that way. I doubt he has any say in where the opium goes or how it gets brought into the city. Some of his friends are from that side of things. It seems to attract young head-the-balls—you know the type. Always wanting to leave their mark, and they do it with a knife, or a gun. He has a few of them on the payroll."

"My kind of people."

"And now that I think of it, there was some mention of his associates and dirty pictures."

"Making them?"

"I'm not sure. Down in the Monto you can buy pictures of girls doing anything you can think of. Dirty films now, too, if you can afford them. There's probably good money in that. And if people with money know one thing, it's how to make it into more money."

"Not a bad thing to know."

She was quiet. "So the daughter is missing, you say?"

"She is. You know her?"

"No. I met her at a party when she was a young girl. Very confident, I'd say. Impressed with herself, but sharp enough that you'd understand why. Her mother is an icy ol' bitch."

"It was an odd house altogether."

"Has she run off, then? Could you blame her?"

"I don't know yet. I have a funny feeling about it."

"And do you trust your funny feelings, Tommy?"

"Most of the time. Instinct, the Major used to say, is the body's way of alerting us to something our consciousness hasn't yet processed. Always trust your gut, basically."

"Well, I agree with your Major. Now, have I been helpful, Tommy? Did you get what you came for?"

She had shifted around and gently took him in hand, pushing herself up with her elbow on his chest, fingers circling in the hair over his nipple, her legs spreading around his hips. She smiled at him. He smiled back.

"Not quite yet, Molly."

"Good boy. That's the right answer."

———

DUBLIN HAD TWO BIG UNIVERSITIES, both south of the Liffey. Trinity College dominated the eastern end of College Green, and was one of the cities keystones. It served the protestant population, while University College Dublin, set at one corner of Stephens Green, less than half a mile away, served Catholics. Around these two institutions, several smaller colleges existed.

When he left Molly in bed, Conlon made his way to York Street, at the opposite corner of Stephens Green from University College, and enquired with the porter of the Royal College of Surgeons as to the whereabouts of the library. The man gave him some directions and Conlon found himself squeezing through corridors around medical students and passing classroom doors through which loud voices echoed their serious teachings in rich baritones.

He was looking for a friend of Philomena's from childhood; one Margaret Kendrick, daughter of a bank manager, and studying to be a doctor. When Conlon had placed a phone call to her house, the voice who had answered told him that she would likely be in the library, that this was where she spent all of her free time these days, and if not there, in a lecture somewhere, classes only having resumed a week or two before.

The library was in a large space but felt cramped due to the shelves of books dominating most of it. They towered in long, dark rows all across the center of the room, and the amount of lamps and windows and the skylights all fought against the looming shadows and shade they threw.

There were tables and desks scattered around the room wherever there was space: a line of them against the wall near the door; a cleared area between the shelves where four big desks sat, with a couple of students whispering over textbooks, paper and fountain pens, and a few other desks in nooks and corners.

He found Margaret Kendrick at one such desk. She was wearing a headscarf tied across the back half of her skull, with her fringe tucked under one edge, and smoking a cigarette as she bent over a manuscript. She was as extravagantly red-haired as anybody he had ever seen, with eyes of frighteningly clear blue. She didn't seem surprised to see him, merely raising an eyebrow calmly as he explained who he was and what he wanted.

She suggested he pull a stool over from nearby—it was one of those stools with steps they climb to access the highest shelves in a library, and after its tortured screeching upon the wooden floor turned every head their way and elicited a symphony of tuts, finally he perched on the edge of it as they talked.

She remained unperturbed throughout, and he realized that the raised eyebrow was a permanent thing.

"She'll be gone with that odd church she was involved with," was the first thing she said, when he was beside her.

"What can you tell me about them?"

"I was with her, the night she first met them."

"And how did that happen?"

"We used to meet up every few weeks, because we'd been friends since we were little girls. It's easy to allow those friendships to just slip away as you get older and life pulls you in different directions from one another, but we both felt it was important to stay friends and be aware of one another's lives."

"That sounds nice."

"It was nice. It is nice. She's never any less than entertaining company, Philomena. Both her monologues about her own experiences and her animated responses to episodes from my life are always genuinely hysterical. She's one of those rare people: it's extremely difficult to dislike her, I think."

"So why was this night different?"

"We were in Maisies, which is where we always find ourselves after we've had dinner somewhere swankier and have exhausted most of our funds. It's not a first choice sort of establishment."

"I've been," he agreed.

"There are often groups there, or meetings. Political parties, debating clubs, generally an excess of students and their excitement. It can be quite boisterous. That night there was a small group in a corner. Philomena was flirting with one of the young men in the group."

"Talking to him?"

"Not at that point, no, they were located on the far side of the room. But I could see her smiling over my shoulder at him."

"Was he smiling back?"

She made a gesture like an attempt at a shrug, with less intensity. "The eyes in the back of my head weren't working that night."

Conlon laughed at that, and for the first time, this made her smile.

He said, "If she carried on doing it, that probably means that he was doing it, too."

She nodded. "Men smile at Philomena. Being her friend, one becomes accustomed to feeling invisible."

"But she did get to chatting with this gentleman."

"Of course. The whole group dispersed themselves throughout the room and distributed little leaflets about their church."

"You didn't keep one by any chance?"

"No, they came and retrieved them, having given us ample time to read their gospel."

"And what did it say?"

"They call themselves the Centurions of Light." They both laughed then, and she continued through a chuckle. "There was an odd collision of various belief systems and mythologies included, but only in the vaguest possible terms. Roman words and Arthurian legend combined, but it was also incredibly tedious. I can't properly recollect any details, chiefly due to the fact that I was unable to read after the first few sentences."

"But not Philomena?"

"Oh no, she was the same. We laughed about it. She was just as cynical as I."

"So what happened?"

"Well...our smiling young man approached us."

"Oh. Can you remember anything about him?"

"His name was Alan. Alan Rogers."

Conlon had the photograph before her on the desk in seconds. "Is this him?"

She nodded. "That's him. Where did you get this?"

"Philomena's room. Did she mention she'd been seeing him?"

"Not directly. When I left that night, she stayed on there, talking to him. And when I saw her next, she mentioned that she'd been to a few of their meetings."

"What did you say to that?"

"I wasn't kind, Mr. Conlon, I'll be quite honest with you."

He nodded. "I'm sure she expected no less."

"She brushed it aside and we didn't really speak of it again, but after that she was a bit more circumspect with me. She wasn't as candid or as revealing, and I knew it must be down to her seeing this Alan, and becoming more drawn into their church."

"So she didn't give you any details?"

"Only in snippets, and many of those slipped out without her even realizing."

"Such as?"

"They have a place—a pilgrimage they make, a Holy place, I suppose. She mentioned that. I think—I think she was really infatuated with him. Not many men do that to Philomena. I can't imagine that the religious aspect affected her as much, but I suppose you never know. She talked about this chanting they did at meetings and how she enjoyed that, it made her emotional. That was not the sort of thing I was used to hearing from her."

"When did you last see her?"

"Oh weeks now. She didn't provide any indication that she was preparing to abscond, however. She seemed happy. Perhaps going to find her is not the correct decision, Mr. Conlon."

"Perhaps, Miss Kendrick. But it's my job."

"But surely you have a choice in your situation—which clients to accept, and which to deny?"

"To some degree. When I find Miss Naessens and determine that she's safe and where she wants to be, then I'll make my choice."

"So am I to understand that the Lord and Lady Naessens have engaged you because they are upset she left no record of her intended whereabouts?"

"That isn't inaccurate."

She shook her head. "It's a great wonder that

Philomena turned out as well as she did, given the monstrosity of a home she grew up in."

"Pardon me for suggesting you might be wrong, but, aside from parental neglect or maybe a bit of a strong hand from her father, what exactly was monstrous about it?"

She nodded, as if rebuked. "I understand that someone with your background might regard anybody who was brought up in the manner of myself or Philomena as having been raised in the very lap of luxury, Mr. Conlon, but there are cruelties in a household that you cannot always see, no matter how fine the ornaments are."

"Oh, I appreciate that, Miss Kendrick. That wasn't what I meant. I meant: can you tell me why she might find her family home monstrous? Is there anything specific you know about her life there?"

"Her father is a cruel man. An old-fashioned man. If you sat at the table at one of their dinners and listened to them talk, you might think it was 1885. He might be aware that there is a change coming to this country, but he cannot quite believe it. And he sees Philomena as his property. She will marry someone chosen for her. She will abandon her silly plans to be an actress at a time of his choosing. She will provide him with a grandson. You understand, Mr. Conlon? He didn't beat her, or imprison her. Not that I know of, at any rate. She lived a life that most of the unfortunate population of this city would consider to be opulent in its luxury. And yet she was his prisoner in another way. Her freedom was an illusion and dependent upon his goodwill. And with a spirit as willful as Philomena's, that was always going to end with her escaping, somehow. Although...he does have a hold on her, beyond his money and controlling manner."

"What about her mother?"

"Her mother is different. Their relationship is complex."

"I'm not sure what that means, Miss Kendrick."

Their eyes met. "Her mother is a sot. Her mother was addicted to opium. She is a troubled woman, Mr. Conlon. I believe Philomena had remained there as long as she had out of a sense of duty to her. And whatever strange bond she has with him."

Conlon rubbed at his face. "So. You think that she is better off away from her father, but you're not too sure about these Centurions of the Light. If we assume that she is with them."

She nodded. "I'm sorry. You might have a difficult choice to make this time, Mr. Conlon."

He stood. "Thank you very much for your help. And I don't believe in difficult choices, Miss Kendrick. Every decision, deep down, in your gut, you always know what you want to do. It's just a matter of being brave enough to do it."

"But what if what you want to do is not the right thing?"

"Why wouldn't it be the right thing? Obliged to you, Miss. Bye now."

And he was gone.

8

25 Hours After Purification

IT HAD BEEN RAINING FOR TWENTY MINUTES WHEN Conlon saw the village ahead. They had made it to a point perhaps some ten minutes before that where the sea was visible, off to the south, and Conlon knew that all he had to do was keep it to his right and they'd come upon the town and the harbor and a way back to Ireland.

The morning light had become flat and dull, and instead of clouds rolling in off the Atlantic, it was as if something had infected the sky. Its color slowly greyed until it fairly buzzed with malignancy. There had been goats grazing on the hillsides all along their trek, but they had abruptly disappeared, as though they had been an illusion, and the landscape seemed deserted.

When the rain came, it started off soft; a fine spray that was almost pleasant. Abruptly it was hard and streaking through the air. They ran for shelter and huddled under the bent husk of a dead old tree by a ruined stone wall. The tree was twisted as if in agony, its surface a blackened tobacco dark. That meant that they could just about shelter from the worst of this ferocious downpour if they squeezed close together.

"This isn't how I expected this to go," Philomena muttered and they shared a look and both laughed.

"We'll be in the village in a few minutes. We'll get a boat and be back on the mainland today."

"And what then? You drop me back at my daddy's door?"

"I'm still working it out."

"Well, please, do inform me whenever you reach a decision."

"I won't do anything that might put you in harm's way."

She looked at the rain, and spoke quietly. "You must deliver runaways home all the time. Ones who don't want to be delivered. What could possibly make me different?"

"Most runaways don't have an armed group of pagans wanting to purify them."

"They don't?"

They laughed again.

The rain intensified, falling with a spiteful sting so that they could barely see beyond thirty feet. The air filled with it. They watched the ground they had been walking become saturated in a moment, until it was coursing down towards the town like a stream. It reached the point when it seemed as if the island had absorbed so much of it—like a great sponge—that all it could do was bounce off and away, and soon they might be submerged.

Their tree shelter became more or less useless, the

water seeming to attack from all directions. They huddled together and hunkered closer to the wood and the ground, heads down, faces tight against the continual, angry spray. The tattoo it made on the tree's husk was constant and thunderous. And then, abruptly, it was over.

The sky cleared briskly and the silence that replaced the tumult seemed eternal and ringing. They looked at one another and rose, shaking water from their hair. Conlon's clothes felt wet through in places. Philomena's grimace suggested she was similarly afflicted.

The earth was sodden, squelching beneath each step. He saw a goat only fifty feet away, intent on the grass.

She put on a thick country accent and said, "Sure it's a grand soft day."

He laughed at that. She was an actress, he recalled.

"We're nearly there," he said. "One last push."

They made their way down the slope and she slipped and cried out, sitting upright in the grass and cradling her tummy. He rushed to her.

"Are you—?"

She was breathing in huffed blasts through pursed lips, face creased with pain. "Just—I'll be fine in a moment."

He watched her, feeling helpless, stupid. There was something familiar in the way she held herself.

Her breathing slowed and she raised her eyes to meet his. He said nothing but raised his eyebrows in enquiry.

She said, "I'm with child."

He nodded, his face blank, but his thoughts whirling.

"Do they know?"

"I don't think so. They never—took me, the way they did with the other girls. It would have been obvious then."

"Do your parents know?"

"I haven't told them. I haven't even told the father." She laughed. "You're the first person I've told."

"Well, congratulations."

"Thank you."

"How many months?"

"I'm not sure. Eight, perhaps? I'm lucky I'm not showing more."

"We need to get you out of here."

She nodded, and he helped her up. And choosing his footing carefully, he led her down the hill towards the houses somewhere below.

9

8 Days Before Purification

THE STREETS WERE BUSY AT THIS TIME OF THE EVENING; there were the ragged lines of people waiting for trams, bicycles weaving around the crowds crossing Westmoreland Street, horse-drawn carts rumbling along beside motorcars, boys selling tobacco and newspapers, their voices harsh, nasal screeches over the general tumult. People wearing masks across their noses and mouths to ward off the Spanish flu were scattered throughout, an unremarkable sight in the city still adjusting itself to this plague, just as it appeared to be dying away.

Shadows were just beginning to be drawn longer on the cobbles, but he arrived at Trinity and stood in the warmth of the gentle evening sun, the brim of his cap shielding his eyes so that he could watch the streams of people passing, stopping, chatting.

Viv was late. She arrived in a hurry, a line of perspiration visible on her forehead beneath her hat. He felt struck properly for the first time by her beauty as she walked towards him, the jangle of light in her wide eyes, the way her mouth was upturned at the corners slyly.

"Well hello, Mr. Conlon."

"Hello, Miss Logue. You'd know you were an actress, with your penchant for a dramatic entrance."

"I'm sorry. There was an accident and they blocked off half of Sackville Street."

She was adjusting her skirt, subtly tugging here and there at her coat, tipping a strand of hair away from her face, and this made him worry about his appearance, too—that he hadn't made enough effort, or worse, too much.

"Don't worry, I was enjoying the evening sun," is what he said, all this whirling in his brain.

"It is a fine evening, isn't it? What shall we do with ourselves while you interrogate me?"

"How about a stroll down the canal?"

"I love the canal."

"As any sane Dubliner does."

"Is that some complicated way of informing me that you don't, then, Tommy?"

"I love the canal in the right company."

"The canal it is."

He offered her his arm with a theatrical little bow, she accepted it with a mock-curtsy, and they were off.

They chatted in a general way as they walked. He realized after a while that she was subtly interrogating him—trying to find out about him, without it ever becoming overbearing. In return he asked her about herself, paid attention and showed her that he was doing so with his comments. This was how normal relationships worked, he knew. And the awareness slid like a serpent into his brain: he was no good for any kind of normal relationship, now. He would have to find a way to let this be known to her, when the time was right, before it was too late.

For now, it was good enough to be happy in her company; to hear her laugh and watch her face light up when she smiled, to smell her and enjoy the clever, acute way her mind worked, to feel her eyes on him and know that she was feeling something similar. He had felt nothing like this in years, really.

At the canal they walked for a short while, then sat on an available bench, ducks circling in the water, dappled with the evening sunlight through the trees below.

"So, do we compare notes?" she asked.

"What, are you my partner now? I suppose you'll be expecting a fee now and all?"

"Well, you are aware that thespians are a chronically underpaid profession..."

"It needs to be the real good stuff, in that case. What have you learned, then...?"

"It's not that I've learned anything. It's what I've arranged. We're invited to a meeting, the evening after tomorrow."

"We?"

"Well, I'll need to introduce you. The problem is that they know me, these people—"

"The Centurions?"

"Yes. Sure they've seen me in the pubs and cafés they frequent over the last few months. I've mixed with them and I've made fun of their silly beliefs to their faces and I've persuaded friends to abandon any early interest in it all. They know who I am."

"You'd be hard to forget, that's for sure."

She let a sly smile form for that and went on, "So it was easy enough to approach one of them and then the rest was an improvisation."

"What did you say...?"

"Well, I fell back upon what I know. I gave you a role. I made up a story and invented a character for you."

He made a face but he was unsure of exactly how it looked or what exactly it communicated to her.

She laughed, and put her hand on his. "Don't worry. All you'll have to do is look like you have a terrible temper and act as if anybody speaking to you is liable to make you explode. I'm sure you'll manage that."

He nodded. "In the War I had to pretend to be French more than once. And pretend to be German once."

Her eyebrows arched with surprise. "How did you manage that?"

He shrugged. "I didn't do much, to be honest. Kept my mouth shut, mainly."

"Well, that'll probably work with this. Why would you have to pretend to be French? You were a soldier, weren't you?"

"I was, but I was in a special unit. We had to do some funny jobs."

Her eyes on him, probing, weighing up. She nodded. "Anyway. It seems that they have this island."

He nodded. "I've heard they make some pilgrimage."

"I'm not sure where it is, but they go by Belfast, so I'd be willing to wager it's off the Coast up North. They seem terribly keen to keep it a secret."

"How exactly did you find this out?"

"Well, I had a stroke of luck. When I got to Nelligans, one of my friends—Patricia, she was there the day we met—was sitting with one of their lads. He's been trying to chat her up for weeks and this time he caught her without any of us around to ward him off."

"So you saw your opportunity."

"I did. I acted all upset and teary and worried about my cousin Charlie. He's just back from the war and he's not himself, he keeps getting into scraps with strangers, and then a few weeks ago, he boxed the head off a Brit soldier outside the Brazen Head, and if they catch him he'll be in prison and *oh oh,* whatever am I going to do."

"And that worked?"

"You're forgetting what a talented actress I am, I suspect."

"How could I ever forget that? So he went for it?"

"He'd swallow a brick, that one. And once I had him on my side, it was easy. He told the story and all I had to do was give some details and answer their questions. One of them suggested the island. I was just following along at that point."

He chuckled. "You are a wonder."

"Thank you."

"So what do I have to do?"

"Well, they still want to meet you, and make sure you aren't some sort of lunatic, I suppose. This meeting Tuesday evening—somebody will interview you there, they said. So you might need to answer some questions."

"And if I get through that I go to this island?"

"I think so. Do you think Philomena's there?"

"On the island? At this point I do, yeah."

"What'll you do if you find her?"

"Get her out of there, I suppose."

"Just take her? Do you think they'll just allow you?"

He shrugged. "There aren't really any indications that they're anything but a peculiar little religious group at this point, are there?"

"No, no there aren't."

"But you have a feeling nevertheless."

She nodded.

"Tell me," he said.

"It's silly. I have nothing to base this feeling on, but they just seem off to me."

"Off?"

"Yeah, I know, I know, Tommy. But, it just feels always like there's things under the surface with them, like there are references in conversations and only they get them."

"That's—not—"

"I know it isn't. But trust me: it's based on nothing and on a thousand tiny little things. They aren't right."

"I agree with you. But in my world, I have to be suspicious. It gets so that it's hard to trust anyone. And then you wonder if you can trust how little you trust people—if it's just your cynicism that's the problem. My cynicism. It's a fair relief to hear that you feel it with these people, too."

"Why did you trust me?"

"Why says I did? Maybe I'm still deciding."

She laughed. "Do you think they're dangerous, though? Really?"

Shrugging, he said, "I don't know, Viv. This country at the moment—you never know who'd have a gun, do you? Who's involved in what or friends with who. An organization like this looks alright from outside: it looks like a load of ol' crackpots trying to start a religion and probably fleece people of their hard-earned money, to me. But all it takes is one of them to have a gun and ambitions to be Billy the Kid and things take on a different feeling."

"You'll be careful, though?"

She put her hand on his again, and left it there.

He shook his head. "No, I won't be careful. I'll be Charlie. Cousin Charlie."

He had changed his voice to a more guttural, yet absurd version of his own in order to say the name and she burst out laughing.

"Oh Lord bless us and save us," she said.

Maintaining the voice, he said, "Couldn't you have invented a more original character for me? Like the angry soldier, back from the trenches? Come on, Viv. You must have more imagination than that..."

"I'm sorry, I wasn't aware of your theatrical leanings."

Still laughing, still she rested her hand on his. He turned his over so that their palms were facing and took her hand in his. Their eyes met, he leaned towards her and they kissed. A long, slow kiss, and when they broke apart, both a little breathless, she said, "Haven't they been saying that people shouldn't kiss in public? It spreads the Black Flu."

"Have they? What do you suggest?"

"My house is only five minutes away."

He nodded. "So it is."

As she made to get up, he stopped her with a light squeeze to her fingers. She looked back at him, surprised, and he kissed her again.

"Charlie," she said, "This is not how cousins behave."

10

7 Days Before Purification

HE DIDN'T SPEND THE NIGHT. AWARE THAT THE COUPLE with whom she shared the house would be back soon, he left after a couple of hours. They had not slept together. They had kissed a lot more and he had held her, but mainly they had talked. It seemed that an unspoken agreement had passed between them to take things slowly, to be careful with whatever they were both recognizing was already forming between them.

He hadn't felt quite so happy for a long time; being with her had made him feel good in a way too few things in his life did. He was with her, not wishing he was elsewhere, not thinking about anyone or anything else; just happy to be with her. He was old enough to see that this was a rare thing in life, and for all that he foresaw problems down the road—for life had also taught him that everything good had to end—he was determined to take his time and try to enjoy it for now.

He returned to his flat, and slept deeply and dreamlessly for what felt like the first time in a long time.

He woke late the next morning, which was not like him, and went down to the local grocers, where he purchased some eggs, bread and bacon. He felt unusually cheerful, and chatted to the girl who served him. He had to stop himself from whistling. He bought a newspaper from the tobacconists on the corner, and read the headlines and some of the front page on the walk back to the flat. The War, the Spanish flu, London politics, Fenian gatherings and arrests—it felt like the news had been static for months, the world circling the same issues and problems it had been for as long as he could remember.

He cooked himself the rashers, scrambled the eggs and had them on toast so heavily buttered it looked golden in the light of the afternoon sun when he ate it by the window. He was reading the paper still, but his mind was turning over the case now, questions surfacing, details and angles he felt he needed to check and confirm.

He finished the paper—again, something he did only rarely—and went back out into one of those Dublin days when the sky is a light grey and the heat turns the air torpid and yellowing. He flagged a cab, passing in a clatter of hoof on stone and creaking steel on wood. He observed it as it slowed and waited for him. The horse was sweating in the heat, droplets running in streams down onto the cobbles beneath it, the driver squinting around at him as he approached and nodding when he told him where he wanted to go.

Conlon climbed into the back and settled in, watching the city fade away through the sway and jerk of the cab as they followed the Liffey, then the old road out into the green. Hooves on the road had a hypnotic, blurring rhythm which made him sleepy, his hands idly playing with his cap as his eyes tracked sky and tree line, distant hills and the odd lone cloud. The grey bled into a light blue out here, the smoke and smog of Dublin's chimneys far away.

He was thinking of Viv, and of course it happened; Orla slipping into his thoughts like a knife, comparisons unfolding unbidden and unwelcome, the familiar ache at the thought of her face, a few memories of a rapture that now felt like a dream: their first kiss, the first time she said she loved him, the sight of her across a room with their love a secret known only to them, her body in his arms, the moment she stepped between him and a killer, the sight of her falling, falling away from him.

Viv deserved better than this competition, and so he resolved to ignore it. Often he luxuriated in his doomy memories of Orla—the keenness of the pain they brought him was a reminder of how real their love had been. But not now. Not today, with Viv's scent still in his nostrils, her voice in his head. He just wanted to savor all that a little longer, before Orla and her imprint on him weighed in.

He led his thoughts away, and to the Centurions of the Light. He had known soldiers in the War with interesting religious beliefs. A Canadian Instructor in the Major's Squad had been a Mormon. Conlon had only read about this religion before that, and the instructor, who taught them tracking, knife-fighting and survival skills, had been enthusiastic and honest in his descriptions of the founding and beliefs of his faith.

But to Conlon, raised a Catholic in a society where the Church was a strong, sometimes terrifying, daily presence; and the Church of Ireland was a distant, oppressive organization suitable only for the wealthy, hearing of another religion had been a wonderful novelty, even if his brainwashed heart struggled to take any of it seriously.

Not that he believed in anything anymore. His Catholicism had slipped further away with every single dead body he had seen, every grim mission he had carried out, every perversion and cruelty his business had led him to. He understood that for many men, a few weeks in the trenches meant that they were forced to embrace God, for the alternative was a belief that the carnage was a gruesome act of chance. So they believed because otherwise they knew that the path led inexorably in a spiral towards suicide.

But for Conlon it was the opposite. No God would allow the Somme. No God could permit Gallipoli. They were manmade catastrophes of cruelty and disregard, and he held that belief to his chest throughout the war.

And still these Centurions sounded different. They sounded inescapably like a con man's act, like an invention. Not only that; they sounded like the trick a wealthy man might play on the poor. Capitalize on the ignorance of the uneducated. Exploit the passion and the need for a cause of the young and earnest. Give the desperate some hope. And there was a part of him that couldn't help but want to burn all that to the ground.

But then there was Naessens. Naessens and what Miss Kendrick had told him. And so he was returning today for more. To see how Naessens responded to an unexpected visit. To see if he reacted differently if Conlon pushed him a bit.

The carriage was turning into the long driveway of

the Naessens land. Conlon observed a gardener working on the lawn through the trees.

When they got to the house, he paid the cab driver before he climbed down. The driver squinted at him and asked, "Do you want me to wait, boss? It's a fair ol' walk back."

"Nah, I'll find me way. Thanks anyway."

The horses were already turning, straining to be away, when Martin appeared at the door atop the steps. "Mr. Conlon. You aren't expected, sir."

"No, I'm not. Is your man in?"

"He isn't, no. Off on business somewhere, sir. We're not expecting him back for a week at least."

"Mrs. Naessens?"

"She is here, yes, sir."

"Tell her I have a few questions, Martin, please."

The butler frowned, but agreed, and opened the door for Conlon. "Wait here, please, sir."

Conlon agreed and admired the paintings in the hall while he waited.

Martin returned after a few minutes. "My lady will see you, sir. Please come this way."

Lady Naessens was smashed. She was lounging on a setee, a half empty bottle on a side table, a tumbler sloshing in her hand.

"Ah, it is you. I almost didn't believe Martin. Why would you want to come back here? Silly man."

"I had hoped to speak with your husband."

"Business, Mr. Detective Man, business. It's always business."

"You mean he's away on business?"

"I do mean that, yes. But also that for an instant, I might have hoped that you had returned to see me. Men used to queue up to see me, Mr. Conlon, would you believe that?"

He nodded. "I absolutely would believe that."

"Ooooooh, you charmer. A diamond in the rough. My daughter likes a man like you, with an accent from the slums. A rough man. But no. Here on business. Looking very serious. You have questions."

He sat on one of the chairs nearby as she sloppily filled her glass and, with a pained grimace, took a mouthful.

"I don't think I have any questions for you, Mrs. Naessens."

"You must be suspicious. That's why you've come back—because something has made you suspicious. You think he knows something? Do you? What could he know? Could he? Does he?"

"I just need more information."

"Noooooo, I can tell, Mr. Detective Conlon. They didn't get along. She wasn't what he'd hoped for. Is that what you want to hear?"

Conlon just watched her.

She went on, "He wanted a son and an heir and someone he could take hunting with his boarding school chums, and instead I provided him with a head-strong girl who hated him. No wonder he hasn't shared my bed in years, is it, Mr. Conlon?"

"She hated him?"

"Oh they fought like cat and dog. Screaming matches. If she couldn't be a son, then he was deter-mined that she could at least marry him one, but she rejected every respectable, eligible young man we presented before her. She'd rather lie with the unwashed radicals in her cafés."

Conlon laughed at that, and she caught it. "You see? I was a young woman of wit and charm."

"You still are."

"Oh, my youth has vanished with Queen Victoria. Once you have a child, your youth is gone. You can be a girl no more, Mr. Conlon."

"Could she have left just to get at him?"

"Oh, certainly. Certainly, that would not be beyond her. Headstrong girl. But also, Mr. Conlon: she loves her daddy. She always has." She finished her drink and held out the tumbler in a wavering, uncertain hand, expecting Conlon to pour for her.

He just looked at her.

She gave a visible start when she realized. "I do believe you are trying to shame me, Mr. Conlon."

"Not at all. But I'm not your servant."

"So you don't care if I drink myself into an early grave?"

"You're upset. This is natural."

"For all you know, this is my daily routine..."

"Is it?"

"Not entirely. Once a week or so. When it all gets too much."

"What gets too much?"

"Business. Tension. Loneliness. The loss of one's dreams."

"I'm sorry," he said.

She nodded, pouring, spilling some.

He rose. He was learning nothing here beyond what he had already partially known. This was an unhappy house; a troubled family, like so many families. The girl may have fled because of that, or she may not.

"Thank you for your hospitality."

"You're leaving? But you have just arrived, Mr. Conlon."

"I came to see Mr. Naessens. I'll come back another time."

"How—how is your investigation progressing?"

He saw her reluctance to be alone now, the sudden stark realization in her that she was drinking like this alone in her house, the fact that she could see herself suddenly, as he saw her. And he felt a swell of sympathy for this woman.

He sat down.

They had tea together.

She stopped drinking from the tumbler and asked Martin for a pot of tea, which she and Conlon shared. Their conversation had evolved into something very different. They spoke about her life in a big house in the Midlands before she met Naessens, memories of pastel days and sunlight over fields; her parents and their difficult marriage, a dinner table crackling with tension; her love of painting. She asked Conlon about the war, about boxing. Her questions showed that she was actually listening, so he enthusiastically played along and told her what it had been like, gave her an insight he rarely gave anyone. He even alluded to Orla.

He ate tea with her in their dining room, a chilly, formal space focused upon a dark, long table. Ridiculously, they sat together at one end, a maid carrying trays to them. The food was good: guinea fowl and parsnips with a rich gravy.

Their conversation went on: they were comparing his wartime impressions of France with her memories of trips there. She was witty and self-effacing, and quick to laugh.

When it came time to leave, she offered to telephone into town for a carriage to come and pick him up.

"Does your driver have the day off?"

"He has resigned, apparently. We haven't seen hide nor hair of him for a few days."

"I'll walk, then," he said.

"Oh, come now, it will take you over an hour!"

"I need to walk off that apple tart." He laughed.

He extended his hand, and when she offered her own, he kissed her knuckles. "You deserve to be happy, too. Thank you for a nice afternoon."

She nodded, her eyes surprised and wet. "Thank you, Mr. Conlon. I will be seeing you again?"

"Hopefully with good news, yes."

He moved down the steps into their drive. She stood in the doorway, watching him. The evening sun cast low, long shadows across his path.

"Mr. Conlon!" she called. He turned and squinted up at her. "Enjoy your walk!"

He laughed and turned away.

———

It took him an hour and a half before he passed Kingsbridge Station, the first villages beginning to string themselves into connected suburbs perhaps ten minutes before that. All of the walking put him in mind of trekking during the War, a three day long walk he and Dalton had been forced to make in Turkey, his basic training, the regularity and routine of army life.

He flagged down a carriage and asked to be taken towards Portobello, but when he arrived there and paid the driver, he had second thoughts. Though he felt desperate to see Viv again, he remembered how proud he had felt of the idea that they were being patient, that they were taking it slowly.

So he decided to head back home instead.

That meant that it was still relatively early when he found himself crossing back over the canal into town, the dusk still heavy with a storm that was sure to fall upon the city once night sank in. Removing his jacket and carrying it slung over his shoulder, he followed the canal north, passing courting couples and feeling that sentimental approval you can feel when you are part of such a union, the recognition of kinship.

There were plenty of people out; it was early still and Dubliners were enjoying the warmth of the evening. On Baggot Street he stopped in Everett Hotel and asked could he use their phone. The mustachioed gentleman behind the desk made a strained face as he agreed, and Conlon pushed some coins across the surface to pay for any inconvenience. The man pocketed them and turned away to his paperwork.

Conlon called Barry, but the girl on the exchange told him Detective Barry was out on a call.

"You wouldn't happen to know where exactly, now would you?" Conlon asked.

"I'm very sorry sir, I can't disclose that information."

Something in the way she said that jogged Conlon's memory. "Is that Joyce?"

"It is. Who am I talking to?"

"It's Tommy. Tommy Conlon."

Conlon had taken to dropping in to see Barry. The first time had been at Barry's request, to settle a bet with a colleague about one of Conlon's bouts, but the workings of the office had fascinated him, and he had returned a half dozen times since. The other detectives were by turns respectful and teasing, but he knew that Barry would have vouched for him to some extent, and he had felt the effect of that. Barry was a good, decent man and an excellent police officer, and without him, Conlon would probably be in prison. Their friendship had been one of the most reliable things in Conlon's life since his return to Dublin from the War.

Joyce was the girl who worked on the office reception—their typist, secretary and manager. She was the gatekeeper Conlon had needed to charm his way past to get into the office. It was a good thing she liked Conlon. She smiled whenever she saw him. He could virtually hear that smile now, across the phone line.

"Ah, Tommy, why didn't you say? You sound just like any other bowsie to me."

"Oh, I know, it's not the same without my pretty face to look at."

She laughed at that, then cleared her throat and said in a near whisper: "You didn't hear it from me, but there's a body after being discovered, and Barry took it. You can imagine his excitement."

"I can." It was Conlon's turn to laugh at their shared understanding of the man.

"Primates Hill," she said.

"Alright. I'll drop by. It's on my way home, as it happens."

"Well, isn't that fortuitous."

"It is, alright. Good night, Joyce."

"Good night, Tommy."

Primates Hill was an old nickname for Henrietta Street, because a bishop had once lived there, Conlon vaguely recalled. No bishops these days, it was entirely made up of tenements, some of the worst and most crowded in the city. It was also a good fifteen-minute walk at top speed. Conlon hurried out of the hotel and headed towards the Liffey and hopefully a convenient tram.

When he arrived it was easy to tell which house contained the body, based purely on size of the crowd gathered outside.

There were only gas lamps at each end of the street here, and the other light came from the candles and flickering lanterns in windows, their glow feebly felt through dirty glass, so that the middle of the road was a large dark pool; figures murky and indistinct. But the police had brought lanterns, so the door to the tenement in question was a bright, grim beacon. Two uniformed men stood there, heads down.

Women, a knot of straining children, and a few men in hats were standing at a distance from the door, out in the middle of the street, their gazes all fixed on the same house, their informal group a dark clump in the black here amongst the tenements. He wondered had they been pushed back or were they holding their distance out of some odd form of respect? It could be hard to tell in such a street. He came from one such street, had been born and brought up in one not too far away, and he knew the sense of community among people who lived so close together in such difficult conditions was as fierce as any love. He also knew that these people had a difficult relationship with the police. He remembered the brutal way they had broken strikes during the lockout, the baton charges, the horses, the edge of glee to some of the violence. People here would not soon forget that, and it informed everything, still. These people didn't trust the law as they might once have done, and the sense that many of the officers were complicit with British rule certainly didn't help.

He stopped on the edge of the crowd and a man half glanced his way.

"What's happening?" he asked, trusting in the Dubliner's natural, God-given love of gossip.

"Dead body, so they're saying."

"Anyone you know?"

"We're not sure yet but the talk at the moment seems to be that it's the young lad on the third floor. Worked in a hotel or something. I can't quite place him, I'll be honest with you."

"What happened?"

The man shrugged. "We heard he's his throat slashed like a fecking chicken."

Conlon made a face. "How many bobbies here?"

"Three of them in the helmets. Two G-Men went 'ithin."

"Right. I'll see what I can see."

He moved around the throng and approached the house and the two constables, their helmets tipped low to hide their eyes. He could fairly feel the attention of the crowd upon him.

"Is Detective Barry here?"

The two policemen looked at each other, then back at him.

"It wasn't a trick question, lads. I'm a friend of his. Would one of you mind going and telling him Tommy is here."

"Tommy who?"

"He'll know."

Conlon leaned against the railings and waited.

An old man in the crowd asked him, "Tommy Conlon, is it? I saw you fight. Jaysis son, the sound your boxes used to make'd get you to buy earplugs. Awful loud."

Conlon laughed.

The constable returned. "He says to bring you up. And he says you'd better have a good reason for coming here."

Conlon shrugged and followed him into the tenement.

It had that tenement smell he knew so, so horribly well, and it assailed him the instant he passed over the threshold. Potato water and human waste, the messy, flea-bitten warmth of people without soap or running water, weak tea boiled and boiled again in blackened pots and kettles over fireplaces. The walls were patchy with peeled paper, mold and mysterious stains and scars. He knew the flats and rooms would be spotless but distressingly crowded when their occupants had not been evicted due to a suspected murder. These people didn't have much, but they took care of what they did have.

The dead body was indeed on the third floor, in an attic flat with a sloping ceiling. The detectives had their lanterns close to the body, and the scarlet lake of blood around the corpse shone under the twin lights.

Barry was bending over to peer down at something, the other detective—Canning, Conlon saw, the youngest in their section, and regarded by the others as a hen-pecked, over-educated and under-experienced fop—scribbling away in a notebook.

Conlon stopped in the doorway, not wanting to be entirely intrusive. "Barry," he said.

"You pick your moments, Tommy."

"It's just that I miss you so much when we're apart."

Barry peered around at him, one eyebrow raised. Conlon nodded to Canning, who mumbled a greeting.

Having returned to his poking around, Barry said, "I'm assuming you're in need of something, since you never call on me in a social capacity these days."

Conlon took a quiet step into the room as he answered. "Just some information."

"Is it urgent?"

"Well now. I need it as soon as possible, is that urgent?"

"Ah, but sometimes you get 'need' confused with 'want.'"

Conlon was scanning the room, which was mostly bare. The room of a poor man, without much in the way of possessions or luxuries. A couple of books on a wooden crate, upturned and acting as a bedside table. A photograph of a girl's face, smiling beneath a fashionable hat on a sunny day. The girl's face stopped Conlon, and he stared at it, then took a step towards it and stared some more.

"Tommy?" Barry said, a note of confusion in his voice.

He knew her, the face, from a different photograph. Where—it was her. Philomena Naessens.

Certainty landed in him and he strode across the room to make sure, past Barry, who said his name again, and leaning over the dead body to see the waxy, still face of the Naessens' driver, drained of color and slack now, eyes open and dark as marbles.

He stood up straight.

"What's going on here, Tommy?"

"I know him."

"You know him?"

"We met—a couple of days ago."

"Who is he?"

"He's a driver for the Naessens."

"Naessens...Lord Naessens?"

"Yeah."

Barry looked at Canning.

"A driver, you said? A coach driver?"

"No, a motorcar. He picked me up at home and drove me out to their house, then took me back afterwards."

"Naessens hired you, did he?"

Conlon looked at Barry, an eyebrow raised. "Let's just say he wanted a chat, shall we, Barry..."

Barry nodded. Canning's scribbling was growing more feverish.

Conlon said, "Somebody cut his throat?"

"Looks like it," Canning said. Conlon and Barry both looked at him.

Barry looked at Conlon again. "Would you be privy to any information that might shed some light on the whys and wherefores of such an occurrence, Tommy?"

"I can't see how it could be connected to my case, Barry, to be honest with you."

Barry's eyebrows were high on his forehead, his glance lingering. Conlon shrugged.

"Unless you know anything interesting about Naessens," Conlon said.

Barry nodded. "Well, now."

He looked at Canning. "You'll be alright while I escort Mr. Conlon down, won't you?"

Canning said, "I'll be grand, boss."

Conlon took one last look at the driver, his stilled face shining pale in the room, and turned out and back onto the stairs, sinking into shadow.

He and Barry descended in silence and went out the back door. The garden was a small patch of overgrown grass and compacted dirt, studded with tiny cigarette butts, black in the night, the houses behind looming over it, dull light through their muddy windows.

Barry took out his pipe and went about the long business of filling and lighting the bowl. Conlon watched him, silently, waiting. He found this ritual of his friend's comforting. Whatever madness this country and this city and their lives were steeped in, Barry always had time to light his pipe.

"So...Naessens. The man has a lot of friends, Tommy."

"People like his money."

"They do, sure, and his pull in London and at the castle. We turn a blind eye to some of his friendships, I'd say. Not like we've been ordered to do so, no, nothing quite that obvious, but..."

He had lit the pipe now, and balloons of smoke escaped and fled upwards into the darkness.

"His daughter is missing."

"And you're looking for her."

"I think she's mixed up with this religious group. The Centurions of Light, they're called."

"I've never heard that name, and I'd be unlikely to forget a mouthful the likes of that. I'll ask around for you."

"I'd appreciate it."

"And she knew that poor fella?" Barry asked.

"She did, yeah. He told me himself."

"Were they close?"

Conlon shook his head but then screwed up his eyes. "Maybe closer than he let on."

"Would there be any chance these Centurions were cleaning up a mess?"

"Maybe. I've a bit more digging to do."

"Do they seem capable of that?"

"I don't know, Barry. I have a friend who's arranged for me to meet some of them. So far it's all second hand. They sound awful odd. But murderous? I don't know. We both know that there's been a lot of blood spilled because of God."

"Gods," Barry corrected him.

"Something doesn't smell right, to me, that's for sure."

"That worries me, with you."

"But I need to find out more, I need to be certain."

"And then the fighting starts?"

Conlon chuckled. "Hopefully not."

"It always does with you, Tommy. You seem to attract it."

"I just want a quiet life."

They both laughed.

"You'd die of boredom," Barry said.

"Chance'd be a fine thing in this place," Conlon said.

"One day..." Barry sucked on his pipe, "We'll look back on these years of slaughter and fighting with wonder, that we were so accustomed and calm through it all."

"If we survive, Barry," Conlon said, and patted his friend on the shoulder. "If we survive. I'll be in touch."

"Tommy."

11

26 Hours After Purification

THE VILLAGE BELOW WAS SMALL. PERHAPS A HUNDRED inhabitants, at most, given the number of houses. A harbor as big as the settlement itself, as bright as a sweetshop window, boats of varied colors swinging on the tide. The structures were squat, huddled together against the sea and the wind, only a few taller buildings facing the seafront. On the outskirts there were farms, sheep scattered, fields rolling and bisected by walls and fences. They watched it, through the rain. It was a light spray now, swirling and hooping in the air.

"Can you see any people?" she said. "I can't see any people."

He pointed beyond the harbor out towards the sea. Two boats were splitting off, heading in different directions across the chop of the grey waves, their wakes white in the shape of a widening V.

She squinted, then said, "I can't see that far without my eyeglasses. To be honest with you, Mr. Conlon, I can't see the details of that town without them. It's a bit fuzzy to me."

"There are two boats heading out. One of them is a fishing boat. The other one I'm not sure about. It's bigger. It might be the one that brings supplies back and forth, post and the like."

"But no people in the town?" Her anxiety was audible.

"I can't see anybody moving around. But there are lights in windows. It's raining. It's probably not ever that busy, except when there's a boat in the harbor. We'll find somebody, don't worry."

"I'm more worried that they're already known to the Centurions," she said.

He looked at her.

She shrugged, apologetically, aware of the paranoia. "They have influence around here, on the mainland, even. They pay people."

"I understand. We'll keep our noses down. But we can't sneak through here."

"We could try."

"At night, we could. But we can't wait. They'll be here soon."

"You can't keep fighting them."

"No. I had the advantage the first time. They weren't expecting what happened, at all. The second time they sent amateurs. This time it'll be different. We need to move."

He held out his hand and she took it, both of them moving down the hill. She was jumpy, her head jerking around, her fingers tight with tension in his hand.

"It's alright," he said. "It'll be alright."

The rain grew fiercer. It swooped and scalded

against their backs as they went. The sound of the waves against the harbor wall was thrown to them on the circling eddies of the wind, a scrap of paper, then gone.

The first house they passed was a farmhouse. There was no light through the windows, no sign whatsoever of habitation, although the yard was tidy and well-maintained. Almost a hundred meters on, after a handful of other houses, they were in the village itself. The dirt was flattened and compacted into something like a road. There were flowers in window boxes, clotheslines; empty and wobbling in the wind. Lights dim through net curtains. He didn't want to barge in on some poor family and ultimately drag the Centurions, surely armed and intent on violent retribution, into their lives. So he passed a half dozen houses until they reached a spot where the street opened out onto a wider area, the harbor off to their right, and the largest structure on the island faced it across a cobbled expanse of ground.

A copper plate by the door read "Harbormaster." He pushed inside, into a hallway, painted in bright pale blue, and a man and woman sat in an office through another door. A fire cracked in the hearth behind them, the windows were frosted, lamps fighting the grey of the rainy day outside. There was a typewriter before the woman, but she was leaning back, sipping tea from a mug. The man had his mouth full of bread, a newspaper open on the desk in front of him. They both looked up, eyes wide in surprise, at the intrusion.

"Hello," Conlon said. "We need some help."

12

6 Days Before Purification

"WELL, I HAVE TO SAY, TOMMY; YOUR COSTUME IS JUST right."

Viv looked him up and down, smiling and nodding.

He had chosen the plainest, most worn clothes he had in his flat, the kind of things he would wear if he was to paint a wall or fix some furniture: dull colors, patches flattened and thinned by age and use, shapes fallen away. He looked like thousands of young men on the streets of Dublin, men with only the clothes they were wearing, the clothes they wore every single day and tried to wash by hand in tenement washbowls, in cold water, with no soap, then wore through hours of crushing manual labor on the docks or in a brewery or a warehouse.

That was a look and a man he understood well, so he found it simple enough to replicate. Her enthusiasm made him smile, for he liked to see her happy.

"Viv...that's the easy part. It's the talking that might be a problem."

"Sure don't talk much. They're used to me talking ninety to the dozen. Let me do that and just stay quiet."

He nodded. "I can do that."

"So, just so you remember. You're my cousin, Charlie. You're only back from the War. You're a bit shell shocked. That's what they call it, isn't it? A nervous condition?"

"So I've heard."

"And you've an awful temper. Fly off the handle at the slightest provocation. And you beat up a soldier outside a pub, and you need to get out of town for a bit."

"The Brazen Head."

"What?"

"Last time you said the pub was the Brazen Head."

"See? You're a natural. You already know your character."

She put a hand, tenderly, on his wrist. They had met at the corner of Georges and Dame Street, and crowds moved around them, workers returning home in the evening. It was sunny, dipping just behind the buildings but retaining the warmth, which shimmered up from the cobbles and flagstones.

She said, "I'd like to kiss you."

They looked around at the people.

"I don't know when I'll see you again."

"They're not taking me tonight, are they?"

"You never know!"

He shook his head. "Even if they do, I'll see you before we go to this island, I promise. I'll get away."

She nodded. "We need to be going, then."

She talked as they walked, and he realized she was nervous, and that this was her way of coping.

"It's good though, this story, because you won't have to lie, really, you'll just use your own experiences and leave out some parts and they won't know any different, will they? If you get asked where in France you were fighting and what happened to you, you can tell the truth, can't you? I was trying to make it easy for you with that, so I was."

On she went, talking in a pleasant stream, as they made their way along Camden Street, passing the Theatre De Luxe and Earley and Co, finally passing through the arch at the side of a Haberdashery he had never looked twice at before, and crossing a little court-yard at the back.

Here were the Centurions, he thought. Three young men were sat around small tables, in the last of the evening sun, their jackets slung over the backs of their chairs, smoking cigarettes. Instantly he knew they had been soldiers.

One of them spoke with a Welsh accent, "What's your business here, love?"

"I've brought me cousin," she said, and Conlon noted the way she'd thickened her accent. "He wants to volunteer."

"Volunteer? This isn't the army."

Another young man cut in. He was a Londoner. "Leave it out, Davies. Have you already cleared this, ma'am?"

"I have, so I have." Conlon almost rolled his eyes at how thick she was laying it on.

Two of the men were giving him hard stares, and he stared straight back.

"Who'd you speak to?"

"I think he said his name was Mills? It was in Nelligans."

The men exchanged glances and the Londoner said, "That'd be Mills, yeah. In you go then, love."

He indicated the door. She and Conlon passed them and went inside.

Inside was a warren of small rooms off a larger room —what had been a storeroom, with dark brick walls and a stone floor worn and marked from the passage of thousands of barrels. The smaller rooms were occupied for various reasons—there were bedrooms, a stove, what looked like a printing press, desks and typewriters. The larger room had some long, battered tables at one end, with tatty camp stools scattered around them and scuffed metal plates and mugs of the type Conlon knew from his time in the War haphazardly spread across their surfaces. Two young men in dirty aprons were clearing them, chatting quietly as they worked, tossing them into a big bucket filled with grey water in one of the side rooms.

At the other end a meeting was in progress; a couple of men in sharp suits stood, addressing a group of perhaps two dozen who sat attentively on more camp stools. The group was mostly male, though there were a few young women in the audience, judging from styles of hat Conlon could see. Behind the men a blackboard was marked with names and times. He and Viv shared a glance and slowly headed for the meeting, which they realized was breaking up, as the first people began to stir, place caps and hats onto their heads, and stand up, stretching, jiggling life back into their legs.

One of the men looked their way and Conlon saw him recognize Viv, and felt an unmistakable urge to protect her, followed quickly by the realization that he was playing a part, and he had to be mindful of that.

As they got closer the man nudged the other one, who had been turned to the side, chatting, and Conlon saw his face clearly for the first time. It was the man Philomena Naessens had been involved with; Alan.

He was in charge here. He took Viv's hand and kissed it. His smile was playful, eyes sparkling with attempted charm. They plainly had not met before. The first man introduced them and then he was quiet, observing.

Conlon and Alan eyed one another. Conlon could not decipher his accent—it was Irish, yes, but it sounded somewhat like the Irish accents he had heard many times attempted by English soldiers, trying to tease himself or Mossy in France. Like an actor, putting it on. He listened as Alan and Viv said hello, and had some introductory pleasantries, and then Alan looked at him.

"So this would be your cousin, would it?"

"This is Charlie."

"And he's in a spot of bother?"

"He's managed to get himself in trouble. He needs a place to stay for a while. Away from here."

"And he can't go to England? Or America?"

"I can't afford America," Conlon said.

Alan nodded. "England? Plenty of jobs for a strong lad like you in England."

"I was in the army. I—I had to get out of England, too."

Alan and the other man exchanged a slow sidelong look.

"So you have problems controlling your temper, Viv tells me. That seems obvious."

"I get angry. I don't really...think."

Alan laughed. "But you're willing to work? To work hard? To do what you're told to?"

"I'll do anything. I don't mind hard work."

Alan nodded. "We need workers. We can help with your temper, too. There are plenty of ex-soldiers working with us. You'll be right at home."

Conlon nodded, shifted his feet. It was easy to look and act awkward, like he didn't know what to say or how to act; the undereducated, scarred soldier. Easier than having to talk and pretend.

Viv filled in the silences and the two men laughed at her wit.

Alan said, "We'll be leaving tomorrow. You can meet us here in the morning. Seven. Some of our lads will want to chat with you before we go to Avalon, but you can come north with us and they'll see you there."

"Do I need to bring anything?"

"Just yourself. A few changes of clothes. A willingness to work hard. We can use a man like you, Charlie."

Conlon nodded again, not making eye contact. There were a few more minutes of small talk, with Viv again taking the lead, then he shook hands with both men, and then they were leaving, crossing the yard again and back out into the streets of Dublin.

It felt like surfacing to him, bursting out of the water for air.

They were quiet until they were a certain distance

away, and then he said, "I'm not sure how long I can keep that up when I'm with them."

"I thought you were marvelous. Keeping your head down, the way your eyes were on the floor the whole time—it worked very well. We'll have you on the stage yet!"

"That was Philomena's Alan."

"Was it! Oh my, we're getting close now."

"We are. You were—amazing."

She looked at him. "I enjoyed it. Working with you. I didn't really have to act."

"Just lie."

"Sure that's all acting is. Lying with style."

They laughed.

"So you're leaving tomorrow. This is the last I'll be seeing of you."

"For a while. Not too long, I hope."

"Where are you taking me then? It's tea time, after all."

"We'll see if we like the look of anywhere."

They walked north, turning up Dame Street, bustling with trams and pedestrians, and crossing College Green. When she realized they were going to the Red Bank Restaurant, she looked at him with a sort of horror. "They'll never let you in dressed like that."

He laughed. "I think we'll be alright."

At the door, the Maître D', one of those older men who has been waiting on people for so long that he makes his profession look like an effortless pleasure, greeted Conlon with warmth and familiarity.

"Mr. Conlon, it's been too long. How can I help you? Would you and the lady like a dining room?"

"That'd be fine, George, thank you."

He could feel Viv forcing herself not to gape.

George led them through the Grill Room, crowded with men in groups, past a lady's dining room on the first floor, and up to the second floor, split into private dining rooms. He took Viv's coat and hat, ushered them into a cozy, candle-lit dining area set for two, and said he would return in a moment.

This was one of Dublin's finest restaurants; expensive, with French chefs, a Gridiron Grill, famously good oysters, and three floors of dining rooms.

"Well. Aren't you full of surprises," Viv said.

"Have you been here before?"

"Of course not. You can't afford this."

He shrugged. "I did a job for the owners. An employee went missing."

"And this is how they pay you?"

He nodded. "Not bad, eh?"

She laughed. "Not bad, Tommy."

———

AFTERWARDS, they took a tram and a short walk in the fading evening back to his flat. They both knew what this meant without having to acknowledge it. When she looked around the spartan furnishings, her only comment was that the bed was small.

He apologized, and she said, "No. I like it."

Then she began to undress after they had kissed, and he closed the curtains.

———

IN THE MORNING, he made them breakfast. Drinking tea and eating buttered toast, she watched him pack a bag full of work clothes, and he could feel her nervousness. The night before had been intimate and easy in a way neither had really been expecting, and everything felt more serious and solid between them than it had done only a few hours previous.

When he was packed, and she was rinsing dishes and brushing crumbs off his small table, he took a pencil and a sheet of paper from his desk and wrote down two names and numbers. Pressing them into her hand he said, "I'll be fine. But in case you don't hear from me after a week, you place a call to this number."

He pointed to the first name and number.

"You ask for Mossy and leave your number. He'll get back to you quickly enough if you mention my name. Tell him where I've gone and that I said to call him."

"Who is he?"

"An old friend."

"From the War?"

"From the War. If anybody comes around, connecting you to me because of anything I've done, you run. Don't go home, find a friend's place to stay at or a boarding house. And you phone this man." He pointed to the second name. "He's a peeler. He's a good man. You can trust him."

"You're scaring me now, Tommy."

"I know. I'm sorry. I'm sure I'll be fine. But I don't really know what I'm walking into. And I need an escape plan. You're it."

She nodded. He knew the responsibility would help her, give her some sense of involvement, to stem the helplessness she was feeling. He took her in his arms for a few moments and held her, then they kissed.

"I need to go," he said.

She nodded.

They parted on the quays and he watched her walk away, wondering how long it would be until he would see her again.

13

27 Hours After Purification

THE MAN AND THE WOMAN IN THE HARBORMASTERS' office were effusive in their kindness: fussing around Viv, the woman taking her off to fetch her a change of clothes; the man seating Conlon before the cracking, glowing fire, wrapping him in a thick towel, giving him a mug of hot tea; their questions quiet and sensitive to the ordeal the young man and woman had suffered through.

They seemed unsurprised by the references to Avalon and the Centurions, sharing a wary look at the mention.

"We don't have much to do with them," the woman said when Conlon asked if the Centurions ever came to the island. She had returned with Philomena, dressed in heavy trousers probably a size too big for and a huge cardigan, a scarf tight around her head. She sat on a chair beside Conlon and, now that they were in the proximity of heat and sheltered, both of them were shivering.

The man said, "The wireless is busted, but we've a boat that'll be here in about an hour, and we'll get you on that and back to the mainland."

Conlon said, "The wireless is busted?"

"The man coming to fix it should be on that same boat."

"I could take a look at it."

"It's ancient, son. He's fixed it so many times I'm not sure how it works anymore."

Conlon nodded. He was so tired. He needed a few days' rest. He needed a doctor.

"I need the lavatory," he said. "And do you have any bandages, please?"

"Are you hurt?"

"I cut myself. I need to change the dressing."

The woman brought him an old military medical box and the man showed him where the lavatory was— out in the back yard. The lines of white rain whipped him as he made his way the few feet across the cobbles to it.

Inside, the light bulb cast a yellowy light onto the scratched, spotted mirror. But the room was clean, smelling of disinfectant and soap. The water by the bowl looked clean, the facecloths beside it crisp and freshly washed.

His face was hollowed out, stubble exaggerating the darkness under his eyes, beside his mouth; he looked haggard, exhausted.

Partially undressing, he removed the crusted, dry bandage he had thrown together the day before. The wound was sealed, scabbing already. His fingers gingerly tested the flesh around it. He dampened a facecloth in the bowl and gently washed around the wound, probing at the ridges of the slash as he did so. That caused pain, but it didn't have the tight, pressurized feel of infection. Satisfied, he wadded some bandage over the cut, then wrapped long strips around his stomach.

Panting, he sat on the toilet seat, waiting to feel better. A pang of absolute longing for Viv rose up in him. The memory of her body underneath his, their eyes locked together. He sat there a moment longer before rising and making his way back into the office. Philomena was eating a bowl of porridge, and another had been set out for him. She was listening to the woman talk about life on the island, growing up there, how it could be in winter. Conlon watched her ask interested, careful questions, and listen to the answers attentively, while the woman talked and talked. He looked around for the man.

The woman noticed. "He's going to see if any of the fisherman haven't gone out today, so we can get you over on a boat now and don't have to wait."

Conlon nodded, thanked her, and went on feeling uneasy. All the while they were sitting here, the Centurions were closing in. How reluctant they would be to use violence when they got to town wasn't something he was eager to determine.

He didn't want to put these people at risk. He presumed there were children in some of these houses, perhaps old people. At the same time, he harbored a sneaking suspicion that all wasn't right here. Not quite enough to do anything about it, but enough of a gut feeling to mean that he was remaining alert, even if all he wanted to do was put his head back, close his eyes, and rest.

He sat there, feeling the warmth of the fire lulling him, struggling to fight it, weakness chipping away at his focus and resolve. Sleep came in those misty, seeping moments where consciousness and unconsciousness blended and he was only aware that he had slipped out when he was awake again. He would shake his head in order to rouse himself, blink rapidly, and then settle back, and a moment later he was drifting sideways and away from the world, the two women's conversation and the steady crackle of the fire a soothing backing for his snoozing.

The man returned perhaps fifteen minutes later— Conlon could not be sure, time swimming in an out of focus for him alongside the waking world—and he and the woman again shared a glance Conlon, still trying to fully wake, struggled to decipher.

"Right, so I've a fisherman who's waiting to take the two of you across the sea, if you're ready," the man said.

Conlon and Philomena looked at each other; she was up and coming to help him when she saw how unsteadily he rose. He made sure he had his feet under him, again blinked himself alert and then they followed the man back out towards the harbor.

The door was open and Conlon could see by the blue of the sky and the warmth of the light that the weather had turned, the rain stopped. Philomena was a few steps ahead of him and he heard her say, "No—" as she went through the doorway.

Men. Centurions.

He should've known as soon as the man had said the wireless was broken. Too tired. Not thinking.

Centurions.

One of them had already grabbed her, a rifle dark in his hand, and another was turning into the doorway and towards Conlon, and he was back-pedaling into the house, away from them. The woman behind him screamed, and he shouldered past her, back out towards the yard with the toilet. A bullet exploded wood from a door frame into the air above his head. He heard shouting from outside, Philomena screaming for him to run.

Across the yard he went and over the ragged wall of stones there and he saw them closing in, two men, one from each side. He should have seen them instantly, as he came out of the door, but he was slow, weakened, his senses dulled.

The one coming from his left shot, a revolver shaking in his hand, and the bullet whined off the stone and was lost in the sky. Conlon had ducked under it and he lost his footing and tripped, turned that into a roll and came up only a few feet from the man, who was waving the gun towards him, saying something angry Conlon couldn't make out.

Conlon hit him. One punch, a right cross. The man went over backward and Conlon was already lifting his revolver and turning when a rifle shot creased the side of his head. It was like being clubbed. The impact spun him around and he fell onto his side. His hands and feet were scrambling as soon as he went down, desperate to be up and oriented. The sky and earth wheeled in a ring around his vision. He was unsure whether he could stand, and his attempts to lever himself up resulting in his crawling and hitting the stone wall head first.

Blood was coursing down into his ear and onto his

neck. A hand—his own hand—grabbed one of the stones in the wall and pulled him up. Men approached from multiple sides. Guns.

His hearing wasn't working as it should be. He raised the pistol and shot one of them and then he felt an impact. The back of his head. The first one bowed him. He clung to the wall and somehow stayed up. His vision was dark. He felt so tired.

Clearly, he heard an English voice, "Fucking hit him again."

A second blow. He fell to his knees, consciousness a tenuous, fragile thing now.

Hands on his shoulders, somebody dragging him up by the front of his shirt. He struck out on instinct. An elbow into the man behind him. The sharp crack of a nose breaking. He threw something like an uppercut using the momentum from the elbow at the one holding his shirt. Felt that in his knuckles, the clacking of the man's teeth when Conlon's fist took his jaw.

More of them coming. The one he had punched kicked out, sweeping his legs. He fell sideways and was seeking equilibrium when he saw the rifle draw back. It hit the side of his head, just where the bullet had stung him.

Darkness.

14

5 Days Before Purification

CONLON SPENT THE FIRST FEW HOURS OF THE JOURNEY TO Avalon in the back of a lorry with a couple of other young men, none of them really talking as they drove north to Belfast, where they stopped for petrol and were encouraged to get out and stretch their legs.

The lorry had a canopy stretched over the back, like an old-fashioned covered wagon from a cowboy story, with a sheet rolled down at the rear. Conlon had arranged the edge nearest to his place so that he could look out at the road behind them, and see some of the places they had passed.

The petrol station was on some road on the outskirts. It was a muggy, grey skied afternoon and they had just missed a shower. The puddles were evaporating on the forecourt. Across the street there was a short terrace of houses, beside it a squat, functional looking depot of some kind.

He hadn't been in the city since a couple of fights

during his boxing career. Belfast had always produced good fighters, and was, in many ways, a far superior boxing city to Dublin, so it had been important for him to come up and show his pedigree. He had two fights in ten days, winning the first in two rounds, the second in just over a minute.

Belfast fighters were tough and gritty and technical, and the trainers he had met had impressed him with their sharp eyes and acute observations. He could hear a harsh Belfast rasp in the first fight encouraging his fighter to exploit Conlon's lazy jab, and Conlon knew that the coach was correct. He relied so much on his speed and power that some of his fundamentals had grown slack—laziness about his form creeping in.

It ended up being irrelevant; he knew after his first few punches landed that his opponent was afraid of his power, and the first smart combination he put together had put the young man down. But after that he was much more careful to ensure his form was solid, at least, his flaws not so apparent.

He remembered those days in Belfast fondly, training at a gym near the docks, staying at a City Center hotel, fish and chips on the nights after his victories. It seemed a different life to him; before Orla, before the War, before everything else, good and bad, that had come his way.

The driver returned from paying for the petrol, and yelled for them to get back on board. Conlon was up first, and helped the other two on. They thanked him, then all three slumped back to their places and the lorry resumed its shuddering, noisy passage northwards. Conlon watched as they skirted the city and then were out on bumpy, battered country roads once more, fields and fences and walls and trees flickering past. The grey of the early afternoon faded into bright blue skies and burning sunshine.

He could smell the sea before he saw or heard it, and the lorry stopped right on the dock. A fishing village, with a putrid fish market's stink rising into the summer evening, boats long since returned from their harvest swinging in the water, and much activity around one vessel in particular.

Conlon and the other two were quickly put to work, unloading the crates and bundles from the back of the lorry and carrying them onto the boat, where they were added to a small mountain of provisions and equipment in the center of the deck. Sacks of potatoes, cans of salt, shovels and boxes of nails, cement, bricks, books, bags of clothing; a huge assortment of different items bound together by thick rope.

Alan appeared then, dressed in a uniform of sorts; a khaki shirt with epaulettes and matching work trousers tucked into heavy boots, a flat cap in a darker shade of green. A red band wrapped around his upper arm. Conlon noted that most of the men on the dock wore variants on this outfit, but Alan's epaulettes held yellow bars, indicating rank of some kind. His bearing was different here, too. He stood more upright, his chin pointed slightly upward, eyebrows swooping down. The relaxed, ingratiating young man from Dublin the day before was gone. Conlon wondered if this was because he felt puffed up by the underlings surrounding him or if it was just that there were no women here to impress.

Alan led him and the other two across the dock to a spot where men were carrying bundles wrapped in tarpaulin to the boat, like ants in a procession, bowed beneath several bundles, tied together. Conlon could tell, from their size and shape, that they were rifles.

Two men were directing the operation, leaning with studied calm against the low dock wall. Like Alan, they had yellow bars and red bands around their arms. When they looked up at Alan's greeting, Conlon noticed that they were identical twins.

"Lads, these are the Hastings brothers, Val and Norman. They handle our security. They need to meet any new arrivals."

The twins were already up and scrutinizing the men as if they were livestock at an auction. One of them was peering into the earhole of the big lad with the Midlands accent, the other prodded the runt from Meath.

They both looked at Conlon.

One of them took a step toward him. Conlon looked in his eyes and did not break eye contact throughout their conversation. Although both twins had pimple scars on their cheeks, this one had a knife scar from the corner of his mouth down his jaw as well. It made his pinched little face look infinitely crueler.

"What's your name?" the twin asked.

"Charlie."

"You a soldier, boy?" He sniffed at Conlon and turned to his brother.

"This one looks like a soldier, dunnee?"

Cockney accents on them.

"I was in the army alright," Conlon said.

"Oh yeah? Where'd you fight?"

"France." No point giving them anymore than that.

"The Somme. Probably just up the way from us.

And now—you do what we say. You eat when we say eat. You piss when we say piss. You understand?"

"I understand."

"How many Bosch did you kill?"

"I don't know. A few."

"A few? You can't say how many?"

"Four," Conlon said.

"Did you bayonet any of them?"

"The first one."

The brothers looked at each other. "That'll do. You might be useful, at some point."

The one behind said to Alan, "They're all fine."

Meanwhile his brother was still glaring in Conlon's face. Finally, he said, "See you later, Private."

Conlon nodded, and he was directed to helping carry the last barrels onto the boat, forgotten by the Hastings.

It was another twenty minutes or so before they were all onboard and ready to depart, then an hour or so on the water, the craft heaving over cutting North Atlantic waves, at least a quarter of the passengers vomiting over the side. Conlon had a strong stomach and solid sea legs, and he found a cubby and napped as they went.

He awoke to shouts that Avalon was visible. He stood and watched as it grew larger, an island like the mound of a hill cropping from out of the sea, a flattened peak just off center, some buildings and a road near the jetty they were approaching. Darker areas stubbled further inland: woods, surrounded by green and yellow squares he could only just make out; what he assumed must be farmland.

As soon as they had docked, he was detailed with

helping to carry more cargo off and onto the dock. There were horses and carts here, a big building with wide doors like a warehouse, a few smaller cabins and cottages. They loaded up three carts into piles tied down with tightly strung rope and then they were marched up the road as evening darkened the sky.

The road was a dirt track. Well-worn and pitted, it cut straight into the interior, then wound around the hill that sat forbiddingly near the very center of the island. The fields here were farmed and rudimentary rock walls separated them. Further off, around the steep slopes, the woodlands climbed and hissed in the breeze off the sea.

They passed a couple of stone cottages, set far back from the road. Then they were at the main settlement— Avalon proper. It was a village, a sprawl of buildings on either side of the road. Houses of various sizes, a few big barns and workshops, and at the far end from the road, a sort of compound. They passed it and all of the new recruits strained their eyes. There was a big house, made of brick with a proper roof, and it seemed to have been fashioned with polished wood and it shone in the dusk, lanterns already hanging from two posts at either side of an arched doorway in the center of the wall that surrounded it. Most of the other buildings were like those all across Ireland: stone hovels, basically, with thatched roofs.

Beyond the compound there was a common area that initially made no sense to Conlon's mind: a bowl sloping down to a stage, like a Greek amphitheater. Then they were at their quarters—a long, low barracks, like many he had known in the army. Only here they had no beds. He was given a pillow and some blankets in a roll, and told to find some space on the floor.

Once they had all laid out bedroll and dumped their meagre possessions, they were corralled back out and into a nearby barn, where tables had been laid out and they were given bread, gruel-like soup and water to drink.

It was dark now, and the people who were moving them around—all men wearing the red sashes around their arms—were mono-syllabic and elusive. Conlon and the other young men spoke little, eating in the automatic way of the exhausted worker, in need of fuel.

Just as the first of them were finishing, both of the Hastings twins arrived. They had a little retinue of men who trailed behind them, all with the swagger that being around power could bestow upon the weak and impressionable. They surveyed the men and then one of them gave a little speech—they were to get a good night's sleep because the next morning they'd be up at dawn and would be expected to work hard.

Conlon stopped listening once he realized it was a standard speech designed to show authority and set general expectations. He eyed the men. Each had a fresh-out-of-the-army look. A couple had that hollow-eyed face he knew from men suffering with severe shell shock. There was a glassiness to them, like they saw through everything, their eyes focused on something only they could see, which was disconcerting. They carried rifles on their shoulders, and both of the twins had a pistol in a holster on their belt, like an officer would.

He had been counting how many armed men he had passed as they were marched across Avalon and he thought there were at least two dozen, which made this much harder. He would have to find Philomena, get her out of wherever she was being kept, get both of them across the island to a boat, and then across the sea to the mainland. All with a small army after them.

And it was obvious here, in case there had been any doubt—the Centurions were dangerous. So many guns, so much serious organization, so much obvious money to back them. Whatever they were doing, it was illegal, and highly profitable.

He was already thinking about creating a diversion of some sort. He would need time to get a lead on them. Confusion would be a necessity. It would be difficult to outrun them from here.

If he was alone, he could do it. Pick them off, use the landscape: it was what he was best at. But with Philomena—if she was indeed still alive, if she was willing to come—it would be a case of moving as fast and as far away as they could.

The Hastings twins left, their posse trailing in their wake, and within twenty minutes all of the men— "serfs," the twins had called them—had been directed into the outhouse to wash and use the latrine. Then they were in their beds and it was lights out. Just like the army.

———

CONLON SLEPT for a few hours and woke to a symphony of snoring and mumbling in the dark. He carried his shoes out and dressed near the latrine. It was still and silent out here. A faint breeze carried the scent of the sea over the latrines' stink. He crept around the outside of the barracks. A guard smoked near the front door, shuffling his feet in the dirt. Another dozed, mouth open to the sky, on a chair nearby. Conlon retraced his steps around the structure—the snoring from inside was so loud he could hear it out here—and made his way back towards the village by looping around on one of the hills that cradled it.

It had been built in a valley of sorts, with the amphitheater the lowest point and the barracks at one end. There were a few lanterns hanging outside the buildings and throwing a dull glow in a halo above the rooftops.

Conlon squatted and watched, listening, every twenty meters or so. Guards wandered up the main street in pairs. Their sharp London accents carried up to him, all vowel sounds without words or meaning. Their feet were silent on the dirt road. He watched them for a few minutes. They walked from one end of the street, turned, then back the way they had come, chatting throughout. They barely looked around them. Their talk was loud, so if a squad of soldiers had been approaching, they would likely have heard nothing.

As sentries, they were woeful.

That they had become complacent would be his only real advantage. This was their domain. They had no enemies here that they knew of. Whatever he did would need to be fast and hard if it was to work, but they would be slow to respond, because they were not accustomed to any resistance. He could use that.

He moved on. The walled compound that dominated the entire community had more lanterns around it than the rest of the village combined. He assumed that if Philomena was anywhere, she would be here.

Their leader—the "Caesar" they spoke of in hushed tones—would likely be sleeping within those walls, too.

He moved around the building on the hillside, eyes searching the walls and the windows. He could climb the stonework easily enough, he thought. The windows would be easy to breach. There was a guard at the front gate, and at least three others inside the walls, that he could see: one on a circular patrol, tracing a path around the building, a couple more stationed near the front and back doors, with chairs. Already he was visualizing—this was always how it had worked for him. His mind made projections, possibilities, and he mentally played out scenarios. He could see himself doing this stage readily enough.

As such, he had a momentary desire to do it now—steal inside, kill a few of the guards if he had to, find Philomena and get out of there. But he wasn't even sure if she was in there. He needed to know more. The unknowns in this situation were what would kill him.

He watched the building, snooped around the village a little longer, observing angles and lines of sight, easily avoiding the guards. At one point he could clearly make out their discussion, which involved one of them eulogizing the beauty of Lillian Gish and recounting the entire story, shot by shot, of one of her films, which he'd seen in a picture house in London a few years before. Conlon let them pass by and then he struck out, at a brisk jog, across country towards the sea. He wanted to track the distance to the coast, mentally factoring in the time the girl might cost him.

Once he got there—the moon dimly picking out a cliff top perhaps five meters above the clatter of the waves, which were pale lines of movement below—he followed the shore until it dipped into a dark beach for a half mile or so. He stopped when he could make out the light of the little pier and marina ahead. That was work for another night.

He turned around, taking a different route back, and was asleep in his spot on the floor when the whole group was awoken only a couple of hours later.

HE SPENT the morning helping to clear an area of wood, a hatchet in his hands, felling trees, then carrying them across the clearing he was created to pile them in a huge roll for other serfs to take to the carpentry shop, somewhere in the village. One of the Hastings' underlings came around as they ate a lunch of hard bread and broth and asked if any of them was a good shot. They needed somebody to help with hunting.

Conlon put his hand up, and he and another young man, a Scot who said his name was Don and hailed from Aberdeen, were led to the armory. It was in an outhouse inside the compound. Rifles racked along the walls, boxes of ammunition, other locked strongboxes against one wall, containing things he could only speculate about.

Conlon picked an American made Enfield; a rifle he knew very well. He was given two magazines, and felt their eyes upon him as he loaded, checked the action of the bolt and the sight, and pocketed the spare magazine. Don went for an older Lee-Enfield, and then they were told to head for the southern end of the island, where the rabbits and game birds were plentiful.

"Anything will do, mind," the Centurion said. "Lotta 'ungry mouths 'ere."

They set off, and for the short walk through the hills, Conlon could almost forget the circumstances and enjoy the day for what it was.

Don chatted to him sporadically in a clipped, wry grumble. He was a decent shot, too. He had grown up shooting pheasant and grouse and the occasional deer, he confirmed on their way back. He had taken two wood pigeon and a rabbit.

He cast his eye over Conlon's haul—five rabbits. "Where'd you learn to shoot, then? You've hunted rabbits before?"

Conlon shook his head. "I learned in the army. The only thing I've ever shot before is men."

They shared a glance and both laughed.

Don dared to ask: "Why're you here, then? Ye don't believe all this mumbo jumbo, do ye?"

"I need a job. I got in trouble."

"Aye, me, too. Hard t' avoid trouble since I got out th' army. So I end up here. Some of these wee radges gimme the willies though."

When they arrived back at the barracks, their hunting prowess was received with great raptures and joy that rabbit stew would be dinner that night. The game was headed for Caesar in the compound, apparently.

Their success meant that they were asked to go out again the next day.

The rifles were taken away and would need to be collected in the morning. Conlon slept soundly in the barracks that night, aware that he could use the freedom of movement to do the exploring he wanted the next day without having to risk any exposure at night as he had previously done.

He and Don hunted together in the morning, then split up after they had stopped to eat. Again, Conlon enjoyed a moment of unexpected peace, sitting on a rock in the sun, eating cheese and slices of apple, drinking tea from a thermos flask, while Don smoked cigarettes, sat against a tree nearby.

"It's not too bad, eh?" was all the Scot said to him, and Conlon agreed.

When they agreed to part, he spent a short time hunting, shot a couple of rabbits to add to the wood pigeon he'd already taken, and then headed north. He wandered into the little harbor, acted like he was lost, and cast an eye over the boats, the sheds and the situation with sentries.

A handful of serfs were unloading fish in boxes from a boat, two others were working on an engine, and a lone guard nodded to him from a chair near one of the cottages. The game—a line of dead animals tied, swinging, to the stick over one shoulder—together with the rifle in his hands made his status clear, and apart from that nod nobody paid him any mind.

He was able to stroll through, take in the details he needed to, and walk back into the hills. Then he wound his way back towards the barracks, staying off the main road, memorizing sights and quirks of the terrain as he went.

The next day there was a sense of anticipation amongst them. People sat near him at breakfast now. His hunting had given him some status among the serfs. The men chatted as they ate. They were preparing for something called "Purification," a ceremony, of some sort. A few of them had been tasked with constructing something for the stage in the amphitheater—some sort of table used to display something. They weren't finished it yet. Others had been told they would be helping the fishermen today—more food was necessary for the celebration. There was hushed talk that Caesar would be addressing them.

The importance of all this was underlined when Conlon and Don went to collect their rifles, after breakfast. One of the cooks was there, and he said they were to stay out as long as they could and get as much game as they could. They needed to start putting food aside for the Purification ceremony. Conlon asked if they had a cold storage room and the cook told them to take their kill to the building Conlon had been told was the Machine House.

The cook, with a heavy Belfast accent, told them there was a cold room in a basement there and also a Fridgerator Machine, which was powered by a generator, the only one on the island.

They had a bad morning's hunting, and agreed to head towards the coast on the other side of the peak, in search of fresh territory. Things improved there, as the weather took a turn, a chill breeze suddenly cutting in off the sea, followed swiftly by a stabbing rain.

Conlon had already shot a couple of hares and a woodcock, and Don had taken two grouse. They sheltered under some trees as the rain worsened, then in the subsequent sunshine, Conlon took another couple of hares, seemingly everywhere on this side of the island.

They stayed together all day, and Conlon enjoyed the quiet companionship. It reminded him of the War; the enjoyable aspect of the camaraderie, of Mossy and

Dalton and the other men in the Major's Unit. The way they had trusted and relied upon one another. Their quiet humor, their stoicism. No real agendas, no rivalries—they were together, death was close, they needed one another for support, for laughter, for everything.

He wondered if Don would come under suspicion when he made his move, and decided to distance himself from him over the next two days. His preparations needed to be made, and it would be necessary for him to move around the island alone. Better to make his excuses and do that.

30 Hours After Purification

CONLON AWOKE WITH HIS HANDS BOUND BY ROPE, TIGHT behind his back. He knew it was rope from the coarse feel against his wrists, the slight give when he strained a little. His head pounded; a blank, pulverizing ache right at the top of his skull. He had been clubbed with a rifle butt, he remembered. The wound in his side was numb, at least. His face was pressed to cold wood floor. The world was swinging.

He kept his eyes closed, allowing himself to make sense of it all, allowing strength to gather in his limbs. He was alive. They had been caught.

It took him a moment to work out that the swinging was the movement of a boat on the sea. There were men in the room with him. A cabin? The boat. English accents. Where was Philomena? If they got him back to Avalon and into the compound, he was dead. Mossy would not be here for days, if he ever came. In their hands, he wouldn't last beyond a day. He had killed a handful of them, he knew their secrets, Caesar wouldn't allow him to leave. He was being brought back for execution.

He listened. Three distinct voices in this room with him. Others would be outside. Which craft had they taken? One of the yachts maybe? Philomena must be somewhere else onboard.

He had to decide. Could he reclaim her and both of them escape? If he left her, would she be dead when he returned? Would any of them even be here when he returned?

He was injured. His powers of recovery had always been good, but he was up against armed men in a confined space upon the ocean. He wasn't sure how many. He assumed he had little time, given that there were only a few hours travel between the two islands.

His priority had to be escape.

If he was able to escape and survive, he could regroup and return. Bring Mossy with him and they would decimate the ranks of the Centurions in an afternoon. The question then was: would Philomena still be alive when he came back? Even before that, he realized, the question was whether or not he would be able to get off this boat alive enough to make it to shore and come back for her.

But lying there, a part of him could not accept any of this. That part of him that would not accept when things did not go his way. The part of him bruised by what had happened with Xavier and Orla and unable to countenance a loss like that ever again. That part of him that used the skills he had developed, skills which enabled him to hurt and kill and destroy and do things most people would never be able to do—to right wrongs, and punish those who preyed upon the weak. That part of him was insisting that he try, now, that he get past these men, out of this cabin, and get her off this boat. If he failed, he would die. But he had faced death many times before. And the one thing he had learned was that he was extremely hard to kill.

He strained against the rope: harder, a sustained flexing of the muscles in his arms. Then relaxed. Then again. He spent a few minutes on this alone until the rope started to feel looser around his wrists. Then a few more minutes.

The men were still talking, one grumbling about something from his past. Conlon listened for a moment, then twitched enough that they would notice. Then he groaned. Their conversation died mid-sentence. Silence in the cabin.

"He's waking up."

Movement.

"Careful, he's dangerous."

"Should we get Hastings?"

"We're not bloody children, Hopkins. He's tied up for God's sake."

Tentative steps on the floor near him, booming through the wooden flooring against which his ear was pressed.

"What are you—"

"I just want to see if he's—"

"Teddy, it's—"

Hands on his shoulder, trying to roll him. He stayed limp, a dead weight.

"Give me a hand, one of you."

More steps.

"I don't think you should be doing that."

"Shut up, Hopkins."

"You—"

Two pairs of hands now. They wrenched him up and as he was turned, Conlon braced his legs and exploded straight up and into them, tearing one arm free of the ropes as he did so. One of the men fell heavily onto his back, the other kept a hold of Conlon's arm. The third remained seated, eyes and mouth all wide, round pools of shock in his pale face.

Conlon dipped, away from the man's grasping fingers, and arced a huge overhand right into the center of his face. He hit the wall, and before he had even bounced back, Conlon had pivoted from the waist and punched him again, a hammering uppercut which clattered his teeth together and knocked him out before he landed.

Conlon turned. The second one was rising, a knife in hand, his eyes narrow. The third was trying desperately to get out from behind the table. Conlon feinted left, towards the door, then slammed the sole of his foot hard into the knife-man's chest. He made a desperate slashing cut at the air as he flew back and his body barged into the third, just standing from his attempts to escape the seating area. They both sprawled over the table, an octopus of writhing limbs. Conlon was on him already, pinning his wrist to the table, prizing the knife out of his hand. He shifted his grip and drove it in one fluid movement into the soft flesh where jawline met ear. The man's eyes flickered blank instantly. A sheet of blood sailed across the room when Conlon pulled the knife free.

The third was whimpering in the corner, hands

pressed together as if in prayer. "Please don't kill me, please don't kill me."

Conlon looked at him, used the bloody knife to slice through the rope wrapped loosely around one wrist, and said, "If I see you outside that door, you die."

The man nodded. "Thank you thank you thank you, you won't, you won't."

Conlon was turning. He had that feeling that battle had always given him. As if his blood felt thick, strong; and the surge of excitement had awoken him—all weakness gone, his senses opened up, the world something he saw and comprehended and shaped to his will.

He opened the door and looked up a short set of steps to what he assumed was the wheelhouse. His view was just of the ceiling, wood strips darkened by time and smoke, sunlight glowing through some aperture. So it was earlier than he had been assuming. He had not been unconscious long.

No talk, no movement, although he assumed there would be somebody present.

He stepped out, trying to be as light and silent on his feet as possible, and took a careful stride, ducking down as he placed a foot on the first step. Then he went up in two bounds, springing into the wheelhouse. Only one man was inside, leaning on the wheel, his eyes on the waves. He looked at Conlon with shock and shouted, "Help! He's loose!"

Conlon moved for him but there were already figures rising from the deck and the first was coming in fast. Conlon set himself and met him with a short knife strike, hard into his gut just below his ribcage. The man uttered a grumble of barked pain and slipped downwards, eyes aflame and rolling. Conlon allowed him to fall, stepped over him with a short glance at the cowering figure by the wheel, and then burst out onto the stern.

Three men here, one still rising, two already moving towards him. They were all shouting, a gun pointed at him, and he knew there were others coming from the fore.

Where would she be? He took a step forwards, away from the wheelhouse, fearful of somebody coming over the roof at him.

The big one made his move. He swung a haymaker with a huge right fist. Conlon parried it, feeling the impact sharply on his wrist, and tried to pivot, but the man knew what he was doing, and he was incredibly strong. He smothered Conlon, his other hand at Conlon's elbow, turning them together. Conlon took a step back and stamped down at his knee, but the big man bent his leg away.

Gunshots, the deck erupting with splinters, a voice yelling, "Cease fire!" as they turned together, fighting for control and balance. Their eyes met for a moment, and then Conlon's left was free, the man pawing for it in the air. Conlon needed only a fraction of a second and he torpedoed an uppercut into the big jaw inches from his face. The man was out on his feet, but his legs had not yet received that signal and he still held Colon's arm, swaying ever so slightly.

Conlon's eyes flicked across the deck over his shoulder, the man approaching along the starboard, rifle levelled at him, Hastings crouching beside another man, both pointing pistols, atop the wheelhouse, the other two at the stern. Hastings was speaking and he and the other gunman both took aim.

Conlon swiveled, ducking behind the huge bulk of the big man and the shots hit him, at least three of them. He cried out, head thrown back, and slumped forward, onto Conlon. He felt the weight pressing into him suddenly, tipping him backwards, and tried to step away but there was nowhere to step, the gunwale biting into his leg, the man's weight tumbling into him now and he felt himself going over backwards, the ocean rising up.

He gave himself to the fall.

The shock of the cold water struck him instantly, the other man's body lost in the waves, and even with the swirling weight and confusion of the sea tugging and pushing at him, he knew they would be shooting at him.

Kicking hard he dove into the black toward the seabed. He could see the white trails the bullets left in their wake as they twisted through the water before drifting to the bottom. He arced away, forcing calm upon himself, knowing he had to stay under for as long as he could and get as far from the boat as possible because all of their rifles would be ready for him as soon as he surfaced. He kicked and kicked and stretched and then shot upwards with great pulls, just his head surfacing, a huge breath, a quick look, then back down.

He was headed towards land.

He kicked back and went as far as he could again. Pushing, straining, forging through the water until his lungs ached and his muscles burned and he had no option but to surface. That or take a mouthful of salt-water and die.

This time he came up and turned. Great lungfuls in gasps, turning, searching for them. The boat was perhaps fifty or sixty meters behind him. The men were all looking around, yelling, rifles pointed in every conceivable direction. He went under again. Everything hurt now. His lungs burned. His muscles tore at him. The water felt thick as treacle and he had to force his heavy limbs through it. The cold was sinking deep into him, too, the shock of the ocean battling against the heat of the exertion. He was so exhausted.

As always in these situations, his will to live was a metronome that drove him forward when he could scarcely consider moving forward. It was automatic. He would not die. He would not die. He would not die. But always, underneath that was the thought of how nice and easy it might be to just let go. Just let go, open his mouth and drift away.

Orla.

He would not die.

He pushed and pushed, far beyond what he thought he could do, then pushed a bit longer. Only then did he surface again. He didn't even look for the boat now. He needed to get to shore. It was still horribly far off. He went down again and a part of him shut down. He would do this. He would not die.

This time when he came up for air, he stayed on the surface and swam for shore, the great gulps of air he took in more beautiful than any breaths he had ever taken. He was close now, and able to move faster this way.

He heard shouts from far behind and thought that they had spotted him. He pushed and pushed. The beach ahead felt very close now.

Something buzzed in the air very near his head. They were shooting at him.

He went down and kicked under the waves but he could see the seabed now, gently sloping upwards towards the coast, and he was too tired to drag himself through with the weight of all that ocean fighting him with every movement.

He surfaced and gave it everything he had.

He could hear the gunfire now over the sound of the waves. They had one very good marksman. An occasional bullet would whine through the air close to his head like a mosquito.

Shooting with a rifle at a target—a small target, just the head and shoulders of a swimmer—over a hundred meters away from a boat, with all the movement of waves, was no easy task.

Suddenly he could feel the roughness of pebbles and the craggy tendrils of seaweed around his cold, near-numb hands. The beach was meters away.

He stayed low for as long as he could, the gunshots still barking across the surface of the water towards him, and then stood at the last moment and ran, splashing and streaming water from his limbs, across the sand towards the dunes.

A fusillade of gunfire. Sand kicked up around him.

He tried to sprint but his limbs felt impossibly heavy and he could not summon the energy to surge at all. Each step he expected that bullet to find his spine but then he was atop a dune and he dropped and rolled down the other side. He lay there panting.

They might be coming, he knew. He had to move. He forced himself to stand. Inland.

16

1 Day Before Purification

HE HAD HEARD THE MEN TALKING ABOUT THE COMPOUND.
Some of them had been inside for various reasons. It
was where the girls were kept, was the talk. At least four
girls at the moment, they said. One of the men had seen
a blonde being led to the Machine House as darkness
fell, he whispered to the others. She looked drunk, and
one of the lieutenants had been leading her.

His main memory was of her beauty. So young, so
pretty, her hair...he said. Pale skin in the moonlight.
Lipstick.

Another man said that they made films in the
Machine House. The main purpose of the generator was
to power the lights and the cameras. So they speculated
that they were making pornographic films. One of the
men had seen a Spanish film on leave during the war in
France he said, where a girl had fornicated with the devil.
He actually used the word fornicated. Conlon listened to
all of this. They had all seen the many erotic cards and

pictures that circulated among soldiers at the front in the war. Could all this really be just a front for the production of illicit pornographic films? Was that where the Centurions got the money for all of this? This question had been troubling him. An operation of this nature would demand an enormous amount of money. There was no obvious economic output here—they exported nothing, made nothing that he could see, produced nothing. And yet they bought supplies back from the mainland regularly, kept the generator running, maintained an operation in Dublin. All of this consumption came at a cost. The money for all that had to come from somewhere.

He was surprised that there could even be that much money in such an enterprise, but the only other possible source of so much revenue was a wealthy benefactor or two.

Over the past few days, he had traversed most of the island and made his preparations. He had planted a pistol, ammunition, and a couple of grenades, all stolen from the armory, where he was now trusted enough to basically come and go as he pleased, along what he had planned as his route from the village to the coast. Wrapped in cloth, concealed in a hollow behind a tree, he could grab them as they moved without much of a pause. He knew which boat he was going to take and had prepared a spot near a beach in which to conceal it. He was ready to go, aside from a couple of last minute details.

But he needed to know where Philomena was. He needed to be sure, so that when he broke his cover and took her—when he had to use violence—then it was as part of an escape. If he acted before he was ready, all was lost; he would have to fight his way out and he would not get another chance.

That day, he double checked everything and spent a long time surveilling the compound from cover in the trees on the edge of the settlement. He was already aware that it was the most heavily guarded building on the island. Guards changed regularly—all Centurions, all armed. They chatted little; maintained focus. The twins checked up on them often, and he knew the men were largely fearful of the twins, whose upbraiding of what they considered ill-discipline could be cruel and spiteful.

But it changed at night. Fewer guards and a slight sense of lower standards and relative relaxation. On previous evenings he had witnessed men wander away from their posts to chat to other sentries, men nod off in chairs and men reading magazines. He felt like he could perhaps get inside at night.

He had still never seen the Caesar the men were certain was installed inside the compound. None of them had even seen him.

———

HE WENT OUT THAT NIGHT. He had done it a few times at this point and understood how to move around unde- tected. The guards were sloppy and far too sure of themselves after dark. They had no enemies here.

He watched the compound for a long time before he moved in. The first time he had observed it he had marked four guards altogether. But he had miscounted. There were five. One on the front gate, one on a route around the interior of the walls, one on each door...and a fifth up on the roof.

He had spent hours watching the one on the roof over the previous nights. They switched shifts at two in the morning, and the replacement usually made it perhaps twenty minutes before he dozed off. He was the only one lying, in a sort of jerry-rigged sniper blind, near the chimney, and Conlon knew how easy it could be to fall asleep in that sort of position.

He would climb up after the sentry he was replacing had descended. He would set himself up, smoke a cigarette, turn and survey in each direction. Then he would settle down, always looking over the central street at the heart of Avalon. And his head would slump down onto his arm.

Conlon watched the process tonight. He gave it six minutes after that and then he made for the settlement over the ground. Scaling the wall around the compound was easy. He crouched at the base a moment, waiting, allowing his ears to fill with the quiet swell that made up the natural night sounds of the island, then ran for the building.

The door here was never locked. He had seen sentries come and go and never use a key, or knock. But still he felt nervous. Opening a door to a building where he did not know who or what, really, was inside. Here be monsters, the Major would say, when they faced an operation with too many unknowns.

He opened the door quickly and was faced with an anonymous hallway. For a moment he stood there, knees slightly bent as they would have been had he been in the ring, facing an opponent. He listened. Then he crept forward.

The door at the far end of the hallway opened into a larger space: a big staircase rose up to one side, doors off into various rooms, ornaments and books on shelves, ornate decoration. Electric lighting. Not what he had expected, and it reminded him of the Naessens' mansion, which was oddly disconcerting.

Still no people. He crossed the space to one of the doors. Peeked around the frame into a murky, deep space, and then went in.

It was a studio. There was a huge camera, semi-covered with a tarpaulin of some sort, its large eye unblinking as he passed it. Lights tottered on rickety-looking stands, their heads bowed down towards what he recognized must be the set. There was a chaise lounge, draped with a large throw. A bed was shoved off into a corner, too. He passed by and into a smaller room. Stocks, handcuffs, whips, a sort of crucifix on a rack, shining in the gloom.

He cocked his head and stood, listening. His dominant feeling was nervousness now, and he trusted that instinct. He had pushed his luck enough tonight. He was not going to rescue Philomena now, even if she was here. The plan was for tomorrow, and he would stick to the plan.

He retraced his steps, swiftly, as quietly as he could manage. Back over the ground, slipping over the wall, circling around the sentries patrolling. Lying then among the snoring men, he thought about the next day. The mysteries of the ceremony, the violence he would cause.

He did not sleep for some time.

17

2 Days After Purification

IT WAS TRICKY. HE MADE IT—BY HIS OWN RECKONING—A few staggering, limping, grimacing miles across country before doggedly following a road he crossed until he found a house. The sun was setting and the breeze off the sea carried the familiar smell with it. He remembered how much he had missed the smell of the sea when he had been at the Front; the first real awareness that he had missed home. And only when he had been waiting for a troop ship back to England.

It felt a thousand years ago now.

He saw the house a long while before he reached it. The country was flat here, rolling gradually up toward the coast and the mounded dunes. A cottage, set back, some modest vegetable patches stretching out behind it, an automobile parked under a wooden porch. He virtually collapsed into the kitchen as soon as they opened the door to him.

A young couple, the girl pregnant and red-cheeked,

the man bespectacled and wary. They let him sit, she gave him water; a sandwich; a sliced pear. The husband found him some work clothes and took his own ragged attire, still sodden with sea water, speckled with yellow sand and stained with blood. Then the husband, barely able to control his eyes from constantly straying to the cupboard where he plainly kept his gun, looked at him expectantly for an explanation.

Conlon told them the barest facts. They knew of the Centurions. Everybody in the area did, but they were good Presbyterians, and stayed away from such people.

"There are rumors that they perform pagan cere-monies, alright," the girl said. "But few believe such talk, except for the taigs—" She caught herself at this, and Conlon laughed.

"No offence taken," he said. "And it seems the taigs are right."

"They can't be doing that. So close to us. The consta-bles visit them, don't they?" She looked queryingly at her husband. His expression suggested he was uncom-fortable at the question.

She was warm but had a sharpness evident in her comments. The husband, who made sure to tell Conlon that he worked at a local law firm, relaxed once Conlon gave them some detail about himself and disclosed his service in the War. Any Irishman—even one from the Fenian cesspool that was Dublin—who had served in His Majesties Army was a friend of his.

Conlon liked them immediately. Honest, good people. He had got lucky. Once their guard was down, they pressured him to stay for dinner and to spend the night. He insisted he needed to return to Dublin. The Centurions had people there, he said, and he was worried about his loved ones. The husband said that he would drive Conlon to the station, in that case, but he suspected that he would have to wait a night for a train.

"They'll be looking for me. They might not even come this way, but...I can't have you leave your wife here alone."

"Well sure I'll be coming, too," she said. "But first, we'll get you fed."

She talked as she cooked, her husband hovering around and performing small tasks that would not interfere in the main production. She told Conlon how she spent the time when her husband was working in town: how she'd painted and furnished the nursery, how she'd planted and picked all of the fruit and vegetables in the surrounding fields, many of which would be in the stew they would be eating. At the same time, she sprinkled in a fair helping of questions for him, all of them obviously delivered via her jaunty, rapid-fire approximation of subtlety: was he married? Did he have a sweetheart? Did he have a dozen siblings, as most Catholics do? Was Dublin really as filthy and diseased and crime-riddled as they had heard? Was he scared at the Somme, and on, and on.

They prayed before dinner, and then her stew, served with a loaf of crusty bread, was delicious.

He had thought, sitting there, waiting for the food to be served; the aches in his muscles just beginning to hum with renewed pain as the adrenaline that had powered his escape ebbed away, that he must lack something that these two had. The ability to be happy with a life as simple and blessed as this. Was it their faith? Did belief in a God he could not see the way they did allow them to enjoy this quiet, the purity he could feel here? Could he live here with a woman, as this man did, his contentment obvious?

He thought of Viv, and how happy he had felt in their time together. The complicated nature of his relationship with Molly. And then, of course, inevitably, with an almost wearisome predictability: Orla. He could have lived here with Orla.

All the while Conlon felt an uneasy sense of the pursuit that must be heading his way, and as soon as they had finished eating, he made it clear that they needed to leave.

All three of them piled into the car and drove together—not to the local station, but all the way into Belfast. Conlon dozed off not long into the drive.

He woke and drifted off again as the roads bumped and swerved past. He heard them plan to stay overnight in a posh Belfast hotel, as a final treat before the baby came, and the girl fret that her dress wasn't nice enough, and the man's soft attempts to reassure her.

They awoke him from what had become a deep sleep at the station, telling him he needed to hurry, the last train was leaving. For an instant he was blank in terms of where he was and who they were and what exactly was happening. And then it dropped into his memory, liquid filling a vessel. He roused himself, physically shaking his head, thanked them; and ran, limping into the station, up a platform, and onto the train.

He was alert for twenty minutes or so inside his carriage, monitoring his fellow passengers, watching suspiciously as people moved up and down the corridor. When the ticket inspector came and he bought a ticket—with money the couple had pressed into his hand as they bade him farewell—he gave it another few minutes before falling once more into a doze, face on his shoulder, shoulder pressed into the window, Ulster passing by in the darkness.

————

IT WAS after one in the morning when the train arrived into Amiens Street Station. Conlon had found himself awake somewhere in the north of the County, watching as the coastal towns he knew flickered by, the Irish sea a black noise off beyond the occasional scattering of lights. Then the dimly yellow-lighted city itself; the swell of suburbs, houses and factories; parks and pubs, the odd motorcar and even more odd pedestrian, moving like a fugitive across a road.

He was aware how it gave him comfort, just to see this city. Fighting the Centurions in their island was one thing. He was a warrior, he could fight anyone, anywhere. But fighting him in his city was another thing.

The train was about half full, and a dozing crowd roused themselves and extinguished cigarettes into blackened ashtrays as they shuddered into the station. Conlon remained seated and allowed everyone else to file off, busying himself with his shoelaces, adjusting the strap on the bag the girl had given him for his still-damp clothing. He estimated that if they were looking for him, the only definite the Centurions had was stations like this one. After all, they did not know who he was. The identity he had given them had worked, he had told nobody any different, and all they had to go on was a physical description and that he was from Dublin. He had recognized Caesar, but Caesar would not have known him, and he doubted the old man had even seen him.

So he was sure that their only hope of catching him would mean that they would have their people here looking for somebody who matched his description. Once he vanished back into the teeming sprawl of the city, they might never find him.

But he also knew that eventually they would trace him back to Viv. Once they started asking questions of themselves and any interactions anyone had been through with him, she was soon to be mentioned. Alan would remember her, and whatever forces they had in Dublin would be directed her way. He should have thought of that before he left, but he had not foreseen things going as badly as they had. He had underestimated the size of the Centurions operation and their determination to stop Philomena from escaping. He had also overestimated his own capability to evade their pursuers, with a drugged girl on his arm and nursing an injury.

He had told her to run if anybody came asking about him, but if anybody did come now, it would already be too late for her to run.

He did not waste time being annoyed at himself. It was useless, and he had no energy for it now. At some point he would go back over every detail of the last twenty-four hours and evaluate what he could have done better. But now he had to be disciplined. He had to put aside all of the things that were gnawing away at him. The decisions he made that didn't work. The choices that didn't pan out. He had to let them all go and try to be practical. His first priority had to be Viv.

He felt responsible for the danger she was in, but at

the same time, he was confident he would get to her first. He was less confident of getting Philomena back now, and unsure of what to do about the whole situation. He would report back to Naessens when he could.

He stood, stretched his arms, rolled his shoulders, and climbed down onto the platform. He was about halfway along the train, which seemed to be humming, like a runner breathing heavily after a race. The last of the disembarked passengers were just turning into the station hall. Some rail staff were near the engine. Smoke and noise in the air, the lighting in bright pools amidst the heavy black. Conlon looked around and moved towards the station. His eyes were active. He checked behind him, eyed the windows of the darkened, still train a couple of platforms over, and watched the entrance to the station hall carefully. He wished he had a weapon.

He felt it as soon as he came into the station hall. Eyes on him. There were people around. People waiting for passengers, workmen hauling sacks and crates onto trolleys off and dragging them across the concourse, couples reunited. A man in a uniform was locking up the ticket office. Two policemen chatted, leaning and smoking together in thick clouds, nearby. His eyes flicked rapidly over all of them. A man over near the closed café, wearing a pale hat and a long coat. His eyes were down when Conlon looked his way, and Conlon knew.

He maintained a relaxed pace, not betraying anything as he moved towards the doors out to the street. Another man detached himself from the shadows as Conlon neared the exit, this one in a cap and shirt sleeves, and darted out through the doors ahead of him, as if in a hurry to catch a tram. Both of them, Conlon thought. They would wait until they were away from the peelers, and then try to take him.

But then—all they would have was a description. No picture or photograph. Presumably neither of them had actually laid eyes on him. They might trail him first.

He was thinking too much. He needed to be definitive.

He emerged from the station, went down the steps at a clip. A few horse-drawn cabs were clopping away, an automobile puttering loudly around the corner. The yellowy streetlights gave the men ample amounts of shadow to work in. Conlon was going to make it easy for them.

He went towards the Monto.

The one who had left the station ahead of him was on the other side of the street, perhaps twenty meters in front. Without wanting to turn, he assumed that the man in the pale hat was behind him, following at a similar distance.

He thought about what he had seen on the island. What they had done to that girl.

He turned sharply, into a side street. Then, spying a vacant lot with a sign advising the imminent construction of a new house up ahead, painted in a shaky hand, he kicked the fence open, and stood in shadows in the lee of the building next door. He listened. It was late—early, really—and the city sounds were distinct and lonely, rising up into the night sky: hooves and the rattle of a carriage a few streets away, the insistent roar of an engine along the quays. Music contained behind walls and windows.

And there: footsteps. A spatter of them, then slowing; ceasing. The one ahead had realized that he had stopped walking and run across the street. He imagined they were both approaching now, slowly, prepared.

They came around in front of the fence a few feet apart, making it easy for him. He breathed, confident the shadows were concealing him.

The first one stepped through the opening in the fence and Conlon moved. He did not hold back. He was brutal, decisive. A cross into the center of his face, always his best punch. The man's nose snapped, several teeth crunched inwards, he stumbled back, off his feet, his hand out for something to keep him up. The second one was in the way and Conlon was already moving at him as the two Centurions mashed together. He threw the same punch, this one hitting him in the jaw and breaking it with a shockingly jagged crack, his hat sailing off into the night air with the snap of his head.

The first was reeling, what looked like a blackjack in his hand. Conlon hit him again, a left hook and then an uppercut thrown with all the whip a torqueing of his hips could give it. The man was unconscious before he hit the ground.

The other one had recovered his wits and he threw a punch, a sort of wide overhand with his left. Conlon rolled his shoulder to take most of the knuckles, and it hit, then grazed his temple. He ducked under the follow up and came up with a short left to the same, broken jaw. The man screamed in pain and staggered. Conlon followed him and hit him with two sharp rights and down he went. This one was conscious but dazed, his eyes unfocused. Conlon knelt, and put a palm around his throat, then waited for him to come back.

"Tell them I'm going to burn it all down. Their

church. If they're still there when I come back, I'll kill them all. Tell them."

He heard the sharp click of the hammer as soon as he finished speaking. He turned his head. A third man, a man he had missed, was aiming a pistol into his face. Conlon was dead.

The shot was loud, echoing, and made him blink, but somehow he still lived. The gunman fell forward, a wound high in his back. Conlon looked around him, frantically. Who had shot him, who had saved his life?

He knew that the gunshot would draw people. There would be Metropolitan Police here in moments. He rose, head turning and eyes scanning, and was gone.

18

Purification Day

THERE WAS MUSIC. THAT WAS WHAT HE HAD NOT BEEN expecting. Drums, but not like a military tattoo; more of a tribal rhythm. Steady, heavy, in the background as they were all led out of their bunkhouse and through the village to the amphitheater.

Torches lit the whole place—burning bunches of sticks daubed in oil, planted atop metal poles. Dozens of them ringing the stage. The audience, composed mainly of serfs and some Centurions in lines closer to the front, stood in relative shadow, looking across at the platform.

The platform was centered around what looked at first glance like a table. But when you focused on it, it was evident that it was an altar of some sort. Its countertop was thicker than a regular table, candles burned at each corner and there was a pale sheet or fabric draped across it. And before it, placed on the ground at the foot of the stage—a camera. They were going to film this. Two Centurions fussed around the machine, consulting with one another every few moments. This was just another thing for them to sell, Conlon thought.

There was a feeling in the air that reminded him of the War: the anticipation of waiting to go over the top—an eerie, queasy sense of expectancy. Something big was about to happen, something that might, at the very least, alter one's view of the universe and your place in it. It made him want to run. Part of him did not want to see what these people were capable of. And yet: he had a plan. He was close to finding her, to getting out of here. All these days spent preparing.

After a while, a man in a robe over a suit climbed onto the stage. The audience instantly quietened. Conlon had never seen him before. He had a military bearing, and spoke to the crowd the way an officer spoke to his men: with an assurance and ease and assumption of his power and position that came, in Conlon's experience, purely from breeding. He was middle-aged, English. He spoke of the Centurions, their beliefs, their sacrifices, the way the world was heading for what he called a new Dark Ages, and how they would be prepared. How when the time came, they would be ready to swoop in and save English civilization.

Conlon stopped listening to the words, his senses instead attuned to the men around them, counting the guards, noting how alert they seemed, which ones looked young, which ones might be weak.

The man on the stage had introduced somebody and Conlon had missed it. But now he realized it was Caesar. The men rose to applaud him.

He was an older man, and this time Conlon vaguely recognized him. The Army. The Major. He had been at their camp in France at some point, he was sure of it. A big man, balding, with wispy strands dragged across his pate and a neatly trimmed moustache of the type favored by officers of a certain generation. Conlon was sure he had been a general, a colonel; somebody high in the chain of command. He tried to dig out the memory, find missing details, but it was not there today.

He watched what transpired on the stage. Centurions led on a girl. She was young, perhaps in her teens. Long, tumbling red hair. Her face was made up, clumsily, and it gave her soft look a grotesque edge. She was dressed in a robe or gown. Her eyes were glassy, unfocused, as if she had no idea where she was. She allowed herself to be led onto the stage, and then they ripped the robe from her, exposing her pale nakedness to the audience.

A stir went through the men around Conlon. Many of them had not seen a woman for weeks, never mind been with one.

He wanted to look away now.

She was directed back to the altar, like a child at mass, and one of the Centurions took hold of her neck and forced her down. Conlon was aware he was holding his breath.

She was lying on her back on the altar now, and four centurions held a limb apiece, spread-eagling her. She did not struggle, or buck, or kick. Whatever herbs or chemicals were in her bloodstream were doing their work well. She was docile, at peace.

Conlon was aching to intervene. He knew what was about to happen; or at least what the end result would be. You could feel it in the air, the thickening of coming violence. Some of the men around him must feel the same. They must. What was it that was making them stand and watch, so obedient, so cowed?

He felt a mixture of rage and revulsion. At these men, at himself. If he acted now, Philomena would be lost, he knew. But. He could not just allow this girl to die.

Yet—he had to allow this girl to die.

Caesar had a knife shining in his hand. A long blade; curved and polished. A ceremonial dagger, of the type you saw in plays and motion pictures. A dagger from a storybook. It was held over his head, in both of his hands. He was chanting, saying nonsense words. The girl's face was turned towards him but from this angle it was impossible to tell if she was looking at the man.

Conlon looked down.

He knew from the stir that went through the crowd that it was done. He kept his head down for a moment.

They were bleeding her somehow, blood cascading in a crimson rope from her fingers out of a wound in her arm, collecting in a bowl.

All of this was horrifying enough, and Conlon had seen no little horror in his life. But what scared him was the facial expressions of the men on the stage. There was a sort of amusement in their eyes, an almost child-like glee. Boys pulling the wings off flies.

None of them believed in any of this, did they? It was surely all for show. They used these girls—for sex, to make their films—and then they dressed it all up in this concoction of mythology and religion to feed it to their illiterate, common workers. Who accepted it because they were desperate and lost, or shell-shocked and broken.

Conlon glanced around at the serfs, eyes wide as they watched the stage. Exploited and used by wealthy men. Grateful for a home and a purpose where people weren't trying to kill them.

After a few minutes and another murdered girl, he made his way to one of the sides. The Centurion there looked annoyed, but Conlon said, "I need a piss" and the man let his pass. Conlon headed toward their bunkhouse and instead looped around, retrieving a pair of long hunting knives and a grenade from the bushes where he had stashed them, wrapped in wax-cloth the day before. He moved uphill slightly and paused, crouched in the darkness outside the ring of light around their stage.

As soon as Philomena was led on, he moved, surging forward.

The Centurion closest heard him coming but could not see him in the darkness until it was too late. Conlon slashed his throat in a quick motion, barely pausing his run, and then he was past him and bursting into the light. Five strides and he was on the stage.

Nobody reacted for a second and then one of the Centurions there bundled Caesar backward, as if Conlon was a bomb about to explode. Another one jumped on Caesar, shielding his body from Conlon. One of the others stepped out, as if to tackle him, and Conlon, still moving fast, buried one of the knives high in his stomach, and left it there as he passed him.

The two Centurions who were leading Philomena were both wide eyed as they realized he was heading for them. Each clutched one of her arms in a hand. One released her, and she sagged towards the ground, her eyes sliding sideways. The man was fumbling for his pistol and Conlon was already on him, a single slash of the blade across his upraised arm followed by an arced overhand left. The other man still held her arm, and he tried to twist behind her. Conlon took her arm and pulled her to him, pivoting and smashing the entire sole of his foot into the Centurion's abdomen. He was thrown backwards.

They understood what was happening now—there was uproar from the crowd, and Centurions rushing towards the altar. Conlon's plan meant he had to get her out and to his first stashed rifle, perhaps a hundred and fifty meters through the hills.

Two men coming at him. No guns yet. None of them wanted to hit Caesar or any of the other important men still huddled together nearby. Conlon released her arm and spun, switching his grip on the knife. Then he took two steps, slipped the swing of the first man, and severed the tendons behind his knee. He screamed and clutched at his leg, violently bending up like a salmon before writhing down onto the ground. The other man was more composed, but Conlon went for him, using the knife for a feint, making him dodge to avoid it—clumsily, and straight into a hard left hook.

Philomena had remained upright, blinking around her. Conlon turned, put one arm around her back and primed the grenade he slipped from a pocket. He tossed it across the altar softly so that it bounced close to where the men were crowding around Caesar. The familiar cry, "Grenade!" and everybody dove away, down, hands on heads.

Conlon was already gone, moving with the girl into the darkness, his route to the concealed boat memorized.

He gave it between thirty seconds and a minute before they got organized and brave enough to follow him, depending on how much damage the grenade had done.

At his first stash, he pulled out the rifle and ammunition, gently allowed Philomena to lean, keening faintly, against a tree, and kneeled, aiming back the way they had come.

He heard them. They were many, angry and confident. They thought he was unarmed. They were not going to sneak through the countryside, and try to take him by surprise. That wasn't how the Centurions of Light worked. They were blatant and loud and, frankly, stupid. They didn't know who he was or what he was capable of.

He was patient. When the first group came into his sights, dark silhouettes against the glow of light from the amphitheater, he waited until he was confident he could take at least two, and then he opened fire.

Three shots and three men down.

He and Philomena were already moving. They would be more cautious now. That should give him and Philomena enough time to make the coast.

What worried him were the men who would have been sent out in other directions and could cut them off. Not by design—none of them could possibly know which direction Conlon was going in—but by accident. The men would move fast, although he hoped that the knowledge that he was armed and that he could shoot would negate that.

Philomena was slowing him down. Whatever they had drugged her with, it was still coursing through her, and she slipped from consciousness—when she could plod along, held up by him—to a sort of stupor, when she was a near dead weight.

It took longer than he had expected, but they encountered no random Centurions as they went. Instead the problem was navigating with her in the darkness. The moon was a sliver high in a cloudless night sky, offering little glow, but the difference of covering this ground alone, moving quickly and confidently, and covering it with a girl hanging from his arm was immense, and the reality was steadily draining.

The last five minutes and few hundred yards were tense. His senses were straining, expecting the sound of the men at their heels, expecting a shot from the dark. He could hear the sea, rumble of the waves, and then they were there, the sting of the salt on the breeze.

He left her sitting on the beach, eyes open but unfocused, the night an infinite black ceiling. As he was dragging the boat out onto the sand, hearing it score a path, she stumbled to her feet and he saw that she understood, she knew what was happening. He helped her aboard, wrapped the thick blanket that he had stashed inside around her shoulders. Her eyes seemed to find his face in the dark, but he couldn't see her properly to tell.

It was then that the shot came.

Thunderous even over the surf. He felt the sting and the clipped impact. In his side, just above his hip bone. It had grazed him but that was enough to hurt and make him bleed. He swore, doubled over sideways against the sudden stab of pain. Another shot, lost to the waves. He was already unslinging the rifle from his shoulder and he advanced slightly and fired twice at the spot where he had seen the muzzle flash.

Another shot from a few feet to the right and he fired at that, too.

Then they were coming from the tree line. Three men, he thought, blurred forms against the sand, screaming war cries as they came. The first had a bayonet pointed at Conlon's chest.

Conlon moved sideways, staying in the waves, water splashing just above his knees. That slowed the Centurions down and Conlon met the bayonet with a sideways swipe of his own rifle, then turned that motion into a crash of the rifle butt into the man's jaw. He splashed back, away.

The second came at him with a hatchet and Conlon slipped under the clumsy swing and split his nose open with a two-handed slam, the rifle now his club. He slung it back over his shoulder and pulled the knife from his belt.

The third had a knife, and they performed a brief, frantically merry little dance in the surf, until the man slashed at him and caught him, low down on his pelvis, only a few inches from where the bullet had tagged him. Conlon twisted and in the same motion snaked out a hand and grasped his forearm, and then planted the blade just under his ear.

He looked around, the three bodies bobbing, already in the sway of the sea, limbs hidden in the foam, one of them trying to get back to the beach.

The boat was perhaps twenty meters out and he had to rush after it, wade-walking until he had to swim. He took almost a minute to find it in the dark and the massed surges of ocean before pulling himself messily, soaking, aboard, arranging the oars, and began to row them away.

19

3 Days After Purification

VAL AND NORMAN WERE SENT TO PICK UP THE KILLER from the Aerodrome. It was a blinding afternoon, the sun a hot, startling white in a perfectly sheer sky of blue. They had their shirtsleeves rolled up, caps in their hands to fan themselves as they lounged by the car, watching the activity at the base, not holding back their sneers.

It was odd for them to be around soldiers again, even if this was an RAF facility. Men in uniform, that feeling of order and discipline they had worked hard to instill in the Centurions with mixed results. The papers they had been given had granted them an entry, and both had enjoyed the feeling, driving up in the gleaming Morris Cowley, producing the letter and being waved through the gate, sentries eyeing them incredulously.

All this having only arrived in Dublin that morning, into an audience with Plutarch and Caesar at the

Clarence Hotel, right on the Liffey, a sluggish and stinking strip of river they could see through the window during the dressing down they were given by both men. Once that formality was out of the way—the Hastings twins knew how to handle a dressing down from their betters, heads down, faces serious and remorseful—they got what they had driven down from Belfast for.

His name was Tommy Conlon. A solider, he had been hired to find the girl. Neither of which really explained to the brothers how he had been quite so deadly, how he had managed to kill so many of their men, and escape them even when injured and in the middle of the ocean.

Caesar explained, with that air of infinite boredom he adopted when he was certain he addressed children, that Conlon had been specially trained. The Major, he almost whispered. As if those words would mean anything to the brothers.

Conlon had been chosen for a special squad. Conlon was a supremely talented killer. Conlon was adept in survival. Conlon was an excellent tactician with a particular knack for improvisation. Conlon was, to quote one of his old comrades, the best soldier he had ever seen.

Val and Norman shared a look. Norman stared at Caesar, right in the eye. "Just tell us where 'e is. And I promise you we will go and fucking kill 'im."

Both of the older men laughed at that.

It was already decided. There was a killer coming, chosen specially to deal with Conlon. The Hastings were to pick him up, provide as much assistance as was necessary, and not to get in the way.

They argued, of course. Well, Norman did. Val kept quiet. He had seen Conlon up close in a way Norman hadn't.

"We don't need some facking outsidah. We can sort him out."

Plutarch said, "But you didn't sort him out. How many of your men did he kill?"

"We didn't know he was coming. This will be different. War, pure an' simple. We know war."

Plutarch nodded. "You chased him across two islands, didn't you? And him dragging a drugged girl on his back, with an injury? And he still killed half a dozen of your incompetent men, and managed to escape, somehow. I think it's quite evident that he knows war, too."

"Just tell us where to find 'im. He'll be dead before your assassin even gets 'ere."

Caesar intervened. "He almost killed me, you jumped up little shit. I saw him. Did you see him? Did you? He was so fast. Moving, men dead in his wake. Alone on our Avalon, and he did that to us? Did you see? Did you?"

Norman nodded and looked at his own lap.

Caesar continued. "We will not get into a dogfight with him on his own territory. We will make enquiries; we have men here already. If he falls into our laps, so be it; we can move against him."

"Some of the men we posted at the station had a run-in with him the other night, did you know that?" Plutarch asked them.

Both twins shook their heads.

Plutarch nodded. "He let two of them live. Broken

bones. He was a boxer, you see, before the war. Extremely handy with his fists."

Norman tried one last time. "He'll have made 'is move before this killer even gets 'ere, though. When is 'e arriving?"

"Today. You two have to pick him up."

"Blimey. You got him on a boat fast."

"He'll be on a plane. You're meeting him out at the new Aerodrome."

And so here they were, watching soldiers work as builders, a huge hanger going up before their eyes, constant streams of men swarming in various directions, bearing steel and tools, yelling sergeants the ringmasters. At least three other constructions rising out of the ground around them.

They hadn't discussed it, any of it. Norman had been sullen after their audience with the older men, and Val had left him to it. Now, with the quiet, clipped malice that Val knew meant that his brother needed to do something big, something outrageous and terrible, something that could tear up the roots of their lives and had done on a few occasions in the past, Norman said, "So I say we do what the old men want. We help this bloke, we drive 'im where he wants, we do what 'e asks, we wipe 'is facking arse for 'im. And then, when 'e kills Conlon—if 'e can kill Conlon—then we do 'im. Sneaky, like. Bullet in the back. And we take credit for it. Conlon killed 'im, we killed Conlon. Just like that. You with me, brother?"

He was looking at Val, his eyes hidden beneath the hand that was shading them from the sun.

Val said, "Yeah, Norm. I've always gone along, ain't I?"

"Good. All smiles now, though."

They watched an aircraft approaching, a dark spot far off in the blue of the sky that grew until they could identify its wings and the wobble it made on approach. The sputtering hack of its engine split the day.

The brothers shared a look.

They waited until it had bobbed and slid and finally managed to find the runway, losing speed as it rolled away past them, then circled back before they stood and moved closer to the plane.

A solitary passenger emerged. A tall man, well over six feet, with fair hair and pale blue eyes. He was wearing a tweed suit and carried a hat in a matching shade of earthy brown, which he donned as he stood to his full height after unfolding himself through the aircraft's poky door. He carried only a small bag. His gaze found them and he walked over with long, neat strides. Something precise and controlled about him, Val thought.

"You Sharp?"

The man nodded, a slight amusement in his eyes.

"I'm Norm, this is Val. We're to assist you in whatever way we can."

"That will help. I was told there would be a dossier."

Val couldn't place the accent. Posh Scottish? Newcastle? Somewhere up north.

He reached into the back of the car and removed the leather-bound sheaf of papers. He had leafed through it on the drive over. Some details on Conlon, a couple of police reports, a story from a Dublin newspaper, letters from his time in the service. Sharp took it from him, gestured to the car, and climbed into the back, already reading before the brothers had retaken their seats in front.

They looked at one another again.

"I'll need a rifle," Sharp said, without raising his eyes. "Enfield Smelly. Mark three, if you can find one over here."

"We can find one for you. Would you like a pistol, too?"

"No, I brought my own."

He was reading again. They both turned to look at him, and the silence stretched as they watched his eyes move, face blank as marble.

"Where do you want to go, Mr. Sharp," Val finally asked.

"Conlon's house. Smithfield, is it? Shall we?"

———

CONLON WENT HOME, packed a bag with some clothes, washed and ate some cheese and biscuits, and then sat there, the lights off, looking out the window at the street. He set a cup of tea beside him, to keep him awake, but it was almost too hot for tea.

It was as quiet as Dublin could be on a weeknight in summer. No breeze, the still heat gripping the red bricks, the trees lolling under the weight of it even in the dark. It reminded him of evenings in Turkey, when the burning temperature was incessant and he had come to enjoy it. Their sweet tea had made sense then.

The odd man, tracing drunken paths across the cobbles, then a couple of peelers, intent on their conversation as they strolled, were the only humans he saw for hours. Cats ruled, vermin scurrying from gutter to gutter when they had a chance. The barks of dogs carried flat and harsh into the sky.

The milkman broke the spell. Conlon had been starting to nod off when he appeared, just before five in the morning. His cart was almost musical as it rolled over the stones, the bottles singing together as they clanked, the rhythm of the hooves and rumble of the wheels an accompaniment. That summoned the dawn and Conlon watched it sink into the city, a steely grey light that brightened slowly until replaced by a yellow sun before half past six.

People were moving then, starting out for work or returning from night shifts. He joined them, wary and alert as he made his way across town to Viv's place.

Even at this time, the heat was searing in the morning sun, and he stuck to the shaded sides of each street he followed. Sweating, he removed his jacket, and carried it for the last ten minutes of his walk.

A man answered the door to him, in his shirtsleeves, a cup of tea in his hand and expression of guarded surprise on his face. Abrahamson, Conlon thought.

"Is Viv in?"

From behind the man he heard her cry his name and she burst through the doorway and into his arms, wearing a dressing gown of some sort, her hair wilder than he had seen before.

"Oh I could hardly sleep for worry," she said into his neck as he held her.

Abrahamson stood behind her, his mouth forming little holes.

She recovered herself and introduced them as she led Conlon into the hall. Abrahamson, still somewhat flustered, introduced his young wife to Conlon, and they set about making him some tea and toasting some bread. A gramophone was playing music from the sitting room; what sounded like opera to Conlon's untrained ear.

As soon as they had a moment, Conlon looked Viv in the eye and said, "Can you pack a bag? We need to be going as soon as convenient."

She didn't ask any questions, just nodded and made her excuses to her housemates. That left Conlon sitting at the breakfast table with them.

"Vivienne tells us you're a detective," Mrs. Abrahamson said. She had a pure Dublin accent, not as hard and flat as his own, but one he recognized as slightly more moneyed, with its own distinctive rhythms. "That sounds very exciting."

"I suppose it can be," he said. "But it can be extremely boring, too. Walking and asking questions is what it mostly amounts to."

He felt the look that passed between the couple as he chewed on toast after that. The music carried into the kitchen.

"What is this?" he gestured with his head.

"The Mikado?" Abrahamson said.

Conlon shrugged.

"Gilbert and Sullivan. My favorite of theirs. Do you like opera?"

"I went to one in Paris. It was impressive." He remembered the Major's rapt expression.

"We went to London in May for our anniversary, to visit some relatives," Mrs. Abrahamson explained. "Harold bought a phonograph of this. We listen to it every day."

Just as Conlon was starting to worry, Viv reappeared.

She looked entirely ready—made up, her hair arranged artfully under a hat, a summer dress shining in the morning light through the kitchen window and a small case in one hand. Conlon rose, smiling despite himself, to meet her, took the case from her hand, thanked the Abrahamson's as she made some smooth, convincingly banal explanation, and then waited while she took a coat from the stand in the hallway.

When they were outside, turning onto the street, her arm linked with his, she said, "Oh thank God I'm away from that awful shite they listen to every morning."

They walked through the continued bustle and the sunbaked streets of the morning to Ballsbridge, where they took a clattering Number 8 tram out towards Dalkey. Conlon's paranoia had melted away when he found himself in her presence once again, but he retained a low-level wariness, and eyed the other passengers after they had claimed seats in the balcony at the rear of the upstairs saloon of the tram.

The air moved up here, cooling them, but still people fanned themselves with hats and newspapers. A thin-faced man smoking with frightening intensity looked over his shoulder at them, then again, and the third time he did it found Conlon's eyes boring into his own. He gave a start, looked almost as if he might cry and kept his head down until he disembarked.

Viv had been content to fill the space between them with chit chat as they walked, but once the upstairs of the tram had mostly cleared out, she fixed him with a concerned expression and said, "Tell me, then."

So he did, most of it.

He didn't watch her expression as he went through the events of the last few days. He didn't want to see her feelings scroll across her face even as he downplayed the violence. He felt the pressure of her fingers on his arm at certain points, and then, when he had finished speaking, when he had recounted the fight with the men at the station in the early hours of the morning and the mystery gunman who had saved his life, he looked at her.

She appeared stunned, her eyes wide, face rumpled. "Do you think she's dead?" she asked.

"I don't know. They went to so much trouble to stop us. But if we had stayed, they would have killed her on that altar. I don't know."

"But what do you think, really?"

"I think she's probably dead. Killing her would make sense. They'll need to clean up the mess."

"Such things in the world." She shook her head, a look of pained horror on her face. "Men who behave as if it's the dark ages."

He shook his head in his own bewildered agreement. "The thing that made me angriest...it's all the same shite I've seen all over the world: rich men using poor men. Lying to them, manipulating them, using their power to make themselves richer. Somehow it's all just a front for their films or their pictures. I'm not certain, but the Roman stuff, the cult side—it's all a big lie. And the girls, it's like they don't even see them as human."

She squeezed his hand then, and when he looked in her eyes, all he saw there was tenderness and concern. She said, "You said they'll have to clean up the mess. Is that why we're going—wherever we're going?"

"It is. You're the link to them. They'll find you and it's better if you're not around."

"They'll find you eventually."

"Eventually yes. But I won't be around, either. Not like that."

"What are you going to do, Tommy?"

"I'm going to destroy every trace of them."

"What does that mean?"

"Going back. And burning their Avalon into the sea."

"On your own? You can't."

"Not on my own."

"Who would be mad enough to go with you?"

He laughed. "I have one very good friend who is exactly mad enough to go with me. As soon as I have you settled, I'm getting him."

"I'm not sure how I feel about the sound of you getting me settled," she said, one eyebrow raised.

———

IN KINGSTOWN he took her to a small hotel near the center of town, away from the grander establishments which faced the sea. There was a buoyant, summer holiday feel to the area, with couples and families carrying bundles with their beach clothes and people having breakfast in cafés with doors and windows wafting smells into the streets, the azure, cloudless sky soaring above. An appealing, sunny bustle seemed to hang in the bright air, and it all felt very different to the feeling in Dublin, which was always a little claustrophobic in high summer, with its pungent smells, constant activity and crowded streets of tenements.

In other circumstances, this would have felt like they, too, were part of this celebratory seaside spirit, so he tried to banish the furtive sense from their conversation, to help her forget that they were here to keep her safe from the gunmen who would be hunting for them both, to keep things light and easy. She was sensitive enough to catch this, but she went with it, and they flirted and laughed their way from the streetcar to the hotel door. They checked in as a married couple, assuming the names of Mr. and Mrs. Butler. She loved the entire performance, changing her accent, clutching his arm throughout.

When they were in their room, she was forward and forceful in a way that he loved and they were soon in bed together. He knew her better now, there was an understanding between them of how to make each other feel good. Afterwards, they stood together wrapped in a sheet at the window. She leaned back against him. He could see the beads of sweat on her shoulder blade, smell the warmth of her scalp through her hair when he bent his face to her.

They could just about spy the Irish sea in the gap between two buildings, a shifting sheet of dark blue against the lighter shade of the sky.

He ran her a bath—though the thought seemed insane to him, given the heat of the afternoon—then, when she had sunk into it with a groan of exaggerated bliss, he went down to the lobby to send a telegram to his friend Mossy. He asked that Mossy meet him in McFagans the next night or the one after that, a joke between them; meaning they would meet on the street between McPhillips and McFagans, two pubs they knew well, and to be ready for some work. He knew that the meaning behind that would be clear to him. Then he went back upstairs to her.

Walking in to find her naked in bed, waiting for him, was enough to banish any tension or worry from his thoughts.

Afterwards, they ate lunch together in the hotel bar, and neither really liked the idea of most of heavy dishes on the menu. It was too hot for stew or sausages and peas. Instead they ate sandwiches, and she talked about the way some of the suffragettes she knew in the Irish Women's Franchise League were vegetarians, and how difficult it was for them to find food to eat in Dublin's restaurants and cafés. Conlon told her about the food in France and Turkey, and she expressed her dreams of travel.

Hours later, lying together and watching the sunlight fade on the ceiling of their room, he told her he wanted to take her somewhere. To Paris or Rome, Vienna or Venice. When this was over, if they could.

He left her there just as the sky began to drain of light, that pale passage of the evening when night was an insistent promise. He made her swear to stay in Kingstown, and said he would check in when he could, either by telephone or, preferably, in person. She expressed an intention to read on the beach, and held him tightly before they parted.

20

4 Days After Purification

A FEW MONTHS BEFORE, HE HAD FOUND THE WASTREL SON of a widow who lived alone in a big house where Irish-town began to turn into Ringsend. The son had stolen a load of her jeweler and flogged it to pay off some gambling debts before hiding out in Mullingar. Conlon had dragged him back to his mother, then, feeling sorry for the women, refused payment for his work.

She had insisted, and he had instead asked her to always keep a bedroom free for him, because he often found himself in need of a room nobody else knew of. That night was the first time he had availed himself of her hospitality.

He was pleased to see that she had taken on a few lodgers, even as he avoided them, thanking her quietly and retiring to his bed before eleven o'clock, some light still clinging to the sky through the thin curtains.

He slept deeply, tired from his hours with Viv and

still recovering from his injuries. He was the first one at the breakfast table, and she fed him fried bread, thick rashers of bacon and poached eggs with milky tea.

He was gone before anyone else was up.

He jumped onto a tram into town, busy with commuting men in suits, then alighted near Trinity College and approached the men in the shade of a Cabman's shelter to haggle about the price of his fare out to the Naessens Estate.

A few moments later he was in the shade of a cab, swaying and bumping over the cobbles, the horses rhythmic beat rolling over the burble of the city a near enough thing to the pure sound of nostalgia for him. It was hard to fathom on such a beautiful morning that there might be men, right now, hunting for him. Men waiting outside his home, watching his usual haunts. But he had to assume that that was the case. He was still puzzled by the way the Centurion at the station had been shot. There was somebody watching out for him. And though he was grateful, it only served to feed his paranoia. People were tracking him, monitoring him. He hated the feeling. Hunted.

———

THE TWINS WERE SOMEWHAT TAKEN ABACK by the way Sharp worked. He was silent, working things out behind those pale eyes. He made decisions quickly and communicated them simply. He seemed never to doubt or to hesitate. He read the dossier, sitting in the back of the car, then re-read it in the pub near Conlon's home. Then read it again when they were parked near the house where the girl lived. By the time they walked the street where Conlon's mother lived, he had seemingly internalized it entirely.

Val asked him, "If you don't mind me asking, what are we doing? What next?"

Sharp said, "Conlon is clever. He knows that we will be looking for him, so he's gone to ground. He won't be in any of the places he might usually be. He's done this before."

"So why are we here?"

"Getting a feel for him."

"And? Has it worked?"

Sharp grimaced. "He's hidden the girl somewhere. Now he needs to take some steps to hurt your organization. That is what he will be doing. Planning. Recruiting, most likely. And then he will hit you. Hard."

Norman laughed. "He's one man."

Sharp nodded. "He is. So am I. If I had time and resources, I could accomplish an awful lot. He is an experienced killer. A hunter. A warrior."

"You sound like you admire 'im? 'E's just some Paddy who fought in the Somme."

"Read the dossier. You saw him work. He and I have some colleagues in common. I know the training he's had. I understand how he was shaped. I respect him. You should respect him. Otherwise, he will kill you both."

They were silent, their petulance voiding all the words they wanted to say.

Finally, Val said, "How do we get him, then?"

"We have an advantage."

"What's that?"

"One piece of information he does not know we possess. Today or tomorrow he will fall into our hands. And then I will kill him for you."

The twins looked at one another.

Sharp said, "We need a few more men. Two, perhaps three. Men who are good with their fists. Or knives."

"When?"

"Now."

"Now?"

"Yes. Have them meet us."

Norman said, "Alright. Meet us where?"

Sharp gave him the address, and Val suddenly understood. He couldn't help but smile.

———

THE CAB WAS slow and Conlon almost dozed off in the rhythm created by alternate states of jerking and swaying, sat in the warm shade. He asked the driver to let him walk into the house from the gate, needing the exercise to jolt himself awake. Standing in the hot sun, he waited until the animal and the carriage it dragged were gone, its sound fading, then began up the drive, hugging the line of shadow on one side, sweat already layered upon his back, his shirt stuck to his flesh.

The trees shook languidly in the occasional whisper of stuffy breeze that the stillness breathed. He could hear insects, birds. Dublin seemed distant.

He had to knock at the main door when he reached the house. They were unaccustomed to receiving visitors unannounced, and on foot. Martin answered the door looking somewhat disheveled, even panicked. He brought Conlon inside. The master was away, but Lady Naessens might see him, if she was up.

Conlon understood this a moment later. She was passed out on a settee in one of the drawing rooms, head propped on a complex arrangement of cushions, mouth ajar; a tumbler of whiskey half empty beside her. Windows were wide open but it was close and unpleasant in the room.

He was unsure of how to approach this. He looked at Martin for guidance, but the Butler threw him a theatrical shrug as he retreated.

Conlon sat across from her, rubbing at his own face. He spoke her name; a half dozen times. Finally, he shook her by the shoulder. She emerged, blinking, then coughing, and sat up, eyes wide for an instant, before rolling onto the settee, moaning. The tumbler rolled heavily onto the carpet.

It took her a full two minutes before she was sitting, conscious, squinting at Conlon. Her words were slurred.

"Did you find her? Did you find her? Where is my girl?"

"I found her."

"Where is she? Where?"

"On the island. I couldn't get her off."

She looked confused, tearful.

"Where is your husband?"

"He's—"

The door opened and Conlon turned, expecting to see Martin. A group of men entered instead. Conlon was already standing, turned towards the door.

She said, "Who are you? Mr. Conlon?"

Conlon knew the first two were veterans immediately. The way they carried themselves, the scalded look of their eyes. They wore shirts, no ties, no hats. Their sleeves were rolled up. They were here to fight him.

He took a step out into the room, away from the chair, the drunken woman mumbling.

Three more men behind the first two—the Hastings, both of them. The Centurions, then. How had they found him? Had they been watching this house because of the connection to Philomena...?

And then, no. Suddenly he understood.

One of the twins was grinning at him, broadly, smugly. Conlon was done for, that grin said.

Behind them, the fifth man. A recognition passed between him and Conlon. Tall, broad-shouldered. Something neat about his Nordic fair hair and blue eyes. He hung back, watching.

The two veterans circled in opposite directions. Conlon stretched his shoulders and made two fists.

The one on the right, one of those men who would probably maintain a military buzz-cut for his entire life, made the first move—a classic jab on his step forward. Conlon should have retreated but he instead slipped and came up on the inside with a short left uppercut, snapping the man's head back. He took a few steps away to recover.

Conlon turned to the other. He was slight and balding, but light on his feet, moving as if he was held up on invisible strings, a bounce in his step like some odd puppet. He came in straight on, eyes locked, and suddenly stuttered his steps and flew at Conlon from the side. He was very fast. His fist pumped once, and Conlon rolled and turned his head enough to just about avoid most of it, but still felt it graze his cheekbone.

Instinct made him sling a right upwards and it caught the man in the chest, but without any damage.

They spun away from one another.

Conlon took a step back. Both of them faced him now, and he saw the problem. They had chosen men who could fight. The first one felt like he trained people. He had that relaxed efficiency about him, a style honed and practiced down to bare essentials. An instructor. Conlon remembered the grim battles with instructors in France, where he had held back but still been pushed to keep from being overwhelmed.

The other, the puppet, was more unorthodox. His speed and fleetness of foot would make him a nightmare to catch.

Conlon knew that he could beat either of them alone. But he had to fight them together.

They came at him at the same time now. He rolled under a straight from the instructor and the puppet met him with a left hook to the jaw. Conlon staggered and the instructor speared his ear with a jab. He felt the world lurch, his balance affected. The puppet feinted, as Conlon moved around him. Conlon threw a right and the puppet slipped it and caught him with a ripped fist to the body. Aiming for the liver, it had only missed because Conlon had twisted partially away, but it was still a shot with his weight behind it, and Conlon winced as it thrummed through him. The wound in his side, still not healed, opened up anew.

Then the instructor was on him. A one-two-three combination, and that predictable sequence saved Conlon. He ate the first two punches, hard. Blood in his mouth now. But he parried the hook and replied with a brutal left which knocked the instructor off his feet. The small table in the center of the room exploded under his fall.

The puppet moved again, darting in and throwing a punch from a stupid angle. He was low to Conlon's right and he unleashed a sort of left uppercut from there. It should never have been attempted. Yet it worked. The spring in his feet let him bounce around and pull off punches. The uppercut knocked Conlon's mouth shut, and the puppet was already around to his left and throwing another shot, a hard cross which caught Conlon's shoulder. Again, only instinct had saved him, his body twisting and dodging without any conscious instruction.

The puppet kept on moving, and Conlon watched and reacted to his strikes and feints. The instructor was climbing to his feet, blood streaming from his nose and mouth.

Again the puppet came in from an angle. Conlon blocked his fist. He knew now he just needed one opportunity and he could put this one down. The instructor waded in again. Conlon let him make a move, then he shifted his weight and shoved him, with both hands, into the puppet. Both men sprawled into the cabinet against the wall. Vases tottered and shattered against the floor. Conlon struck while they were disorientated, one hard right to the instructor's jaw. He went down again, but was already getting up as the puppet came at Conlon once more.

The puppet feinted, then attempted his strike from the opposite side. Conlon had backed off, and now he waited. I know you, he thought. I've timed you. The puppet tried again; the other side now. Conlon read it and let him feint harmlessly, then smashed a right cross into his jaw. He was unconscious instantly and fell down face first.

The instructor nodded and came at him. He threw a flurry. Two of them got through Conlon's defense, but Conlon threw his own in return. The wide hook he flung as the instructor leaned away tagged his chin, and his hands went up to protect his head. Conlon exploited all the space left defenseless with two mighty hooks to his gut. He doubled up and Conlon could line up his final shot. This time he didn't get up.

Panting, blood beginning to course out of his side, Conlon looked at the twins. The other man stepped between them. He was shrugging off his jacket.

"Very good," he said, holding his jacket up. One of the Hastings' took it, unable to hide the annoyance in his eyes.

"Do I know you?" Conlon asked.

"No, but we have some friends in common. I've heard stories of some of your operations. I've been looking forward to this."

"Friends?" Conlon said. "The Major."

Sharp smiled. "I must say, you do not disappoint. Injured and outnumbered. Still you were too good for them."

He had noticed that Conlon's side was troubling him. He must be favoring his right, or otherwise betraying the pain he was feeling. But it showed how acute his understanding was. He had to be good.

"My name is Sharp."

"I've never heard of you, and I really don't care," Conlon said. "Come on."

He nodded and then he came at Conlon. They

exchanged jabs, blocks, parries. Circled. Sharp kicked the remains of the shattered table away.

When he came forward again, he threw two punches, and Conlon realized that he was astonishingly strong. He slipped the first blow, but the second was a straight to his chest, and it caught his sternum like a blackjack, with a clubbing, horrifically heavy impact. Conlon backpedaled but Sharp was quick in pursuit and threw another flurry. A left caught Conlon's temple and he went over backwards, his shoulder catching on the edge of the sofa. He turned that into a roll and came up on the other side of the room. Sharp was smiling as he moved around the sofa. Aggressive, then. Never on the back foot. Using his size and strength and speed to dominate and overwhelm.

Conlon decided to use that against him and met him as he came around the sofa. He threw an instinctive, rolling, rapid combination of power punches, designed to bring Sharp's hands down and leave his head open for the straight right that would finish him off.

It worked. Sharp blocked and slipped and then his face was open and Conlon hit him. A big right with weight behind it. Conlon was heavy-handed, he always had been. His fists knocked men out. One punch power. This was a right with perfect technique: pivoting, turning his hips, force transferred up through his torso and shoulder and down his strong arm to explode in his fist, straight into Sharp's face.

Sharp took the punch, stepped away, spat blood, and there was that smile again.

"As I said, you do not disappoint."

He came up with an uppercut. Conlon just managed to evade it, feeling it cut past his jaw. Next came a hook to the body he couldn't avoid, buckling him. Another hook, to the side of the head, throwing him sideways, off his feet. A one-two as he stood, throwing him back again.

He was so fast. Somebody that fast should not be able to punch so hard.

Conlon attacked again. Big punches, many of them landing. Sharp shrugged it off, almost disdainfully, and smashed his own blows to Conlon's tiring body. He felt his strength ebbing, the wound near his hip open now and pulsing as it coursed blood down his leg.

Sharp got through his guard with a heavy cross, and Conlon felt the world swing. His balance had been off since the instructor caught his ear, and now vertigo was a swarming incoherence, the ground unstable beneath his feet.

Sharp was still coming. Conlon was thinking. He was losing this fight. He needed to get out of here, regroup. Survive. He had always survived. He won fights.

Sharp came, and Conlon made a deceptive little sidestep, and stamped down on his ankle. It twisted and Sharp growled in pain, swinging away, the hint of a limp in the motion. Swearing at Conlon, his smile gone now, he was a silhouette against the sun in the window.

Conlon launched himself the short distance between them, his body a battering ram, and they exploded together through the glass. He was up before they had even fully landed, trampling the big man under him and sprinting across the lawn for the trees.

Shots came, but he was only meters from cover, his own breath thunderous in his ears, and then he was gone, away, in the cool and the shadows under the green canopy.

"How the fack did that 'appen?"

Sharp had climbed back in through the shattered window. Bits of the frame hung limply over the lawn, a sheet of glass fragments carpeting the grass. He had stopped the Hastings' from pursuing Conlon, with a sharp bark. They stood there, pistols in hand, radiating frustration. Lady Naessens appeared to have fainted.

Sharp looked at the twin who had spoken. "He's a soldier. That is a tactical retreat. We will see him again."

"Come on, let's go after him," one of the twins said to the other.

Sharp was testing his teeth with his tongue and fingers. Conlon had knocked one clean out and loosened another two. He tried to put weight on the ankle Conlon had targeted; pain rippled up his leg and spine. If he hadn't twisted at the very last instant, it would have broken. Annoyance and admiration were counterweights in his mind.

He said, "If you go after him, the best that will happen is hours spent running through fields, chasing ghosts. You won't catch him. The worst that will happen is that he waits, sets a trap, and you both die."

One of them virtually snarled at that. Sharp sighed. "Go if you wish. It will only mildly inconvenience me. To this point, you have been little help."

One of them—the louder, more witlessly aggressive of the two—nodded and made for the opening in the wall where the window had been.

His brother said, "Norm, no."

Norm stopped and stared down Val. Eventually he

shook his head. More contemptuous than disappointed. "You facking coward."

He vaulted through the space and ran off towards the trees, pistol in his hand.

Sharp waited a few seconds and then looked at the remaining Hastings brother. He was watching his twin run, and then vanish into the tree line.

Sharp said, "He will work it all out now. Conlon. About Lord Naessens. We must end this quickly."

Val was lost in his head. He could almost feel that he would never see his brother again. It was a more complicated feeling than he had expected.

Finally looking to Sharp, he said, "What do we do, then?"

"We find a weak point," Sharp said. "And we squeeze."

———

IN THE ROLLING, dappled green and brown ground beneath the trees that ran for a mile or so to the north and west of the Naessens property, Conlon found himself strangely at ease. It was still here but for his passage, the occasional startled animal or bird flickering through the leaves ahead of him. The heat was deep and damp, the moss seeming to seep up into the air from the stones and bark it wrapped.

His injuries didn't cause a limp or affect his senses. Lucky. Some day he assumed his luck would run out, but not today. He determined how many were coming after him, began to angle back south, toward the city and the river, and looked for the best place to ambush the Hastings brother.

He could hear him, off in the brush, trying and failing to be quiet—a sound at odds with the birdsong, and more discordant against the stillness of the green world. The noise and stupidity ruled out Sharp. He couldn't imagine somebody as skilled and highly trained as Sharp would even waste time with a pursuit. It had to be one of the twins. The angry, spiteful one, who had liked to insult the men back on Avalon, most likely.

Despite the insistent pain in his side and the dripping away of his energy, Conlon maintained a pace that meant the twin wouldn't catch him. Then, when he started to alter his route, he knew he needed to deal with the pursuer and finish this.

When he found himself in the thickest copse of trees yet, he recognized an opportunity. He climbed a tree; quietly and quickly pulling himself up into the thick, broad beams mid-way up, using his feet when he was able. Then he waited, crouched and concealed beside the body of the trunk. The stillness, holding himself there, the quiet; it all made him feel the nagging pain in his side again. He grimaced as he felt at the skin around the wound with his fingers.

Part of him—a loud, insistent voice in his head—wanted him to return to Viv and wait all this out. Stay with her in that room for a few weeks and then emerge when this was all over. He could almost feel her on his skin in that bed again, her soft body, her wet, hungry kisses, the way she held him afterwards. The covers clinging to their sweat. He could feel it all. But alongside that, a fixed point in his mind, was the sight of the girl on Avalon, bled to death on the altar. There must be other girls, many other girls. He could not just let that happen.

Hastings came along perhaps a minute later, scanning the ground for signs as he went, his gun waving around like an insect's antenna, eyes narrowed in anger and effort. Conlon let him pass, watching his head bob and turn beneath, then slid down the tree and followed him, staying low and noiseless.

It took Hastings a full two minutes before he realized he had lost the trail. He stopped and stood to his full height, casting looks around him, then stooped to search in the undergrowth, scrutinizing leaves and twigs for signs of passage.

Conlon erupted out of the bushes and smashed him into a tree. His head made a flat, harsh impact noise as it hit. A noise came from his mouth. Conlon had smacked the gun into the undergrowth. Hastings swung a punch sideways, his free hand going for a knife at the same time. Conlon slipped the punch and replied with two of his own. A right cross and then a left hook.

This Hastings was no fighter, and he was already crumpling. His jaw broke with a deep, satisfying crack when the hook caught him. Maintaining the will to live, his fingers had freed a knife from its sheath on his belt, and he was trying to bring it up to use it. Now he tried to shift away and Conlon pinned his wrist to the tree and twisted and ground until the knife slipped from his mangled fingers. Conlon hit him again, two rapid uppercuts to his solar plexus. His breath came out as a bark of air, and then he slumped there. Their eyes met.

Hastings had no breath to speak, but the rage and hate were sparkling in his face. Conlon nodded, picked up the knife and cut his throat. Quickly, firmly. He stepped back from the spray and allowed the body to bump down the tree, eyes blinking, searching for a focal point until life left them, a second or so later.

Conlon wiped the knife on Hastings' trouser leg, then arced it off into the wood. He retrieved the pistol, waited in the silence for the sounds of anymore pursuers, and then he made off.

21

5 Days After Purification

MOSSY WAS THERE BEFORE HIM. EVEN IN THE DECLINING light of the evening, Conlon could see him from the other side of the bridge. He didn't lean against the wall, the way another man might have chosen to. Instead he stood there like a sentry, suspiciously eyeing every passer-by. His dark form was lit by a gas light outside McPhillips, the whites of his shirt sleeves shining in the gathering gloom.

He hated Dublin, hated cities, disliked the crush and sprawl of so many people. He was happy to remain at home, keeping himself to himself. But he and Conlon had fought and bled together, and Mossy loved action. He always came when Conlon asked.

Conlon crossed the Tolka and Mossy exclaimed, "Jaysus, you've been in another scrap."

They shook hands. Conlon was always genuinely glad to see his friend, even if keeping him leashed and calm could be extremely demanding. Mossy lurched between moods and had a propensity for volcanic eruptions of temper, often accompanied by episodes of extreme violence. He was calmest and at his best in combat, and was perhaps the best shot Conlon had ever encountered. Better than Conlon himself. He also trusted Conlon and would stick to a plan while retaining the ability to indulge in some improvisation when his experience suggested it was appropriate.

But mainly, their bond went back to those first days when he was recruited by the Major out of a unit decimated at the Somme, his exploits already legendary to men who had witnessed him. At that point, having joined up in London, he was weary of the way the English spoke to him, the constant prodding and needling for a response, the jokes about Fenians and ignorant bog-men, the officers talking to him with barely disguised suspicion.

He had felt like he was constantly forced to win the respect of strangers. They chided him, teased him, isolated him. And then they saw him fight and they respected him, but that respect was tinged with fear. And though he had fled Ireland wanting to wallow in his own grief, he felt lonely. Lonely surrounded by the men he fought beside, men who he risked his life for.

He had expected the same even in the Major's special group, but after an initial sparring session with Mossy, he had found a compatriot who treated him with a familiar brand of rural Irish disdain based on the fact that he was from Dublin, not based on his nationality. The warmth of that was something he could not forget. Soon after Dalton had joined the unit and they were a little Irish group within the group. Conlon had never had brothers until he met Mossy and Dalton.

"You look like you need a drink," Mossy said now.

"You always look like you need a drink," Conlon replied.

They chose McFagans, found a table near the back, and ordered pints.

"The only thing I like about this city," Mossy said. "Besides yourself, Tommy, is the way this drink tastes here." He had finished a Guinness before Conlon had taken two mouthfuls, and was at the bar for another. "It's too hot for Dublin," he said when he returned. "You need the cool of a good pasture in this heat."

"I thought you moved off the farm?"

"I did, but I bought my own place. Few acres. We've got chickens."

"We?"

"George. My friend."

Mossy had always liked boys as much as girls, if not more so. In the army during the war, many of the British officers had similar predilections, but Ireland was not quite so understanding. Despite his size and fearsome bearing, Conlon had often worried about Mossy's reaction to a jibe or insult getting him into trouble. He had never quite envisioned that the big man might find happiness with another.

"How long have you been there?"

"When did I last see you? Those fellas in Killarney?"

"Three months."

"Three months then. Moved in when I got home and George was already in, picking out wallpaper, so he was."

"What do you do for money?"

"I still have some from the Major's hunting parties."

They both laughed at that.

"And I do odd jobs. Not a decent mechanic for miles. George is a doctor, so he's loaded."

"Well. It's good to hear you're happy."

"How about you? You still courting your widow?"

"No, that's been over for a while."

"Another one who can't compete with your Orla?"

Only Mossy could say that to him, and the fact that he said it while slapping Conlon's shoulder and laughing made that even more obvious. Conlon had no memory of even telling him about her; whether it was in a foxhole or a pub, or if he told him some night while they waited to ambush a patrol in France or Northern Italy, if he was drunk on whiskey or fear at the time. He just did not know. Only that Mossy knew and understood.

"I just met a girl," Conlon said, weakly, as if making excuses for himself.

"She's not connected to whatever you need me for, is she? You always fall for one of the women you meet on the job. Not very professional behavior, if you ask me. The Major would not approve. Remember his view on women? He only liked whores."

"I remember. I met one of his boys yesterday."

"The Major? By 'met' you mean you tangled with him?"

"That's what I mean, yeah."

"Did he give you those bruises?"

"Of course. The Major always could pick a man."

"Is he dead?"

"He's not."

"And you fought hand to hand...? He must be very good."

"He is. Had another couple soften me up first so he

could see what I had, then he came in and almost killed me."

"Will he be a problem?"

"I imagine so."

"Oh I do like this, Tommy. Can you beat him?"

"I think so."

"That'll do me, so. Tell me the rest."

Conlon laid it out. Philomena, the Centurions, Avalon, Sharp, Viv, the Hastings twins, the sacrifices, the pornography, the strange gunshot that had saved him at Amiens Street Station.

Mossy looked upset when he was finished. "Fucking animals," he said.

"So what are we doing?"

"Well. I think Naessens is in on it. I think he had them take his daughter because his driver got her pregnant. I think they murdered the driver and hired me to search for her to cover himself."

"Not realizing that you would actually find her."

"Exactly. So what I did on the island has frightened them. But they think if they take care of me, then it all goes away. I think he told them I'd probably show up at his house to brief him as my client and they could kill me there, and it would all be squared away."

"And what do we think?"

"This is search and destroy, Mossy. We find them in Dublin, we find them on Avalon, we find them wherever they've gone. And we fucking exterminate them."

Mossy smiled with genuine pleasure.

———

AFTER TWO DAYS, Viv had begun to worry about him. She tried to keep her head clear. She read newspapers, the Chekhov play she had been given by one of her instructors, and the copy of Vanity Fair she had read annually since her sixteenth birthday. She went for long, ambling walks along the lengthy harbor wall, she people watched on the front, the beach, in cafés, in busy parks. Kingstown in such sultry summer days was pleasant and bustling, with a feeling of general gaiety. She could lose herself to that when she was out among the people, under the warmth of the sun.

But always she would have to return to the room, and then his absence was impossible to deny. In bed she could not forget what it was like to lie in his arms. The room held his memory for her, and she struggled to overcome that.

She began to construct elaborate scenarios in her imagination. His death. Over and over, different each time. She had a vivid, exciting ability to invent—characters, stories, settings. It had come easy to her as a child and it still did, in adulthood. And usually she saw it as a blessing. As an actress, it surely was.

But now; here, in this room; with Tommy off, in danger, battling a secret army of...whatever they were. Now it was absolutely a curse.

She saw him stabbed in the belly, bleeding to death between his fingers, sagging to the earth in some yard.

Shot in the head by the Liffey, a cloud of blood and bone in the air.

Beaten with clubs and fists by a mob, overwhelmed by bodies, smashing and battering him.

Tortured, tied to a chair, cut and beaten and hurt and hurt and hurt until his body stopped.

Drowned, poisoned, blown up, burned.

She shocked herself with the extent of the violence her own mind could conjure. She shocked herself with how much pain it all caused her. She would tell herself she barely knew him. And yet she knew herself well enough to know that it didn't matter. She knew him. What had happened between them already was enough.

She wrestled with it all for days.

She had nightmares, she lay awake worrying, too hot to sleep, her thoughts circling back again and again to him. Fended it all off and felt it come back to her, relentless as the tide.

She had to do something, or else she would go mad.

———

He had given her his address, just in case.

She took a streetcar and then walked from Stephens Green. The sun was held behind a grey, dulled sky on this morning, but that just made the air clammy with its heat.

It was unpleasant on the tram, even with all of the windows open. She thought it would be nicer on foot, but after a street of walking, she was already awfully sweaty, and she fanned herself with her hat as she went from that point.

In Smithfield, where he lived, she went into a café across from his flat and sat near the window. She had iced tea and half a buttered scone. The heat robbed her of her appetite, so she chewed it without much energy, one eye on his door and the upstairs window. No light or movement while she watched. The red bricks, the blue door and the beige curtains were all she could really see, and they were stolid and dull and almost mockingly banal in the clear hot city air. She had come here in the hope of a reunion, however fleeting, and now she felt foolish and annoyed—at herself, at him, at the situation.

He had said that nobody lived in the ground floor flat, so if she didn't see him, who else would she see? She was also observing the comings and goings on the street and in the café; he had told her that they would be after him, and she was accordingly wary of everyone, but she had no idea what to look for. Unless it was one of the young men she already knew from the Centurions, it could be anyone.

She wanted to scream with frustration. She wanted to knock on his door but that would be too obvious, just in case she was being observed. She wanted to see him.

When she left, she wandered in town for a while. The sun had burnt through the layer of grey and the day was now sizzling onto the cobbles and bricks of the buildings squatting around the Liffey, which gave no sea breeze to lessen the effects of the heat. She took to sticking to the thin strips of shadow thrown by the taller structures, made sure she walked underneath awnings. Then she decided to go home, just to say hello to the Abrahamsons and see if she had any messages.

When she reached the house and had let herself in, closing the front door behind her as she returned her key to her bag, she had a brief, barely perceptible sensation of oddness—as if something had shifted in the space, something she had not even known could shift. The house had a different feeling.

But it was the sort of feeling one shook off because it

was so fleeting and based in instinct, not conscious thought. Only afterwards would it return to her: that her body, her senses had been trying to tell her something.

She walked through the hall, calling out, "Hello?" as she went.

Mr. Abrahamson and Mrs. Abrahamson were both on the floor of the back room. Their mouths were gagged, their hands tied behind their backs; the same ropes pulling their feet up to meet their fingers. They lay on their fronts and both strained up to look at her with wide, imploring eyes as she entered the room.

She cried out in shock and then almost immediately, she controlled herself. Two men were sitting at the table. One of them pointed a revolver steadily at her stomach. Their hats were off and lay casually on the table beside mugs of steaming tea.

Another man was behind her then. He had been waiting in the Abrahamsons' room for her to pass in the hallway.

One of the men at the table stood, picking up his hat. He was very tall, with eyes of cold blue.

"Good afternoon, Miss. You'll be coming with us." An accent.

"I will be doing no such thing. Who do you think you—"

He turned his head to the other man, who pointed his gun at the Abrahamsons. They writhed and cringed away from the aim, livestock in the seconds before slaughter.

She held up a hand. "Wait. Wait, please."

He looked at her with a sad, half smile. "I don't want to hurt anybody here. I don't want to hurt you or these fine people. You know who I want. If you come with us, he will come to us. That is how it must be, Miss. Be practical, I beg you."

She nodded. Words would not come. She wanted to sob.

"What about—?" She gestured at the couple on the floor. Mrs. Abrahamson was weeping, she saw, her eyes reddened with fear and pain.

"My colleague will remain with them until we have left. Then they will be released. You have my word that they will not be harmed."

His accent was odd, but he was uncannily calm and polite. She studied him as he looked to the Abrahamsons and spoke to them. His face was bruised. Cuts on a cheekbone and above his eyebrow. A shiner under the other eye. She knew that Tommy was responsible. She felt a deep sense of doom fill her.

"We are taking this girl," he was saying to her bound housemates, "but we do not wish to harm her. Her male friend, Mr. Conlon, is my quarry. If you go to the police, or inform anyone about what has transpired here, then I assure you, she will be killed. If you can maintain some decorum and control, then all will be well, and I will return her to you, untouched. Does this sound agreeable?"

He chuckled, as if at the absurdity of this situation.

The man with the gun stood. He was younger, and had a haunted, pained look in his eye, she saw as she watched him fit his hat down on a haircut that suggested a long time in the army. The gun was hidden somewhere as he took her arm in a tight, bony hand.

The man behind had moved around her and now leaned against the doorway into the sitting room. He took a cigarette from his pocket, lit it with an extravagant flick of a match, and began to smoke.

The leader said, "Are you ready? We have an automobile."

She nodded.

"I'm sorry," she said to the Abrahamsons, over her shoulder, as the two men led her back down the hall. "I'm sorry."

The automobile was around the corner. She was placed in the back seat, and the leader sat beside her. He gave her a grin. She noticed some teeth missing.

"Did Tommy do that?" she nodded at his face.

He laughed with what seemed to be genuine amusement. "He did. He's a fighter. It will be an honor to kill him."

"You won't kill him."

"Oh, but I will. He's going to be far too worried about you to worry about me."

The car started with the familiar brutal explosion of the engine, and she watched the streets roll by, chewing on her lips, all the way to Camden Street.

22

6 Days After Purification

CONLON USED A FEW PUBS AROUND THE CITY FOR messages. When he was working, some of his contacts knew that they had a good chance of reaching him by telling the barman in Kehoe's or the Hole in the Wall that they were looking for him. Theresa had even used this system in her last weeks of working with him, before she informed him that she found it too difficult to be involved in his life, given what had happened between them.

He'd left it a week or two before he dropped into Slattery's, as ever a busy hum of eating and drinking off the clatter and ringing of Capel Street. Mossy waited outside in the shade, watching the door, knowingly frightening passers-by in the street with his manic eyes and bulk.

The barman, a flinty little Corkman called Ray, saw Conlon come in and nodded, suggesting he had something to pass along.

"Ray," Conlon said. "Been a while."

"It has. There was a Jewman in for you."

"A Jewman?"

"Aye. Didn't know the man. Respectable feller, I'd say."

"When was this?"

"No more than an hour ago. He said it was urgent, and that he'd be in his shop in the South City Markets for the afternoon."

"Jewelry shop, is it?"

"Tailor, so he said. Do you know the man?"

"No, but I know the shop. Thanks, Ray."

Conlon flicked him a shilling, which Ray casually picked out of the air. "Anytime, Tommy. Seeya now."

Together, he and Mossy crossed the Liffey. Mossy asked few questions during times like these, content just to follow along in Conlon's wake, occasionally reacting to some notable instance of Dublin stupidity that struck him as particularly laughable: an ostentatious, florid hat on a passing lady, say, or the cries of the cox as rowers passed under the bridge on the Liffey. He would chuckle cynically to himself, and perhaps mutter something to Conlon.

When they passed under the arch into the covered market hall, busy as it was with shoppers and traders and people enjoying the cool offered by its tiled floor, he did say, "Who are we here to see, then?"

"A tailor was looking for me."

Conlon nodded to the shop, in one of the units halfway along the market.

Seeing the name, Mossy said, "A Shylock?"

Conlon looked at him. "Don't be telling me you're one of those has a problem with Jews."

"No, no. Our next door neighbor is a Jew. Left Limerick after all the trouble they had there and he owns a furniture shop in town. We bought a table off him. Nice discount he gave us. Good people, I'd say."

"You remember Hurwitz?"

"The bomber?"

"That was him."

"I haven't thought of him for a while. He still out there, would you say?"

Conlon shook his head. "He blew his hand off on a job for the Major. I saw him in the hospital in London. He was planning on moving to Australia. He had people there, he said."

"Jaysus, Mary and Joseph. He could blow the sting off a bee and not touch its wings. How'd he blow his own hand off?"

"I asked him that alright." They were standing at the door to the shop now, Conlon's hand ready to push it open. "He said he got distracted for a second, slipped, and boom. He's going back to watch making."

"They'd be fairly good watches, I'd say."

Conlon laughed. "I imagine they would be."

They went into the shop, the bell over the door jangling their arrival. The man who emerged from an alcove near the back of the shop in a waistcoat, hair slicked back, nodded with instant recognition.

"Mr. Conlon."

"That's right. And you'd be Mr. Leventhal?"

They shook hands.

"I'm friends with the Abrahamsons," Leventhal said, and Conlon nodded, remembering Viv's housemates.

"I only met them a few days past."

"They wanted to get a message to you. Men came to

their house, men with guns. They were looking for Miss Logue."

"She's not there, she's safe."

The small man shook his head. "No, no. She arrived home. The men took her."

"She went home?"

"The last the Abrahamsons saw was Miss Logue leaving with these men."

Conlon felt Mossy's hand on his shoulder.

"They have her," he said.

He looked at Mossy. "They have her."

Leventhal said, "I am sorry to give you such awful news."

"No, no, thank you, you've done me a service. If you ever need..."

The tailor nodded and they shook hands.

Conlon and Mossy left and stood outside a moment, the big man watching his friend think, watching him digest all of this, watching him begin to formulate a plan.

"Where'll she be?"

"I don't know, really. They barely exist. They don't exist, officially. They have one building that I know of, but probably a few more that I don't."

"So what do we do?"

"We wait till tonight and then we hit them."

"You sure?"

Conlon looked at him, and Mossy nodded at the look in his eyes. "You're sure."

———

THEY WAITED until half past two in the morning. It was a still, sticky night. People had left windows open, curtains hanging limply in the hope of a breath of breeze.

Conlon had been inside the building so knew the layout and the way in. The courtyard at the front would most likely be under guard, but there was a cellar at the back, and he had asked Mossy to walk by it and evaluate the access before the sun set on the day.

It was an external barrel drop door of the type used in pubs across the city; all the better for rolling barrels of stout off the backs of lorries and straight into storage basements. Easy to breach, and then they were in.

At two, Mossy made his way onto the roof of a building five doors away by climbing out a window on a landing and pulling himself up using his huge hands. A rifle wagged and wiggled on his back, his bulk making it look almost small. Conlon watched from a corner a hundred meters off.

The night silent but for the odd drunk and the footsteps of a patrolling peeler, swinging his baton and failing to notice Conlon, held back in the shadows of a doorway. When he was gone, Conlon moved and crossed a street over, watched for a while from another doorway, and then made his way to the cellar door. He broke the lock with a crowbar, and dropped down into the darkened space. He allowed his eyes to adjust. Light was dimly seeping through the gap at a door at the top of the steps, giving everything a ghostly air.

It was a big room, low ceilinged, and he heard the sound of his own movement echo back at him in the space. It appeared empty but for some crates by one wall, broken wooden chairs piled in a corner as if waiting to be thrown into a fire, and what looked like an old printing press, half covered by a tarpaulin on a table. Conlon lowered the doors closed above him and crouched, listening for a sign that his incursion had been overheard.

After a moment, he moved forwards, slipping the pistol from the waistband at his lower back, the crowbar in his other hand. He checked his watch. Mossy would start shooting soon.

The stairs were brick and pitted with holes and gouges; he climbed them slowly and cautiously, choosing each step with care, feeling himself tense as he got nearer that door. He was through it quickly and at the far end of the big room he had been in for the lecture, when he and Viv had talked his way in. The light was coming in a diffuse spray through the windows, from the moon, hanging summer-large in the clear black sky. Otherwise, the building was dark. And deserted. Not a man in sight. No gunmen, no Centurions and certainly no Viv.

He perfunctorily searched the room and some of the smaller chambers branching out from it, but it had been abandoned. Newspapers, a couple of mugs and ashtrays filled with cigarette butts were all that remained.

He felt a mixture of hopelessness and anger. Hopelessness because he had let her down, and at this point, he had no idea where she was. Anger at himself. For not checking the building. For not watching longer. For not realizing it was empty.

He let himself out the front door, hands up, so that Mossy, watching through a scope from his rooftop vantage, would know that it was him.

By the time he was out on the street, Mossy was there.

"We got here too late?" he said as he approached.

"They've cleared out."

"And we don't know where?"

Conlon shook his head. Mossy put a huge hand on his shoulder, a rare act of obvious warmth. They both turned at the sound of footsteps.

Two men had emerged from a doorway thirty meters away and were approaching. In the gas light, they appeared smartly dressed, one middle-aged, the other in his early twenties, perhaps.

Conlon put his hand to the pistol, and Mossy, noticing, tensed.

"That will not be necessary, Mr. Conlon," one of the men called out.

Conlon peered at him under the streetlights. "I don't know you," he said.

The one who had spoken was short, plumpish, his face carrying weight in his cheeks and jaw so that his head looked to have the shape of a pear. His hair was heavily oiled flat to his head and he carried a rather ostentatious top hat in one hand, expensive enough that it had a gleam to its surface in the artificial light. His clothes too were all fine, obviously expensive, even in the dim light.

The other man was a veteran. Conlon could tell at a glance. His eyes had the hollow, pained look around them. He was thin in that hard lethal way and coiled, ready to act at any instant. The muscle, a bodyguard. The older man was important, or wealthy, or most likely both.

"But we know you. We have an automobile just

around the corner. Would you possibly allow that we finish this conversation there, so that your friend doesn't get us all arrested with that rifle on his back?"

Conlon and Mossy exchanged a look. Conlon nodded at the men, who turned away and indicated that they should be followed.

They were led around the corner to a motorcar parked outside a hat shop. Conlon recognized the vehicle from the front. Officers had been driven around in these, like roman senators carried in litters.

Mossy said it aloud, "Is this a D-type?"

"It is. We've repainted it, and the seats might be more comfortable than you're accustomed to from the War."

Mossy chuckled. "We never got to ride in these over there."

They all climbed in, and Conlon appreciated that the men allowed him and Mossy to sit in the back for their own sense of security. Mossy tucked the rifle at his feet, but kept the strap wound tight around his fist, in case he needed to pull it free and start shooting.

The veteran drove, still having uttered not a sound, and they wound their way through the silent, somewhat eerie streets, across the Liffey to Mountjoy Square, where they were ushered into one of the grand houses on the southern end.

The men took them into a dining room, offering food and drink. When each of them had a cup of tea, Conlon said, "It was you. At Amiens Street."

The older man said, "Well, it was Marr here. He's an excellent shot, as you saw."

Conlon nodded at Marr, who returned the gesture. He had still not smiled, his face an impassive mask.

Mossy said, "Who were you with?"

Marr looked at him. "Welsh Guards. I joined up in Wrexham." His voice was soft, gentle, a contrast to his hardened, tight features.

"Welsh Guards? Did you know John Diggle?"

"Everybody knew Diggers. That Elephant Gun of his."

Mossy laughed. "He could shoot, though."

"He could."

Conlon looked at the other man. "Why? Why are we here? Who are you?"

"That does not really matter, Mr. Conlon. All you really need to know is that we have a common cause. We want to help you."

"'We?'"

"I represent a group of concerned citizens with the resources to act upon our concerns. The organization you are currently battling have been a problem for our group, but we have had no means of addressing them until you became involved."

Conlon stared at him in silence for a moment, allowing it to drag out until it became uncomfortable.

"Tell me about your group," he eventually said.

"We would rather...not reveal too much. We are Irishmen. Patriots."

"Fenians?" Mossy said, without any judgement in the word.

"No. We do not take political action. Not at this time. But we observe. We see our country changing. And we anticipate further, future changes."

Mossy laughed. "This is shite, Tommy. More landowners trying to rule from the shadows."

"No, no. We simply seek to protect our heritage and our culture."

"Like the Gaelic League?" Mossy said.

"We have some aims in common. But we see more of a panoramic picture. And pay more respect to history. Mr. Conlon here may not know or understand it, but we see in him a great Irish hero struggling to protect his people. Cu Chulainn. Fionn Mac Cumhaill."

Conlon, sensing some mockery and a test of some sort, shook his head. "Enough. What do you want?"

"These so-called "Centurions" are a criminal organization masquerading as a religion. A false cult, which is in actuality a convenience trick. We have seen you stand up to them. We have seen you bloody them. We want to help you destroy them."

Conlon and Mossy exchanged a look.

"How do you propose to do that?" Conlon said.

"They have abducted a young lady of your acquaintance. We understand that this is to inhibit you taking any direct action against them, while they in turn hunt you and attempt to kill you. We know where she is."

"Any manpower or reinforcements coming our way?" Mossy asked.

"Our involvement must remain indirect."

"Not even your man?" Mossy nodded at Marr.

"Indirect, I'm afraid. We can supply equipment and weaponry, if you should need. Perhaps some hired men if the situation is serious enough."

"So we get Viv back," Conlon said. "And then?"

"They are already starting to run. There are men involved at quite high levels of the British administration in this country."

"I don't really care about them."

"Yes, yes. You want Naessens."

Conlon nodded. "And their Caesar."

"He is a man whose disgrace is already in motion. We have seen to that. He will run, now. We can give both of them to you, Mr. Conlon."

"How is that possible?"

"We show you where they are, and you do what only you can really do."

"And then we just shake hands?"

"You will most likely never hear from or of us again."

Conlon was silent again. Finally, he nodded. "Sounds fair. Where is she?"

7 Days After Purification

ACCORDING TO THE NAMELESS MAN, AND THE intelligence gathered by his mysterious confederates, Viv was being held in a printers on the edge of the docks.

Conlon and Mossy watched and assessed it through binoculars from the windy roof top of a Milliners a quarter of a mile away. It was the first day in weeks that the sun was hidden by the sky, and they had come here as sunrise prized loose the grip of the night, presenting a chill morning and a promise of the Autumn.

The printers was a detached, squat red-brick structure with wide bay doors and high walls enclosing a yard, barbed wire curling along the lips of the wall and the flat metal gates. There was a guard visible, sitting atop a porch on a folding chair, nodding off with a pistol in his waistband. They watched the building as the sun burned through into the morning. Another man left the printers, smoking and heading towards the river.

"Who were they?" Mossy said, almost to himself. "All of this makes me feel uncomfortable. These people who hide in the shadows, pulling strings. It makes me want to break things."

Conlon chuckled. "I know. To me, they sounded like...another cult. Annoyed that a false cult has moved in on their turf. And these lads might be genuine, and they might have Ireland's best interests at heart—"

"I doubt that," Mossy spat.

Conlon nodded in acknowledgement. "But they're just more little men wanting control. They see us as a way of getting what they want, like Xavier and all the petty little tyrants fighting for streets, for bookies, for floozies, for guns. They don't care about Viv or about the Naessens girl or about all the other girls these Centurion fucks have destroyed. They just want things the way they want them."

"But they can help us," Mossy said.

"They can. So here we are."

They were silent a while.

"How much time do we have? How long do you want to watch?" Mossy asked him, his exasperation evident. He had never been a fan of reconnaissance.

"We need a few hours at least, to estimate how many there are. You know that, Mossy."

"Can't be going in blind," Mossy growled, impersonating the Major.

They both laughed softly.

"Could be a dozen men in there," Conlon said. "Sure there must be ten rooms, at least. Presumably a big printing press, so a space in a workshop for that."

"No idea of what sort of weapons they have. If your

friend who gave you a beating is there, you'd say he'd have them ready."

"Yeah."

"And we can't go in heavy, not knowing where your lady is."

They were quiet, watching.

Conlon said, "I know how to do this."

———

BARRY MET them at the Point Train Depot on the North Wall at midday, only a short walk from the printers. Conlon and Mossy had bought fish and chips from the nearby Italian chipper that served hungry dockworkers and were sharing it from some greasy newspaper while sitting on the Quay, legs dangling above the blue of the river, tidal swells still burrowing through its surface this close to the sea.

Barry strolled over and said "Give us a chip, mister" in perfect imitation of the many Urchins filling the city streets. Mossy tossed one over his shoulder without even looking around and Barry snatched it out of the air and had disappeared it into his mouth before he even sat down beside Conlon. He made that huffing sound to indicate that it was a bit too hot inside his mouth, arranged his coat as he sat, removing his hat and straightening his oiled hair with one hand.

"Tommy," he said. "I've been waiting for a call."

"That inevitable call that somebody's found this one's body?" Mossy asked, mouth full of cod, gesturing at Conlon.

"Good to see you, too, Mossy," Barry said.

He extricated his pipe from a pocket and set about filling the bowl.

"Have you found anything out about that murder?" Conlon asked him.

"The Naessens' driver? Nothing. Lord Naessens is away on business. His wife has been laid up with influenza when I've called upon her. Their butler isn't much help. I can't believe you've called me to inform me that you've managed to solve my case for me, now Tommy."

"What about the Centurions of Light?"

"Ah now. I asked around. Lots of whispers. They seem to be connected to a company that imports books, and lots of the lads at the station have heard the name, but details are scarce, I'd say. I'm waiting for a call back from a friend at the Castle for an off-the-record chat about them."

"They're bad news," Mossy said.

Barry looked from him to Conlon.

Conlon nodded. "The religion aspect is a cover. It helps them recruit—loads of men back from the war who work for them. A little army. Workers, soldiers. Men with nowhere else to go, no skills except they can shoot a rifle. Some of them are on the run, AWOL, maybe from the law. Mercenaries in charge of them. And girls. Young girls. They make dirty films, photographs. They have an island off the coast up north, it's all set up there. A little film studio, a barracks, loads of guns, electricity, the whole thing. Girls kept locked in cells. Murder, Barry. They kill some of those girls."

"You're joking me."

"You know I ain't."

"Did you find Philomena Naessens?"

"I did."

"Did you get her out?"

"I did. But they tracked us down and took her back."

"You need to tell her father."

"Her father is one of them."

"Jesus, Tommy..."

"A few of the bosses are businessmen, British landlords, that sort. They're in it for the thrill."

"Have you got any proof for me? I can't just be making wild accusations without any—"

"There's a printers five minutes from here. I think it's their Dublin base now. Go in there with a few officers, you'll find enough evidence to let you arrange a raid on their island."

"What are we looking at? Even that needs a story..."

"Lots of guns. You tell the Castle boys that there's a cache of guns, rumors it's Fenians...they'll be here before you finish smoking that pipe."

Barry rubbed his face. "Alright. You can't be coming in with us, then. You know that."

Conlon nodded. "Go easy though. There might be a girl there, a prisoner. Maybe other girls, too, with these people."

"That one's a friend of yours?"

"She is."

"It'll take me an hour or so to arrange. What'll you two be doing?"

"Watching the show for once. We'll see if we can pick up any strays."

Barry nodded, took a long, deep, soulful suck on his pipe, and stood. He settled his coat around him. "It's never boring, Tommy, I'll give you that."

He tipped his hat and was gone.

———

CONLON AND MOSSY watched the raid, almost two hours later, from the rooftop. They felt the tension and heard the silence as the constables massed, huddled across the road from the printers, out of sight around a corner, and then broke onto the building like a wave, batons raised in anticipation of violence. Some gained ingress through the front gate, another group went in at the rear. They watched the door open a crack then swing in under the pressure of the men. There was a great deal of yelling but they heard no gunfire, inarticulate shouting and screams rising into the afternoon sky.

Barry was right in the middle of it, the third man in the door, and he was perhaps the last man who emerged, ten or so minutes later. By then a cluster of men sat handcuffed just inside the gate and they had also seen four young women led out to a waiting carriage.

Uniformed men were in and out, carrying crates, boxes and files; conversing with Barry; filling the back of a lorry; smoking on the curb and filling out sheets that were clipped to boards.

When a fifth came out, Conlon recognized her as Viv. She squinted in the light and covered her eyes but aside from that, she seemed fine. Barry raised a hand in his direction, but he and Mossy had agreed to stay away.

Mossy looked at him. "You see anyone else you recognize?"

"No. No Hastings, no Sharp, no Alan, no Naessens, no Caesar. The important ones are somewhere else."

"Running?"

Conlon shrugged.

It took almost another hour for Barry to find time to come to them.

"I have to make it quick," he said. "You weren't wrong. Twenty-five rifles, enough ammunition to start another rising, a fair few cases of dynamite, loads of pamphlets, some of their smut...and the four girls. Two of them are opiumed to the eyeballs. Your Viv is fine, asking for you."

"So, what now?"

"We'll question some of these amadan and try to find out more about your Avalon. We need to talk to the girls, too. And then I have a fair bit of paperwork to do. Come to the station at about nine tonight and we'll have a chat and I'll release her to you, alright?"

"Thanks, Barry. Nice job."

"Well, thanks for the tip. Made me look like a genius."

"Sure I'm just letting everyone see you the way I see you, Barry."

"What, as your skivvy?"

They both laughed. Barry nodded to Mossy and was off to his paperwork.

———

WHEN CONLON ARRIVED to collect Viv, Mossy made his excuses and disappeared into the night to do whatever it was that Mossy did. They had agreed to meet the next afternoon in the usual place to plot their next move. Conlon knew Mossy was keen to hunt down as many Centurions as possible, but he was tired of the whole case today, weary of the moral rut it had dragged him through, exhausted from the days of fighting, alertness, worry.

He just wanted Viv in his arms, and to forget about it all. But the niggle of Philomena Naessens was there, deep down, digging into his conscience with an angled, sharp elbow. He tried to ignore it.

Viv made that easier. Her smile when she saw him gave him a flush of goosebumps, a lightening in his stomach. They rushed back to his flat—him reasoning that with the Centurions on the run, they had better things to do than come after him—and into his bed together.

Afterwards they told each other what they had been through, her curled inside his arms, his nose nestled in the nape of her neck, their fingers interlocked. She was quieter than he had seen her, unable to shake the fear and the coldness of what had happened to her. Being brought so close to the violence that some men were capable of inflicting in the world could make a person doubt every certainty that they had. He had seen it so many times already in his life, seen people react in every way imaginable. Some imploded, some were strengthened by their own survival.

She was a big personality, but that was no guarantee of anything. Violence—evil, even—was so implacable that it could rock the strongest human to their foundations, could strip them down until nothing recognizable remained.

When she had moved in his arms and kissed him hungrily, he had not felt any difference in her. She was as vital and passionate as before. But now, she seemed altered; slightly strange and brittle. He let her talk, said gentle, comforting things; made her laugh and held her close.

Finally, they slept.

———

SOMETHING AWOKE HIM. It was still dark, the summer dawn perhaps an hour away, the city silent beyond the bedroom windows. Viv's body was warm beside him. He cocked a head and listened, just barely raising his ear from the pillow.

She whispered, "What is it?"

"I heard something."

"I think I did, too."

He shushed her and they both listened. Nothing. The silence elongated, but now it felt loaded, pregnant with something dangerous.

He remembered this feeling from sentry duty in the War. Your fears filling in the darkness, loading the wind with imagined peril. But at the same time: he trusted his gut.

He laid a hand on her shoulder and slipped naked from bed. His floorboards were creaky, so he took one step towards his clothes, piled by the wall, his pistol somewhere in the tangle, and then the door exploded inwards, kicked by somebody.

There were men in the room, a gun pointed at the bed, Viv shouting in alarm and scuttling out, dragging the sheets with her.

Conlon was behind the door as it bounced almost off its frame and he put the sole of a foot to it and battered it back the way it had come. One of the men—the second—was struck in the arm and thrown into the first, whose shot found the floor. Conlon was on him then, chopping down at the gun and skittering it away, then following through with a shoulder charge and slamming him towards the windows. He sprawled against one, and the glass broke with a jagged crack.

Conlon had already pivoted and hit the second man, who was recovering his balance in the doorway, with a huge cross right in the center of his face. His nose broke with a ripe, satisfying crunch, and down he went.

There was another man behind, in the hall, levelling a gun at Conlon. Hastings.

Conlon jumped out of the doorway as the shot came.

The man near the windows had recovered and he grabbed Conlon in an attempted chokehold, his forearm tight under Conlon's chin, already cutting off the air. Conlon struggled but his naked foot found no purchase on the rug, which rolled away from him, and the floorboard was no better. The man was strong; a big man with a laborer's brawn.

Hastings stepped into the room.

Viv was moaning against the wall, hiding her body under the sheet.

Hastings smiled.

"I'll give that arse Sharp this—he knows how to plan a trap, he does. He said you'd come for her after the raid and then we could just follow you wherever you went to get your end away. He was so confident he didn't even need to see me kill you. Night night, Conlon."

He raised the gun, pressed the barrel to Conlon's forehead, and tossed a glance Viv's way.

The shot punched a hole in the glass of the window and another in Hastings' hand. His gun jumped spinning into the air, as he cried out, blood splashing from his ruined knuckles. Mossy, Conlon knew.

Conlon reacted before the gun had even struck the floor, throwing all his weight backwards and driving the big man who was choking him into the wall between the windows. The impact released his grip and Conlon drove a sharp, hard elbow into his eye, then slipped away from him, turning and pivoted two big right hooks into his face. He staggered, waving a mauling paw towards Conlon, who leant away and then darted in to make a ruin of his face with a rapid series of punches with both hands, his feet planted, power and adrenaline flowing up into his fists.

Hastings had recovered some of his poise and drawn a knife from his belt. He held his gun hand up, a bloody mess.

"You—fucking..." he said as Conlon advanced towards him.

He was quick; an experienced knife fighter, Conlon could see. He held it before him like a fencer and it waved continuously as they moved, in side-steps in the small space.

Hastings moved first, a tiny shuffling half step bringing him in, and Conlon had to arch away and fold an uppercut under the knife strike to clack Hasting's teeth together like a shutting bear trap. Instead of folding, Hastings shifted his grip on the blade and caught the top of Conlon's thigh as he stepped away.

He could feel it; a deep, yelling pain, as they circled again.

And now he felt his anger rise—at this little man, killing at the behest of his lords, killing and enjoying it, killing girls, terrorizing them—and this time he was the one who moved. He slapped the knife hand away and hit Hastings with a massive overhand that broke his jaw, teeth crunching under it.

Conlon grabbed his knife wrist, pinning him to the doorframe with his shoulder. Hastings tried to knee him, and Conlon twisted away, pressing harder with his bulk. He focused on the knife hand and broke Hastings' wrist with a wrenching crack. Then he took the knife and he sank it into the flesh between Hastings' Adam's apple and his chin. Hastings began to sink slowly to the floor, as if sitting for a rest, his knees bending to accommodate his descent.

Conlon stood and watched blood flood into Hastings' mouth, his eyes wide as he struggled to comprehend, a clicking, watery noise like the banging of plumbing dribbling out of him.

When he was sitting, blood still flowing from his throat and in bubbling lines from between his lips, Conlon pulled the knife from him, as easily as he would from a loaf of fresh bread, and Hastings' head flopped heavily forward. Blood splattered onto the floor between his splayed legs.

Conlon breathed, and looked around for Viv.

Her eyes, wide, were filled with absolute horror, the sheet still held over her nakedness for protection.

24

14 Days After Purification

CONLON STOOD AT THE BOW OF THE STEAMSHIP, watching the calm of the ocean lick at the sky. Behind him, Mossy was sitting with his back against one of the barrels that were lashed together centrally, eating an apple, squinting against the sun, a switchblade twirling in his fingers. They chatted sporadically, comfortably, about nothing of much importance, their years of intimacy meaning nothing was out of bounds.

There was no land visible, and barely any wind here. It felt curiously as if they were crossing a lake even though the ship was making steady progress upon such still waters; and cut across the northern edge of the Irish Sea for the western coast of Scotland.

They were hunting the Centurions of the Light.

Conlon could feel how jolly this all made Mossy. His excitement fairly radiated off him, and all his usual short-tempered grumpiness had absolutely melted away.

The benefactors who spoke mysteriously of Irish Legends and protecting their heritage had given them information and provided the ship and its small crew of men who were respectful but kept their distance. All Conlon and Mossy had to do was kill the men they found, and all the crew had to do was get them where they needed to be in order to do that, was how Marr had put it to Conlon at the harbor in Derry.

So the men would leave them alone. Conlon would tell them where they were going, and they would be delivered there.

Three days before he and Mossy had accompanied a unit of twenty RIC men, together with DMP Detective Barry, as they landed on the island the Centurions had called Avalon, from which Conlon had escaped just over a week before. They had approached early in the morning, their small craft stealthy over the waves as it bore down on the dark bulk of the island.

The men were told that Conlon and Mossy were specialist consultants, and on that boat, the simplicity of their preparations, the way they shed unnecessary equipment, told any of the men who had served that these two men from down south were experienced soldiers, and that they had executed raids like this one before.

Dawn was tingling off in the eastern sky as they had waded ashore, Conlon leading, he and Mossy running up the beach with their rifles sweeping the tree line for any resistance, the men's boots crunching as they moved into the woodland beyond the sands.

He had led them back over the land he had hunted in to the makeshift village at the center of the Centurions operation. He knew before they were even in sight of it that they were too late. There was no sound. None of the noise that humanity brought with it, the babble of chat, the hum of the generator, the ring of steel on steel. Just the silence filling in the spaces around the natural sounds of the wood.

Still he took them in quietly, checking buildings for lingering serfs, ensuring all were alert and ready. But there was nobody living. All abandoned.

Barry had been happy enough; they found enough evidence to show the scale of the Centurions' operation to justify this raid and to keep a few men busy for the next year or so hunting down the rodents scattering from the burning house. Most of the equipment has been left behind. The cameras, lights, the sets in the studio. Cabinets filled with dirty pictures.

The armory was locked and fully stocked when they had busted it open. Rows of rifles, handguns arrayed in cabinets, boxes of dynamite and ammunition eliciting oohs and murmured horror from the RIC men who wandered around, rubbing their chins, muttering about German invasions.

And then there was the graveyard.

Conlon had led them there. When he had last seen it there were four graves—all serfs who had died in their time there, they had been told. Now there were perhaps a half dozen new graves with simple markers—Conlon realized that he was responsible for those—and a long trench of newly dug earth just beyond the actual boundary of the cemetery itself. Mossy had been the one who saw that.

A couple of the men began digging and before long they had started to come upon remains—bones and decomposing bodies in sacks, a shallow pit for the sacrificed girls.

Men had retched and vomited while a somber Barry had spoken of the need for a pathologist. None of the remains—the bodies of eight young women, in all—had been pregnant, so it seemed that Philomena Naessens was not with them, after all.

Conlon had placed a telephone call to Lady Naessens once they were back in Derry, and her relieved weeping had only been ended by the butler, Martin, taking the phone from her and thanking Conlon.

His next call had been to the number supplied by the benefactors who wanted him to stamp out the Centurions. Mossy had taken to calling them the "Celtic Gobshites" and Conlon found it hard not to refer to them that way whenever they spoke. But their wealth and the speed with which they made arrangements—money seemingly no object—was undeniably useful.

They already knew about Avalon, suggesting that they had people within the RIC, and Conlon was beginning to suspect that they had people everywhere. Celtic Gobshites perhaps, but influential Gobshites, it seemed.

Their "sources" told them that the group of leaders of the Centurions had fled across the sea for Scotland, and they were arranging for a vessel and a crew for Conlon and Mossy. What else might they need?

And so here they were, only a few days later.

"What did you tell George?" he asked Mossy. The big man had disappeared for a long telephone conversation before they had departed.

"The truth."

"All of it?"

"Oh yes. He loves the details."

Conlon squinted at him. "You've told him everything you've done?"

"I might have forgotten the odd scrap, like. There've been a fair few...but most, yeah."

"Good God. And he's not bothered by any of it?"

"He was a doctor with the army in India. I reckon he's seen his share of awful shite."

Conlon nodded, and looked back at the sea.

Mossy skewered him instantly. "Not everyone sees things like Viv, Tommy."

"I know. You should have seen the way she looked at me. The fear in her."

He shook his head at the memory, trying not to bring up the conversation which had followed.

Mossy said, "She got a glimpse of you going berserker, didn't she? The Major called it that, I remember. I've seen you like that, too. It scared me. Me! She is from that other world that we live in some of the time. She's not from our world, Tommy. My George is, he's been there. She'll recover, she'll forget it all."

"No, she won't," Conlon said. "She felt sorry for me. I could see it in her. This...pity. She said I enjoyed it."

"Well. You do, don't you?"

Conlon turned and looked at him. "Not the killing, no. Never. Even when it is the only option, no, and they deserve to be put down like dogs, no. But the way I feel in the thick of it. I like that."

"It feels good to do what you're good at."

"It does. And she saw how good I am."

"After I'd saved your arse with a fairly stupendous shot, to be fair."

Conlon laughed. "It was a great shot."

"Ah sure it was good of him to oblige me and put his

hand right into view. And good of them to decide to kill you when they did. I was getting tired of waiting."

"How did you know?"

"Ah Tommy...you would've known if you hadn't been so focused on Viv. It was all so easy. Laid out for us like cheese in a mousetrap. So I used you the same way."

"Did you tell George about all that, too?"

"I did of course. He wanted all the details about how you fought three men in a small room, unarmed. I believe he thinks I've made you up."

"Well, I got a scar for my troubles, that's not made up." Conlon lightly patted his thigh, tightly bandaged over the stitches just below his hip. It had opened on Avalon, and still he felt the flat pressure of the closure, the slight drag in his step.

"Another for the collection," Mossy said. "And this scar here?"

He tapped his chest, indicating his heart, and despite himself, and the misery that consumed him whenever he thought of Viv, Conlon laughed.

Mossy smiled to have created that response. "Did you tell her about Orla?" he asked.

"Not really."

"So that means that you did. You mentioned her?"

"I may have acknowledged that she had existed, Mossy, yes."

Mossy shook his head. He started to speak, stopped himself, and shook his head again.

Conlon noted all of this and said nothing. That was a conversation he did not have the energy for.

It was another matter at night. Lying awake in his bunk, the sea churning, he replayed his conversation with Viv over and over. Things he wished he had said. What she had said. The way she had looked at him.

They had no time to talk then, with Hastings dead on the floor, one of the other two men moaning until Conlon punched him unconscious, the other a limp rag of meat. Mossy had appeared brandishing his rifle, and through all this a pale, frozen-featured Viv had been dressing, calmly and with intense focus, not speaking, as if she were trying to will herself to be elsewhere.

It had been later that same night, after a call to Barry had summoned DMP men, who had arrived within minutes, then hours in the Castle explaining things—going over it and over it with Barry only ever in the background, offering apologetic shrugs. Only after all that, when they had finally been released, could they actually talk to one another.

They checked into a hotel on Dame Street at around four in the morning, the sky already lightening in the East, seagulls arcing in the sky. As Conlon signed the register, signing them in as Mr. and Mrs. Conlon, and nodded to the concierge, Viv was hollow-eyed, her face a grim mask of shock and exhaustion. She followed him upstairs but already he could feel her withdrawal, he knew not to touch her.

She vanished into the water closet in the room, and when she emerged, he took her place. When he was done, she was sitting on the edge of the bed, fully dressed.

"You need to sleep, Viv," he said, as gently as he could manage.

She nodded and began to weep—a silent, intense weeping, the tears squeezing out of her eyes soundlessly, her body shuddering.

He went to hold her and she pushed him away, shaking her head, whimpering, "no no no no no," under her breath.

So he sat and waited.

Eventually she gathered herself and said, "I never thought I'd see the things I've seen today, or yesterday."

"I'm sorry."

She shook her head in a way that indicated he should be silent, her eyes shut. She would not look at him.

"You hear about these things, you read about them. The War. I lived here during the Rising, for God's sake. But you don't feel it, like this, like all this."

"It gets better."

"No, you don't understand. I saw you. I saw you, how you were. How you are. Like an animal. Tearing those men apart."

"They would've killed us."

"No, no, no. You were..." She shook her head, searching for the words, the feelings. "A few hours ago, I was sure that I wanted to be with you, beside you, until I was old. That was all I wanted when they had me. But now I see that this...this world you've created for yourself creates these situations. You go after people like that, so they come after you. And you're able to hurt them. It's ok if you hurt them. And that's what you want."

"No, Viv. It's not—"

"Tommy. I know. I know you were protecting me. I understand they would have killed us. But I saw you. You-you liked it, somehow. Part of you. And I don't want you to touch me, ever again. I can't—what you did...I'm not like you. I can't take it." She shook her head again.

"Viv," he said, hopelessly.

"You're right, I need to sleep. I'm going to sleep. Please don't leave. I'm afraid, now. I'm afraid of you, but I know that if anyone comes for me, you'll be here and you'll tear them apart. I understand now why they're so afraid of you. I understand how you can do some of the things you've done. God help you, Tommy."

She looked at him then, in the eyes, a deep sorrow and pity there. He hung his head, shame rising in him.

She lay down on the bed, still dressed, and rolled the eiderdown around her form. She was asleep in minutes.

He sat there in the creeping light of dawn. She was right, he had been thinking. She was right.

———————

THE NEXT MORNING, they were polite; wary and stilted like strangers.

He had eventually nodded off in the chair and slept an hour or two. She awoke him when she rose to wash and he was weary as he took his turn after her. He needed a shave and a haircut. He needed a rest.

When they were both ready, they ventured down and had breakfast in the hotel restaurant. It was one of those Dublin summer mornings when the light is steely and greying, sharpening the air and building up pressure between the buildings, the sun lost in a featureless sky, the heat already stultifying in the airless dining room.

He found himself famished after the day and night before. She ate little, but drank cup after cup of tea. They didn't speak. She had made a call on a telephone in the hotel lobby, and he waited with her until the porter summoned her a cab.

He walked outside with her. The driver climbed down, the horse shivering, and then realized there was no baggage and climbed back up, shushing the animal in a thick Dublin accent.

She turned to look at him before she climbed up.

"I'm sorry, Tommy. I just can't do it. I haven't got your strength."

He nodded, saying nothing.

"I'm just a normal girl. I need a normal life."

"You're not normal, Viv."

"You know what I mean," she said.

"Where will you go?"

"I have an aunt in Roscommon. I'll stay with her for a while. I'll send you the address."

"Will I see you again?"

"I don't think so, Tommy. Please, let me know when it's done, so I know you're alright. I'll be sick with worry."

"I will."

She nodded and put out her hand and squeezed his wrist. "Take care, Tommy. Be careful."

He nodded again.

She gave him one last, long, lingering, sorrowful look, and then she climbed up and was gone.

He had watched the horse and cab rattle away and turn towards the Quays, and then he had headed in the other direction, his mood foul, and not improved by the shave and haircut he paid for twenty minutes later, or by the chatter of the barber, determined to tell him his opinion on the flu; on the elections of Dev and Cosgrave; on the Irish Convention; on the Leinster

Senior League; on the change to the recipe to the tea cakes from the bakery on the corner.

He felt furious. No sadness yet. Just anger, a hot, flat feeling of rage. They had taken her from him. All of those girls killed. And now Viv taken.

He felt furious.

———

ONLY THIS VOYAGE and the blue of the sky over the slow movement of the ocean had lifted him out of himself. He was glad when it was morning, and he could stop thinking of her and talk to Mossy and watch the small islands off the Scottish coast begin to pass by, a series of glorious beaches and rocky shorelines yellow under the sun.

The captain told him they were headed into a Loch and would dock at Fort William, then travel by road towards Inverness. The Centurions were somewhere in the Highlands, they knew. Their people in Scotland were searching, apparently, but their most recent intelligence placed a group of the leaders of the Centurions as leaving Fort William in a motor car a few days earlier. They had men at each of the ports and stations, they were told. Caesar and Naessens were still in Scotland.

Usually Conlon would have bridled at all of this—these unseen agents doing the legwork, the obscene amounts of money and influence these Celtic Gobshites were casually displaying, the implicit understanding that Mossy and himself were there basically as assassins, the triggermen who would take care of the leaders of the Centurions. But after everything that had happened over the last few weeks, all he had seen and heard and been through, he just wanted this to be over, and these bad men to be dead. He knew that he and Mossy would have a better chance of making that happen than anybody else would. So he consented to being used.

It also took his mind off Viv, which was no small thing at present. He allowed the feeling in him to kindle his anger and waited for his opportunity to put it to use.

———

FORT WILLIAM WAS slung low and grey at the end of the water, the green beyond it stretching endlessly over rolling slopes and valleys, off into the distance. The skies here were vast, clouds filling the eye but dragged onward by winds, the light changing by the minute.

They were met at the dock by two men, each with his own automobile. Conlon and Mossy were prepared, and climbed into the first, each toting a bag of gear, Mossy's rifle in a leather case which was strapped across his huge back.

Two of the crew took the other motorcar. They called themselves Harrigan and Holt, though Conlon suspected those names were false. They had identified themselves on the first day as soldiers of fortune, who had fought together in Mexico and China after serving in the British army. Harrigan had a deep scar from his hairline to his chin, similar to the one sported by one of the Hastings twins, just missing his eye, while Holt walked with a pronounced limp. They were both perhaps in their early 40s, old for mercenaries, but they were economical in all that they did, and Conlon knew instantly that they were excellent soldiers and extremely dangerous men.

Harrigan did all of their talking in a gentle Kerry lilt that made a telling contrast with his battle scarred face. They were being paid, and being paid well, to do whatever Conlon told them to do.

"How well is well?" Mossy could not resist asking.

"Enough to set us both up for the rest of our lives," Harrigan said, Holt smiling gently beside him and nodding.

"Jaysus, we're at this for free," Mossy said.

"So would it be safe to say that these fellas we're going after are a bit dangerous, then?" Harrigan asked.

"They have men. Some men you may even be acquainted with. So it all depends how many of those men they've taken with them."

"Or how many they're willing to pay when they get to where they're going," Harrigan finished.

Conlon nodded. "Yes. But we should have surprise on our side. And they will have their leaders with them, who are not fighting men."

"Evens, then?"

"Could be. Mossy here is the best shot I've ever seen. I'm more skilled close up. So we'll probably need you two to work somewhere in the middle."

"Whatever you need. We're all rounders, aren't we?" He looked at Holt, who gave a sage nod.

Both of them carried revolvers in shoulder holsters under tan leather jackets and wore trousers tucked into socks high up their calves, with desert boots, as if going on safari. Both favored Winchester 1890s and Conlon had watched them fill bandoliers with rounds on the deck in the sun, smoking endless cigarettes and drinking tea by the gallon. Both wore dark hats: Harrigan in a golf cap, Holt in a fedora much like the one Conlon wore when he felt a flat cap was insufficient. Mossy said little about them, which suggested he had no worries about their ability, and he even discussed rifles with Harrigan at sundown on their voyage. Conlon trusted that they would do their jobs, which was a feeling he had once taken for granted.

Now they commandeered the second automobile, Holt relegating the driver to a back seat so that he and Harrigan were sitting in front. Conlon nodded to them, gave his own driver the nod, and they rolled away with the usual rumble of engines.

Some of the roads they followed that afternoon were pitted and cracked like old bone, and the motorcars juddered and bounced across them. Other times they shot down hillside roadways and crossed valleys in a few minutes, Conlon's eyes taking in the beauty of this wild, mostly empty landscape. The River Ness was sporadically visible on their left, then in the last hour the road wound steadily alongside, and they passed more cottages and hamlets as they drove. Faces were raised from behind stone walls, squinting as the two vehicles noisily passed by.

Twice it rained, brief squalls falling through the sunshine, the grass dry within seconds of cessation.

As the sky began to seep twilight, they saw the sharp twinkle of lights ahead. Inverness, where they would spend that night.

The drive to the farmhouse where they were staying took them through the center of town, with a scattering of grand buildings, the streets already quiet with the hush of evening. Their billet was perhaps thirty minutes beyond the town, and it was still twilight when they arrived, the squat little house a half mile back from the road down a track of mud dried to dust which clouded around the two vehicles as they went.

The man who met them at the farmhouse saw Conlon squinting at the sky and told him that it would only go dark for a few hours, and not until closer to midnight. Like most of the Gobshites' people, he was modest, efficient, nameless. Conlon would have struggled to describe him only minutes after his departure.

Before he went, he told them what he knew. The Centurions were in a house less than an hour away. A big house in the Highlands, owned by a conservative member of parliament, also a prominent Scottish businessman. They had between a dozen and twenty men with them. They had been there for a few days.

The man left them maps, pointed out the food that was in a large picnic basket on the kitchen table and made his excuses.

Conlon and the men ate in agreeable silence, a big loaf of bread torn and slathered in butter with sliced beef; sharing the bottle of whiskey they found in a cupboard, most of them smoking. There was no talk of the plan until Conlon told them that they had better sleep now, they would be up early to observe the house at whatever approximation of sunrise they could find here.

A few hours later, they drove across the silent landscape as the sun stole into the sky once again. They parked far off and walked the last mile across country.

The estate did not really announce itself beyond the usual stone walls that bisected the farmland in the area, but the house was in a valley with more tree cover than anywhere else on the property. Conlon and Mossy crouched and observed it through binoculars while Holt and Harrigan cut across a hillside to check the other side.

There was a guard posted, three motorcars visible, not much else at this early hour.

They stayed until near midday, by which time they had seen the guard change and a few other men emerge, two driving off, presumably into town, another couple head off into the hills with rifles and hunting caps. Conlon knew how to do it by this point, but he wanted to see as much as possible, so he and Mossy waited, watching, and then headed back to the vehicles in the late afternoon. The other motorcar was gone already.

Back at the house, Holt and Harrigan were sitting in the sunshine, having dragged the kitchen table and chairs out into the yard. They were smoking, drinking whiskey and squinting at one another over fans of splayed playing cards.

Conlon and Mossy made themselves sandwiches, then joined them.

Harrigan allowed them to finish eating, then said, "So what's the plan, Captain?"

Conlon and Mossy laughed. "I was never a captain. Strictly a private."

Harrigan nodded. "Aye, but whatever outfit you two were in probably had no rank and file, did it? Some special unit."

"One officer," Mossy said. "You can imagine what he was like."

The four men nodded ruefully.

Harrigan said, "So you fellas were expected to think for yourselves in the field?"

Conlon answered, "Yeah. That's why they recruited us. Improvisation."

"And superior soldiering," Mossy said, with a pitch perfect impersonation of a pompous English officer's accent.

"How would you do this?" Conlon asked Harrigan. "You've obviously had a lot of experience."

Harrigan shrugged, peeling off a card and looking at Holt's reaction to it.

"We can't go at them full on. Even if we plan it perfectly, they have the numbers, and the best we can hope for is a long siege, which we don't want."

"So?"

"So somebody has to get in. I have a feeling that will be yourself, and you already have an idea of how to do it."

Conlon nodded. "I'll go back tonight. Move in slowly. Hide and rest until dawn. That's when you hit them."

Mossy said, "And you'll already be inside?"

"You at the back, elevated, Mossy. You two around the front, maybe one of you in the tree line, moving around."

"How do you get out?"

"Keep your eyes on the front door. I won't be able to take them all in the house. I'll be looking for Caesar and Naessens. When they're dead, I'll be out as soon as I can get out. I'll use grenades to clear a path out the front door. Watch for the blasts and I'll be coming right behind them. I'll need cover to get from there to the trees."

The mercenaries understood and nodded.

"First light in the sky?" Mossy said.

Conlon nodded. "I'll wait for you to start shooting before I move. And one more thing..."

They all looked at him again. "Just so you all understand: these people have killed many girls. Tortured them, raped them, murdered them for entertainment. Wealthy men acting like fucking Gods, thinking they could do whatever they wanted. They deserve worse than a quick death but a quick death it will have to be. Some of the gunmen might just be hired, but they're taking blood money. The wrong blood money. If they're in that house, they can die, too."

Both mercenaries nodded, faces set.

Mossy made an impressed face. "I always loved your speeches."

Conlon couldn't help but chuckle. "Fuck off, you."

25

16 Days After Purification

MOSSY WOKE THE TWO MERCENARIES AROUND TWO IN THE morning. They rolled up from their cots as if neither had been fully sleeping. All three men assembled their gear in silence, smoking and drinking tea, then Holt drove them back towards the big house. The darkness here was absolute, the moon and stars concealed by cloud, the engine noise shatteringly noisy over the black countryside.

Conlon had set off on foot hours before. By now, Mossy assumed he was inside the house somewhere, or poised to be. It did not enter his head that his friend could have been apprehended, or even killed. He had trust in Conlon's ability, had seen him achieve things most men would have thought impossible.

Holt and Harrigan did not have that experience. As they were climbing out of the motorcar, parked by the side of the road two miles from the house, Harrigan asked him: "Is you friend as good as he thinks he is?"

"I wouldn't want to fight him," Mossy said.

"But against all those men?"

"Hand to hand, I've never seen anybody better, with his fists or a knife. And he's angry, but not distracted. If we can create enough fuss, he'll kill every single one of them."

Holt clicked on a trench torch, and Mossy heard the chain pull of a German Dynamo torch from Harrigan.

"No torch for you?" Harrigan said.

"I'll follow you then the light from the house will be enough. You know what we're doing?"

"We know the plan."

"Alright so. Good luck. As soon as I start firing."

"We'll wait. See you afterwards."

They moved off towards the hill to their east, Harrigan and Holt turning on the torches only every minute or so to orient themselves. After perhaps ten minutes of walking, the light from the big house glowed over a ridge, a dull hinting of the day to come.

Mossy told them he was going and split off from the two men to climb another hillside and skirt around the house. He urinated in the open, his eyes on the building below him. He could just discern the source of the light —a sentry posted near the front door, leaning against the wall with a lantern on a post above him. He readjusted himself and continued his progress across the slope. He estimated it was now a few minutes before sunrise, so he hurried the last few hundred yards, tricky over the scrub strewn with small rocks and uneven patches as it was.

Finally, he found a good spot, and took some time establishing his perch. He was in the heather, partially behind one of the many croppings of rock that studded the hills here. He had a view of the back of the house and the western side. Two of their motorcars were also in his field of fire. Laid out around him were his extra ammunition, binoculars and pistol.

He covered the entire area with a sweep of his rifle, ogling it through the scope. Conlon had not shared how he had been planning to access the house, but Mossy suspected he had spotted an access point leading to the cellar. After that it would be about patience and silence.

He watched, waiting. The quiet was soothing. Birds began to sing then, one or two into the dark, like the first drops of rain before a downpour. Mossy looked over his shoulder. A vague wash of light at the horizon. He let it slide up into the sky, the birdsong beginning to swell with it, then he sighted on one of the motorcars and fired a single shot, blowing out a tire.

Within an instant, he heard two shots from the other side of the valley. Holt and Harrigan had shot the sentry, he knew. There was a lull, perhaps forty seconds of silence. Then he heard Holt and Harrigan firing again.

Some of the men had come out the front door, he imagined. He kept his rifle trained on the back door. Two men rushed out, bearing rifles, only half-dressed. He fired twice and both fell.

Within a minute there were gunmen in the windows at the back. They fired a few shots indiscriminately at the hillside, trying to panic him into firing and giving away his position.

The sunrise was flooding the valley now, lighting the back of the house for him.

Mossy adjusted his scope and focused on one of the windows. A lace curtain twitched. He waited, breathing evenly. He saw the barrel of the rifle and fired. It fell back into the room.

The firing stopped. The men inside the house were organizing, realizing that they had enemy rifles on at least two sides.

He wondered how Conlon was doing.

———

CONLON HEARD the first gunshot and waited, concealed in the space under the stairs in the cellar, slightly twisted around a small tower of piled wooden stools and a big dresser. Rodents scurried, scraping around the walls in the darkness but it had been generally silent down here for the past few hours, since the last of the men had gone to bed upstairs. He had a pain in his lower back. The house settled, phantom creaks in the floor, the brick shifting, but aside from that and the mice, it had been quiet for hours.

He had gained access through one of the cellar windows at the side of the house. There were two on each flank, sunken into the ground, with a steep grass covered slope leading onto the lawn on one, and steps to the yard on the other. Having crawled and crouched and rolled across the lower reaches of the hillside to the walls surrounding the house and its manicured lawn, he had sprinted flat out across the garden.

The sentry was around the corner, at the front of the house, and seemingly not very inclined to patrol. That he had determined after watching him from the darkness for almost an hour. He saw the man's head nod forward and jerk back upwards on several occasions. They were not expecting trouble, then.

Conlon had squatted, head cocked, listening, near the house, then he had slid down the grass in the dark, and waited again. Then he had drawn his trench knife and prized the window open with the blade. The metallic crack of the latch snapping had sounded thunderous to him in the still quiet of the night and he held his breath, watching the corner from where the sentry would come. Nothing. He gave it another thirty seconds, then pulled himself up and wriggled through the gap. Then, after delicately closing the window behind him, it was a matter of patiently negotiating the dark of the cellar with his hands until he found somewhere black and out of the way to hide, in case anyone should come down.

When he was tucked into the space under the stairs, he closed his eyes and rested. He had checked his gear already. He carried a revolver, his trench knife—which had a knuckle duster protecting the grip—some extra ammunition, and three grenades in his pack. He knew it would be close quarters upstairs, and suspected that he would use the knife more than the gun.

But he was ready for anything, open to the chaos, prepared to exploit it. There was no tension in him as he waited.

That changed with the first shot.

A few moments earlier, he had realized that it was almost sunrise when he heard the first birdsong. At that point he had readied himself. Those few minutes stretched and elongated. A feeling of impending doom came upon him, rising up in the dark. This had happened to him before, waiting for death to bear so close to him. Thoughts of those he would leave behind.

He was picturing Mossy, alone on the hillside with

the house in his sights. He found himself speculating where Viv was at just that moment; was she awake and wondering about him? And what of Theresa, who he had been trying not to think about these last few weeks. All that they had shared, torn apart—the guilt of it, of the way he had used her.

Molly Devereux, too. He felt a pang of regret for the transactional nature of their relationship, for not saying goodbye to her, never giving enough. His Mam, who he had not seen in a few weeks. Barry, who would have to clean this up somehow. And inevitably, Orla.

He closed his eyes and summoned her face, letting it warm him. The feeling that she had been his, he had been allowed to possess her, and feel the things he had felt, and if he was to die today, in some world they might be together.

The shot rang out: flat and echoing in the valley, seeming to hang in the air and roll for a minute after its first shattering sound. All thoughts of women and love evaporated.

His hand felt for the revolver, the other going to the trench knife. He listened, tense.

There was a brief silence and then a cacophony of feet on floorboards: men thundering down the stairs, shouting at one another, voices in stressed conversation, furniture being dragged around. More gunfire after that first shot. Harrigan and Holt, he knew.

Glass shattered as the Centurions dashed out the windows. A fusillade of shots. They didn't know where they were shooting at yet, firing blind.

Footsteps scattered around above him. They were moving, unsure of where to position themselves, uncertain of how many men they faced, unsure of how to handle a siege in a house like this one.

Mossy's rifle echoed again. He heard the Centurions shouting, a note of panic there. Mossy would miss with few shots. He heard voices shout a name over and over. Their medic, he assumed. Mossy had shot one.

He waited. Nothing on the stairs, the door to the cellar still shut.

Moving lightly, he went up the steps and slammed the sole of his boot against the door. The lock gave with a sickly crack and the door swung open. He was in a big kitchen in the rear corner of the house. One Centurion crouched by the door, below the glass, reloading an Enfield. He began to turn his head to look over his shoulder at Conlon, and Conlon, walking calmly across the tiled floor, raised his revolver and shot him once in the forehead.

He slumped against the door, a clump of bone and brain spattering onto the wood.

Conlon moved through the room, the gun raised. Up here the sounds were less distinct: a general orgy of shouting, the roll of feet, gunfire, bullets burying themselves in masonry or the walls of the house.

He was in the dining room. Here three Centurions knelt under windows as a bullet scattered the last of the glass in the frames and they all ducked down. That was Mossy, Conlon knew, keeping them down as he waited for an opening.

Two of the men saw him, eyes instantly wide with alarm. Conlon shot both of them in a fraction of a second. His shots were efficient. The first man took a bullet in the chest, near his sternum. The second had most of his Adam's apple obliterated and fell, blood spurting around hands that grasped momentarily at the wound before they were still.

The third didn't look, just threw himself across the room, behind the huge dining table and the chairs that were arrayed around it. Conlon could hear him scrabbling, the clatter of his rifle on the floor. The man began blasting under the table legs. Conlon saw the shots explode in the wall a foot from his knee, watched splinters of a chair leg spray across the ground. He took a step and jumped onto the big dining table, shining with a sort of rich mahogany gleam, one step to cross it, adjusting his grip on the trench knife as he went and then he was in the air, hanging for an instant above the man, who was twisted on the floor, still shooting under the table.

Conlon leapt and landed on top of him, driving his fist past the man's head so that the blade chopped brutally through his throat, sending blood in a high arc onto the wall and floor.

Conlon was already rolling away, gun pointed at the door into the rest of the house. He knew the shooting in here would draw more Centurions and when two appeared in the doorway, he shot them both. He crouched near the wall, reloading the revolver rapidly, then stood and moved into the space through the door. One of the men here was alive, struggling with rolling eyes and a mouth seeping blood to sit. Conlon shot him once more.

The area before him was the hall, the largest space in the house, with walls of a pale blue, mahogany shining from floors and doorframes, paintings hanging in each space, and a chandelier swaying from one of the many impacts or rapid passages occurring all around it.

He looked up a curving staircase up to the first floor. Gunfire from up there. Like a smaller version of the Naessens mansion outside Dublin, he thought, evaluating where would Naessens and Caesar be hiding.

Where would the Centurions assess was the safest spot in the house? None of the rooms with windows, and although he would have chosen the cellar, they had obviously opted for somewhere different. Unless the leaders were already gone, and they were too late.

He made for the staircase, head constantly swiveling, eyes active, his awareness at that heightened level he knew so well from so many battles and fights, and then paused. Nobody was coming to deal with him. The violent sounds his fights with the men inside the house had created had been lost in the chaos.

He could help his comrades outside, and end this quickly.

The sounds of the battle from the hills around the house and in other rooms came and went in jagged waves and the occasional shock of noise. He made up his mind, nodded pointlessly to himself and strode into the drawing room at the front of the house. Here, three men were squatting beneath what was left of the windows, glass and tattered curtain around them on the floor in shreds. Two of them, reloading or seeking cover below the windowsills, saw him as he walked in and one was shooting straightaway.

Conlon ducked, still moving, and squeezed the trigger once, firing from the hip, like a gunslinger in a motion picture. The man's brains covered the wall in a fan of gore. The other one was rolling away, and the third, hearing the shots, turned, still standing, from the window, levelling a wobbling rifle at Conlon. As he did so, a bullet from outside punched a hole in the center of his chest and he spun around, falling on his face, his rifle clattering to the floor.

The second man kept rolling, then came up in a ball, fumbling at his gun. Conlon altered course, then shoulder-slammed him into the wall. The gun was gone now, somewhere on the floor. Conlon pressed the man into the wall and swiftly fit his own revolver under the man's chin, then pulled the trigger.

He was already stepping away, the body tumbling after him.

Crouching, he felt on the floor for one of the men's rifles, picked it up, covering the doorway with the pistol in his other hand. Then he moved back out into the hall.

A man at the top of the stairs. He had not seen Conlon, who had time to lead the target, aim, and place a shot dead center of his torso as he came down the stairs. He crumpled and clattered the rest of the way down, to lie still at the foot of the steps.

Conlon crossed the hallway and burst through the door into the other drawing room. Two men were crouched here also, a big oak table on its side between them and the wall where the huge windows had been destroyed by gunfire. One of them had clearly heard something of the shooting inside the house, and he was waiting.

His bullet nicked at Conlon's thigh as he ran into the room, with a hard, heavy impact. That dropped Conlon, his foot moving out from under him, but he twisted as he fell, landing onto his side and already moving, using the angle to his advantage, firing twice with the rifle, killing both men.

An instant of silence then.

He examined his wound. Blood already flowered on his trouser leg in a slowly spreading blot. Probing at the tear in the cloth, he found a jagged gash in the muscle. The bullet had skimmed him but still caused horrendous damage. Blood was rushing out of the ruined flesh, pain radiating up his spine from the area. Gritting his teeth, he shifted himself away from the doorway on his behind until his back was to the wall, slipped the shoulder strap free from the rifle, and wound it tightly around his upper thigh. With a grunt he pulled it taut and tied a knot. Then he used the rifle as a crutch to stand and tested his weight on the leg. He could walk, with a limp and considerable pain, but running would be difficult.

How many of them were left? Eleven were dead in the house, that he knew of. He assumed Mossy and Holt and Harrigan had taken care of a few more.

From upstairs he could hear a pair of guns still; the occasional shot from two different parts of the house.

Two men then, perhaps. And whoever was guarding Caesar and Naessens.

He knew where they were now.

He moved into the hall, wincing against the pain, which flared a bright hot white with each step. There was a door under the stairs, leading to an interior room of some sort. That was where they were.

He leaned against the wall beside it, panting. He took three of the grenades, primed them, shouldered the door open with a tremendous, wrenching barge, and tossed all three grenades inside, then dived back against the wall.

The explosion shook the wall, the stairs, made the

chandelier erupt in a chorus of tinkling glass on glass as it violently swung. He was already moving, gun first through the door.

Two men were splayed dead on the floor, another one wounded, clawing at the wall, groaning. The two at the far end of the room—a wine cellar, he saw—were both brandishing guns. Conlon ducked, firing. They were close together, making it so easy for him. He just had to aim at the mass presented by two bodies, hemmed in by the racks of aged wine bottles. An almost perfect shooting gallery.

He fired four times and after the second shot they were no longer shooting back.

He stood. The wounded man, still groaning, was Caesar. His chin was lathered in a froth of his own blood, his tongue reddened with it. His eyes, glassy and crawling the walls, settled on Colon, who raised the pistol and shot him between them.

He limped to the men who had been shooting at him. One of them was a soldier, dead on his side, his throat gone, blood pooling around him. The other was Naessens. He was on his back, propped against the wine racks, breathing hard, his eyes on Conlon.

Conlon looked down at him. "I should have taken payment up front."

Naessens said, "I wish I'd never met you."

"This is where you've got it wrong, 'my Lord.' You should be regretting all the hurt you've caused and all the lives you've ruined. All those girls you killed. Not hiring me to help you cover it up. That was just stupid."

"You ignorant bastard. Why couldn't you just report back and then leave it be?"

Conlon shrugged. "Didn't you do your research? Didn't you understand who you were hiring?"

Naessens broke eye contact. Conlon could virtually see him ebbing away.

"Where's Philomena?" Conlon asked.

Naessens moved his eyes to Conlon's face again. A hint of a smile there. "Dead. You killed her."

"Dead where?"

Naessens attempted another smile, but the effort appeared to be too much; his chin slipped onto his chest.

Conlon bent down, waited until Naessens' eyes, now a bit dulled and unfocused, had fixed upon his once again, and spoke quietly. "You're dying. You feel cold because you're in shock. You feel weak because your body is using all the energy you have left on keeping you alive. But it won't help. Your heart will stop beating in less than a minute. Then I'm going to burn this house to the ground with you and all your twisted little pals inside it. And still that won't be enough to make up for all those girls you hurt and killed. But it's better than nothing. Nobody except a few people will ever know what happened to you. You'll be forgotten in a matter of months. But I'll know. And whenever I feel a bit down, or life feels unfair, I'll think back to this moment, watching a piece of dirt like you dying on the floor, and it will make me smile. So thank you for that." He stood. "Goodbye."

The shooting had all stopped now. Conlon returned to the kitchen, found in the pantry a shelf filled with bottles of whiskey and vodka. He doused the carpet, and the table and chairs in the dining room and the tattered curtains in one of the reception rooms, took a box of matches from his pocket and set both alight. He waited in the reception room and watched the flame idle a moment then race up the wall, where it leaped like a spider across the ceiling.

He had already turned and in the dining room he could see the table was starting to burn, tongues of orange rippling along the lacquered surface. Not long now.

He turned and walked straight out the front door, his hands in the air, hoping one of his comrades wouldn't shoot him dead.

26

22 Days After Purification

THE LAST DAY OF THE SUMMER, IS HOW IT FELT. AS SOON as night had ebbed away, the heat seemed to rise up out of the stones and the bricks of the city, only the breeze fitfully tugging in from the coast offering any comfort.

Conlon was at Dollymount Strand not long after dawn. He had bicycled there through the quiet streets as light seeped into the sky. He stretched, the bullet slash on his leg still troubling him somewhat, then shadow-boxed alone in the dunes, then descended to the waves to swim out into the Irish sea until his shoulders and chest began to ache, at which point he turned in a great arc and cut back towards the beach.

He had left his clothes and a towel in a little pile halfway up the sand, and as he rose to his feet in the surf, he saw that there was a man in a suit and a hat standing over them, watching him.

Conlon waded in, recognizing him perhaps twenty

meters on. Alan, the Centurion who had been in the photo in Philomena's room, so many weeks before.

He stopped, dripping water onto the dry sand now, perhaps thirty feet away.

Alan raised his hands in a placatory gesture: "I'm not here to harm you. She sent me."

"Who sent you?"

"Philomena Naessens."

And so again, he was being driven out of the city towards the Naessens estate, just as he had weeks before.

Alan drove. It was the same car as before, Conlon suspected, bouncing and swinging on the bumps and corners of the road west out of Dublin. They did not speak, and Conlon knew that the man was thinking about all of his friends and colleagues who had died at Conlon's hands. Not that Alan would do anything to him—he was a middle manager, a thinker and facilitator. But he would be afraid. Afraid that at any moment Conlon might snap and kill him, too.

Conlon turned his head every so often to look at him. Sweat ran down from his hairline in thick beads. He tried not to show that he was aware of Conlon's attention, but his face had a stricken expression. Once again, Conlon thought of all the girls that had suffered on that island. Alan, for all his fear, had an air of victory about him. He had survived, he was going to live. Conlon wanted him to suffer, too.

"Do you remember when we first met?" he asked.

Alan nodded.

"Sorry, I didn't hear you," Conlon said.

"I remember," Alan said.

"You recruited me. You believed my act, and I'm no

actor. You let me into the Centurions, and now the Centurions are gone. I killed many of your friends. So many that I couldn't count them. Do you understand? Because of you."

"I understand."

"Naessens. Your Caesar. The Hastings twins. Dead because of you."

Alan's chin wobbled.

Conlon said, "If I don't like what she's got to say, I will kill you. You were a party to rape and torture and murder, and it just doesn't sit right with me that you simply get away with it."

Alan was crying now, Conlon saw. Tears mingling with the sweat beneath his eyes and upon his cheeks.

"Cry for all those girls," Conlon snarled. "Instead of crying for yourself."

"I never wanted all that...I tried...I tried—"

"What you wanted doesn't matter a damn. What you did is what matters. You let it all happen. You helped it happen."

"I couldn't have stopped them." Alan took his eyes off the road to look at Conlon, desperately, pleadingly. "I was an employee, I had no real say."

"You should have found a different job."

They finished the drive in silence.

———

PHILOMENA RECEIVED Conlon as her father had done. When Martin, the butler, who nodded with recognition at his arrival, led Conlon and Alan into the study, she sat behind her father's expansive, ostentatiously impressive desk in his chair.

She stood when they came in and moved around the desk to shake Conlon's hand. Conlon just looked at her, her hand hanging in the air between them.

Her pregnancy was obvious now, with a dress hanging off her rounded belly. She smiled at Conlon's refusal, nodded sagely, and backtracked around the desk to the chair.

"Please, Mr. Conlon. Sit."

Martin had already melted away, and Alan walked around the desk to take the chair to the side so that he and Philomena were the other two corners of a triangle. He was plainly terrified, his eyes nervously sticking to Conlon as they would if he had led a panther into the study and asked it to sit on a rug.

"You were in Scotland," Conlon said, before he had even settled in the chair.

"I was. I left the day before you arrived at the house and killed everyone. That was you, wasn't it?"

"That was justice," Conlon said.

She closed her eyes in recognition of the comment. She wore a half-smile at all times, Conlon realized. This woman was unrecognizable from the girl he had rescued from sacrifice on the island three weeks before.

"How did you know I was there?"

"A guess. Something has never felt right about any of this. Where is your mother?"

"Sleeping off another bottle or two of whiskey, I imagine. Her joy at my safe return has been complicated by her confusion at my father's disappearance, and she has embraced the bottle with even more vigor. Did he die well?"

"Your father? He died. So: let me see what I have right, then."

She nodded. Conlon looked over at Alan, fleetingly, just to remind him that he had not been forgotten.

"That baby—" he indicated her stomach "—is your father's."

She nodded again, the half-smile intact.

"Did he know?"

"I think he suspected."

"But you let him think it was that young driver's. You had an affair with him?"

"More of a succession of liaisons than an affair."

"Your father had him murdered. Out of jealousy."

"He was an extremely possessive man, Mr. Conlon. He was not accustomed to sharing anything."

"But you like men. You have a lot of men." He looked at Alan again, who stared intensely at his own lap. "And he decided once you were pregnant that he had endured enough, and that perhaps it could get out, about you and him, when the baby came, and that might be a problem with your social set."

"We didn't have a conversation after he discovered my pregnancy. I became a problem, no longer his daughter. He would not speak to me. I screamed and raged at him whenever I could, and he simply ignored me. And then I did it in front of some of his friends, and that was too much. That threatened his reputation, the only thing he really cared about. So they took me to their island. And even there he made sure nobody spoke to me. Alan here, who I am very fond of, was not allowed to even see me. He was determined to eliminate two problems at the same time."

"You and the baby."

"But he needed to make a show: the concerned daddy whose little girl was missing. So he hired a detective from the slums. Who had no chance of turning anything up. That was his mistake, wasn't it, Mr. Conlon? He had lost touch with this country, with this century. The lower classes are rising. They will consume us if we do not learn how to placate them. It's no longer about control and brutality and imposing order. It's about the illusion of freedom, of sharing. It's about using them in a clever, subtle way and allowing them to feel as if they are making their own decisions. If they want a free state, well perhaps they can have one. But the same wealthy people will really be in charge, they just won't care because they will feel as if they chose that. He could not see things that way. He was old-fashioned—in his pride, in his snobbery. He thought you were lesser, somehow. He thought you would be stupid, and he thought you would fail. A flea ridden commoner, who would take his coin. Once I saw you, I knew his mistake. He allowed a wolf in with the sheep. And you've destroyed everything he built. It was magnificent."

"Why didn't they kill you, when they got you back?"

She looked to Alan to finish this part of the story.

He cleared his throat. "The Hastings were sure you would have survived. And we knew there were other people who might know where you were gone. The girl, for one. Who knew how many more? When we spoke to Naessens, and realized that you were the same man he had hired, calls were made. That was when we realized who you were—your military record, much of which is classified, your reputation in the criminal class in this city. And whatever situation we placed you in, you seemed to survive, and we lost more men. It seemed as if you might have help. Somebody we weren't aware of.

They got scared. Caesar, Naessens and even the Hastings. Killing Philomena suddenly became too great a risk. Better to use her if we had to, if the authorities began to pay attention."

Philomena continued, "So they took me with them when they ran. And I had the chance to talk to my Alan again. I knew you would be coming. I saw you on that island. They sent killers after you, and I knew it would only make it worse. I could have done the same, this last week, Mr. Conlon. But I wanted to talk to you instead. To come to an agreement, like civilized people. Enough death, surely."

"So you persuaded Alan to help you escape."

She nodded. "You see, my father was a businessman, but the real money in my family comes from my mother. All she is good for is spending it, admittedly, on clothing and paintings and furniture, and drink. But it is hers. Her family name is old and tremendously respected. With him out of the way, I have control of the family money. The companies, the properties, the investments. And you took him out of the way for me. Now I can reclaim the name."

"And Alan here becomes your front man."

She looked at Alan with a little smile. "My Prince Consort, if you like. We are to be married. He will be the child's father, to all intents and purposes. That should help avoid that scandal my father was so fearful of."

Conlon was quiet, looking from one to the other. "What's your offer, then? I assume you're here to offer me a payoff."

Alan spoke. "Five times what Lord Naessens was paying you. And you will sign a legal document guaranteeing that you will never publicly speak of any of this."

Conlon was silent again. "I don't want your money." He stood. "But you said that it seemed as if I might have help. You were right. Do you think I would even be able to pursue you to Scotland and attack that house without help? You have an enemy, Philomena. You don't know who they are, or even, really what they want, but they know about you. They have the resources. They have the will. And they'll move against you. If I was you, I'd take as much money as I could and get out now. Go to the continent, go to America, or Australia. Start again, and hope they let you be. I have no interest in hurting you, or even this fucking coward. But they will come for you. Goodbye."

He turned and she said, "Mr. Conlon." He looked at her.

She said, "I genuinely want to thank you. You saved my life. You saved my baby. You're a good man. No matter what happens now, no more action will be taken against you by me or by what were my father's people."

She nodded to Alan. He approached Conlon with an envelope.

"I said I didn't want your money," Conlon muttered.

"It's from Mr. Sharp," Philomena said.

Alan nodded. "He was extremely insistent."

Philomena gave him a smile, and he saw the girl he had been with on the island, still in there somewhere under all the trauma and despite the ordeal of her family and her father and her suddenly improved circumstances.

"Goodbye, Mr. Conlon. Again, thank you," she said.

Conlon nodded to her, took the envelope from Alan, and walked out of the room.

27

23 Days After Purification

SHARP'S LETTER WAS SIMPLY THE NAME OF A HOTEL IN A town in County Meath, and the words, "Let's settle this." Conlon, somewhat frustrated by the way it had ended with Philomena and Alan, feeling as if this case had descended into a mess, costing him Viv and wasting dozens of lives and without any satisfaction from anything that had happened over the last few weeks, immediately resolved to meet him.

The next afternoon he took a train to Navan, and from there another to Kells. It was a grey, humid day, the promise of rain in the air as he made his way through the town, its streets quiet. He crossed a Market Square, deserted apart from some boys playing around the two crumbling Celtic crosses in the middle of the ragged, wide space, and a couple of old men, smoking and watching him from the pavement beneath the awnings outside a tobacconist.

He found the hotel on the road out of town which

led back towards Navan. It was old and imposing, painted a light blue, and as he approached, he watched a middle-aged couple climb down from a cab, a teenaged porter bowing and scraping and carrying their cases inside while the man paid the driver and his wife fanned herself against the humidity.

Sharp was sitting in the lounge by a window and had watched him arrive. He had a pot of tea on the table in front of him, and called the waiter for another cup as Conlon walked in. Conlon sat facing him and they appraised one another, without speaking, until the waiter returned with the cup. Sharp poured some tea for Conlon, who poured his own milk and dropped some sugar in.

They sipped at the same time and then, cups back on the table, Sharp smiled. Conlon saw the gaps in his teeth, the black eye still fading on one side of his face.

"You cost me some teeth, you see?" Sharp said.

Conlon nodded. "It could have been worse."

"Oh, a lot worse, I agree. How are you, Mr. Conlon? How is that injury in your side?"

"Healing up well, all things considered. I haven't had much time to rest."

"Did you find the leaders of that ridiculous organization?"

"I did."

"Then they're dead? I assumed so. What a fine little killer you are."

"And you want me to kill you?"

Sharp laughed and drank some tea. "I was hired to kill you. I feel a professional pride in my work, and failing in this particular assignment might affect my reputation among the kinds of men who are interested in hiring agents such as you and I."

Conlon just watched him. Sharp liked the sound of his own voice. So many men like him did. Conlon allowed him to talk.

"But on this occasion, I must say, it is something more than that. I felt a professional admiration for you. You exceeded my expectations. I heard that you were a scrapper and a survivor. But you are so much more than that." He shrugged. "And I...I cannot have you remaining alive when I took a contract. It would niggle at me. Every time I looked in the mirror and saw these ridiculous holes where my teeth should be. Every time I felt a twinge in my ankle. Every time I thought of this shit stain of a country and its hideous little people, I would feel regret that I had allowed you to live. So. Today you will die. But it will be a fair fight. A man of your accomplishment deserves that much from me. Guns, knives, fists? I allow you to choose, Mr. Conlon."

Conlon looked at him. "You're just another grimy little lunatic—like the Hastings twin I killed in the woods—only you have a nicer accent. You enjoy it. Killing people. I don't. But I'm going to enjoy killing you."

Something flared in Sharp's eyes. He controlled it, quelled it, breathed deeply.

"I propose we meet tonight at—"

"No, fuck that. We do it now. You need to be dead."

"Here? Don't be ridiculous Conlon, it's—"

"There's a cemetery. An ancient one, I saw it on the way in here. It's next door. Now."

Sharp sat, watching him, a mixture of disbelief and that rage in his eyes again.

"You're not in charge here, Sharp. Get up and come with me now or I will stab you in the eye with a fucking teaspoon."

Conlon stood. Sharp huffed and puffed, his cheeks actually tensed and hardened with fury, and suddenly did the same.

Conlon walked out of the lounge and through the lobby, where the man and his wife were still checking in, and out into the street. It was dormant and almost silent. Birdsong from the trees, the rattle of a distant horse and cart. No movement, no people.

Sharp followed him and they looked at one another, then Conlon moved along the pavement, past the end of the hotel's frontage to follow a long, high stone wall.

Perhaps thirty paces on he turned and passed under an arch and through the heavy iron gate into the old cemetery. It felt like stepping into another world. There were stone steps leading upwards to the burial ground itself, which overlooked the road but was partially shielded by a line of yew trees gently shivering, set back from the wall and throwing a darkness over the whole site. It was overgrown in places, the mixture of grave-stones and crosses jutting from the ground, swamped in areas by weeds and grasses.

Conlon walked on to a spot close to the interior, away from any tombstones or obvious graves, beneath one of the big yews. The smell of moss and green fertility hung in the close air here.

There was nobody around.

Conlon took off his jacket and, folding it, placed it on the ground, his cap on top. He turned to see that Sharp had similarly removed his hat and coat, and was rolling up his shirt sleeves, exposing thick forearms.

Conlon looked at him. He had played this fight out mentally many times since they had last tangled, in various different scenarios. Sharp was perhaps the most dangerous man he had ever faced in hand-to-hand combat. He was incredibly powerful, deceptively fast, and could take a punch, but Conlon knew what he could do to win. Their first fight had shown him.

"Shall we?" Sharp said, with a grin. His confidence was key.

Conlon nodded and walked forward. Sharp met him, aggressive as ever. He threw three big swinging punches, his anger at Conlon's attitude driving him to inflict pain early and decisively.

Conlon dipped and slipped, Sharp's blows missing, the last fist a mere inch from his chin. Conlon moved beneath it and came up with a mace of a left hook into Sharp's midsection, which staggered him sideways.

Every punch had to count, Conlon knew. All big shots. Do damage with each blow.

Sharp pawed at Conlon, but Conlon had pivoted away on his heel. Sharp grimaced and advanced again, as Conlon retreated under the yew tree. Sharp threw a right cross, and Conlon parried with both forearms and threw his shoulder into Sharp's sternum, knocking him off his feet.

Sharp said, "You've learned some new tricks."

He feinted this time, but not very well. Conlon was watching his every movement, and he anticipated the right hook even as Sharp feinted to jab with his left. So Conlon was already moving around him as Sharp's right sank into the air and Conlon hit him with two rapid uppercuts, one with each hand, snapping his mouth shut and his head back.

Sharp let out a roar of anger and frustration now and swung a blind backhand that Conlon met with his elbow. Something cracked in Sharp's fist and he groaned.

"That was a finger breaking," Conlon said.

Sharp charged at him, a huge overhand right coming from deep. Conlon swayed away fast and Sharp's big fist shattered itself on the yew tree instead, and he threw his head up, howling at the impact.

"Probably a few fingers," Conlon said, backing off. Sharp cradled his right hand, panting now.

"I thought—you wanted—to fight me," Sharp said through shuddered breaths.

"Hit and don't get hit," Conlon said. "That's fighting."

Sharp came on again, but he was protecting his hand. Conlon let him swing, then swing again, and circled him, then threw his own right cross. He knew he had broken Sharp's jaw with the punch, felt the truth of the impact, heard the crunch of it.

In their first fight, he had slowed Sharp down by street-fighting—going for his ankle when Sharp was prepared for a pugilistic contest. Now he let Sharp come at him, swayed under the first punch and replied with a jab to the body, then parried the second and delivered a speared hook to the ribs. He took two steps away, and as Sharp rushed to follow, Conlon side-stepped and collapsed his right knee with a kick which was more stamp, most of his weight behind it, his leg twisting at an appalling angle.

Sharp let out a growl of pain and his fingers grasped at empty air as he fell.

Conlon was already on him, one arm around

Sharp's neck, locking his chin inside Conlon's elbow, the other pushing forward on the back of his head. Conlon's legs were wrapped around Sharp's hips and waist.

Sharp realized instantly what was happening and tried to buck and push himself up, but Conlon's weight kept him down, and his useless right knee meant that he could get no leverage. He tried to kick them along the ground backwards, to smash Conlon against something—a tree, a gravestone—but the moss and grass here was damp from the shade, and they barely budged. He tried to claw at Conlon's face but one of his hands was a broken claw and the other could not reach Conlon's face, which he had turned away. Sharp slapped uselessly at his neck, his ear, his head.

Conlon squeezed constantly, powerfully, clinging to the bigger man like a leech, clamped to him, constricting him, his arms forcing his airway closed. Sharp tried finally to grab the arm under his chin but he had little strength left now, blinking at the day around him, aware that he had lost, that he was about to die.

Conlon whispered in his final seconds, "You lost your temper, Sharp. Didn't they teach you to fight calm? They only way to kill a man who's your equal without weapons is to strangle him. You should have seen this coming. But you lost your temper."

He squeezed for perhaps thirty seconds after he thought Sharp had died, just to be sure, then he disengaged, and kicked himself clear.

He stood and dusted himself off. He took Sharp's jacket and laid it against the foot of the tree, then dragged his body over to it, laying his head upon it as if he was napping. He closed Sharp's blue, alarmed eyes, then put his hat over his face. He arranged Sharp's hands behind his head and crossed his legs at the ankle. Then he stood and admired the picture he had created.

Sharp was an English tourist, enjoying a nap in the cool beneath a yew tree.

Conlon donned his own jacket and cap, turned on his heels, and headed back towards the train station and Dublin beyond.

28

82 Days After Purification

HE MET VIV IN MAISIES, WHERE HE HAD FIRST SEEN HER those months before, when he had spent an age watching her from over a book as she played queen bee of her group, unaware of where their meeting would take them both, ignorant of the joy and pain to come.

It was a grey, windy Autumn day with steel in the air, and after a brisk walk from his flat through a city that felt quiet, as if awaiting the next steady step on the road to the violence everyone knew, deep down, was coming, he was first to arrive and took the same table he had occupied on that previous occasion.

He felt uncommonly nervous. Few customers sat near him; two old ladies had a hushed conference at a table between him and the door, but aside from that it was all solitary diners, reading newspapers, dragging out tea and smoking.

She was there only a few minutes later and their eyes met as she walked in.

She looked fashionable in a dark blue tunic over a gored skirt and a white blouse, her hat tilted down almost over one eye, high-heeled ankle boots giving her an inch or two of height. He rose when she came across the room, and they had an awkward moment, neither sure if they should embrace, shake hands or exchange kisses to the cheek. He pulled her to him and held her a moment, then they avoided one another's gaze as they both sat.

The waiter came before she was even settled, and they ordered Eccles cake and a pot of tea, and then there was an instant of silence as they regarded one another across the table.

"You look well, Tommy," she said.

"So do you," he replied, though in truth there was a strain in her face that he had not seen before. He wondered how much of that was down to her ordeal and the aftermath. "I was surprised to get your letter."

After he had sent word to her aunt's house that he was fine, he had expected never to hear from her again. Instead, this week she had written to him to let him know that she had returned to Dublin, and she would like to see him.

"I didn't want to leave it the way we did," she said. "I was upset and afraid. I'm sorry for the things I said, Tommy."

He nodded. "Thank you. But you don't need to be."

"No, I do. You saved my life, Tommy. You're the bravest person I've ever met. I was just afraid. I'd never seen anything like it—any of it."

She shook her head, bewildered by the memories of violence.

"I understand. It was a difficult time. They were

horrible people we were involved with, doing awful things."

The waiter returned bearing a tray—their cake on two cake plates, svelte cake forks, a pot of tea and two cups. She poured for them, in silence, and they added milk and spooned sugar, the ritual of it all comforting in its banality.

"Are you back in Dublin for good?" he asked after they had both taken a first mouthful.

"No, I'm just here for a few days. Just some matters to attend to that I couldn't do by letter. Sure the village only has two telephones."

They laughed, the children of the city, united in their gentle, knowing scorn for the simple country folk.

"How are you coping with that, Dublin girl such as you are?"

"Oh, I've adjusted. It's all about finding the rhythm. Life is just slower down there. The days are slow, the weeks are. I struggled when I got there, and I was very upset, crying all the time. My nerves... But then I found the rhythm. And it's calming, Tommy. I allowed it to calm me."

She looked at him and reached out to take his hand.

"I was in bits when I got there because of what happened, and the violence, and the fear, but because of you, too. Worried sick for you, but even when I knew you were ok and it was over, I cried all of the time. My aunt was so concerned for me."

"I'm sorry."

"And I've come here to say a few things that I need to say."

"Alright."

She took a breath and gave him a brave smile. "I'm

to be married. I met a young man, at mass with my aunt. He's a widower and a veterinarian."

Conlon felt his breath stop but controlled his face. "I —congratulations."

"Thank you."

"Is he—" He could find no words adequate. "Does he—"

"He's a gentleman. He's kind."

"He's what you need?"

"Maybe he is."

"So no more acting?"

"Oh, well, there is a theatre in Westport. So maybe in a few years. We've talked about children."

"Of course," he said, quietly.

She squeezed his hand so he would look at her.

"I wanted to say this, not write it down. I love you, Tommy Conlon. I've never loved anyone before. When I left and knew it was over, I felt pain so sharp it was like I was sick. I woke up with it every day, for weeks, and cried and wanted you. But being away gave me time to think about it over and over."

She began to cry and stopped to dab a handkerchief at her face, then drink some tea. Then she continued, "When those men came to kill us, and you stopped them—I was in shock. Seeing you do those things. But after, when I could feel exactly how much I missed you when it hurt every time I thought of you, I looked at it another way." She squeezed his hand again. "That's who you are. I know. You're brave and fierce and strong. You do things nobody else could do. I—I... tried to tell my Aunt about the Centurions and Philomena and Avalon, and it just sounded silly, like Tir na Nog, like a fairytale, and I...I just gave up. But you did it. Only you could. I understood that when I was away from you."

She stopped again, and drank some tea. He did the same, though the numbness creeping out from his chest meant that he could taste nothing.

"And you have to do that. You need to, because you can, because who else can? And...and...I know you've loved other women. Orla, you mentioned her. And I know many other girls have loved you. Because you're— I've never met anyone like you. There is no one like you. Women will always be bowled over by you. But you need to be you and do what you do, and no girl like me should stop that or get in the way or make you worry that they might get hurt."

"But that decision is mine to make," he said, annoyed at some assumption she had made that he could barely articulate.

"Whether to do what you do?" she said. "Of course it is. And you've already made it. But you can't decide if I'm to be allowed to share that with you. You can't make me live a life where I spend every day wondering if you're coming home this evening, Tommy. That's not fair on you or on me. And putting you in any other life... I can't picture you in a factory or a shop. Can you?"

They were quiet, thinking, then both laughed, some-what mirthlessly.

She said, almost in a whisper, "I think somewhere inside, you know that I'm right."

He nodded. "But you don't have to leave Dublin. I won't bother you if you're here."

"I know you won't. But it's painful. Being here today —I've been crying again. I have no idea how I'm holding it together in this conversation. Everywhere reminds me of those few days we had. I thought I would be with you forever, and have your children, and be happy. And then that dream was smashed and I realized I was thinking like a child. I want that memory to be precious, of those days, when we were falling in love."

He squeezed her hand this time.

She gave him that brave smile again. "If I was here, and I knew you were here...I'm not strong enough, Tommy, I'd be at your door and in your bed in no time."

He hung his head. He had not expected this. A reconciliation? Maybe. Coldness, perhaps. Not this. This was worse than anything he could have imagined.

"So you go and live with a man you don't love?"

She winced at that.

He said, "I'm sorry, Viv. That was mean."

"I deserve mean. I thought I was big and complicated, but I'm not, not really. I need a simple life, Tommy. A small life. You're not small. You could never be small."

She released his hand, and conversation, somehow, moved on, to other, more normal areas. They drank tea, and ate their cakes, and finally, she announced she had an appointment. He went outside with her, and around the corner, where they would take separate paths. She turned to him.

He pulled her to him, and said, "I love you, too."

They kissed; one long, deep, lingering kiss in a doorway.

When she pulled away, blinking, she said, "I think of you every minute of every day, Tommy Conlon. Thank you for everything. Goodbye."

She began to walk away.

"Goodbye," he said.

He watched her walk until she turned to corner, then he leaned back against the door. He had that feeling of freefall for an instant. He knew he could go after her. She loved him. He could stop her, make her stay, make her his, probably. But he had realized something when she had mentioned Orla. These last few months, he had been missing her, yes, mourning what he had lost. But that always led him back to Orla. And that was a wound that still hurt more than any other. More than Theresa, more than Viv.

Orla.

Losing her had changed him, and he was still recovering. He felt as if he would never be truly better, as if no woman could ever truly hope to replace her or make him feel better. When she had said that she thought of him every minute of every day...he did not feel that way in return. But Orla—he thought of her all the time. When he saw a beautiful woman: he thought of Orla. When he thought of marriage: Orla. Happiness: Orla. When he heard a song of love: Orla. He could not shake her, or even get close to shaking her. She was part of him, and at this moment, it was her face in his mind that stopped him from pursuing Viv as she walked out of his life.

He closed his eyes. Then he knew where to go and what he needed.

He turned, buttoning his coat against the wind off the river as he headed south toward it. He walked up the quays and then crossed over Carlisle Bridge. The river was high and colorless and rolling with currents. Street hawkers shouted about their wares.

He continued on, and stopped at the door. A servant answered, recognizing him.

"Is she here?"

"Yes, sir. I'll tell her you're here."

He waited, the sounds of the city at his back.

The servant returned and he followed her up to the flat. The street noise became dulled, and the scents of the home above enveloped him as he ascended.

He saw her feet first, coming around through the banisters, as she waited in the door on the landing to greet him. Then the hem of her dress. She was standing in the bedroom doorway, as she always did when he visited her.

Molly Devereux smiled at him. Conlon smiled in return.

IF YOU LIKE THIS, YOU MAY ALSO ENJOY: DEATH IN THE HOLLER

LUKE RYDER BOOK ONE BY JOHN G. BLUCK

MURDER, ADDICTION, AND REDEMPTION COLLIDE IN THIS ENTHRALLING SMALL-TOWN MYSTERY.

Kentucky Game Warden Luke Ryder is an alcoholic on the verge of losing his job. But when a Louisville gangster is found dead in small-town Kentucky—on the first day of muzzle-loader hunting season—his luck may be about to turn around.

Asked to help with the investigation by County Sheriff Jim Pike, Luke works on the case while also confronting his addiction and using his innate detective skills to uncover clues and track down the killer.

Along the way, he discovers that the murdered man came to the Holler for a specific reason—a reason that might connect to a larger conspiracy. Suddenly, solving this murder is the perfect opportunity for Luke to prove his worth and become a deputy sheriff.

The true question is...can Luke Ryder find the killer before something more menacing comes to the holler?

AVAILABLE JULY 2023

ABOUT THE AUTHOR

David Michael Nolan was born and brought up in Dublin, Ireland.

He studied English Literature and Film Studies at University College Dublin and is obsessed with movies, comics, books, rock music, soccer and boxing—many of which find their way into his writing.

Currently, he lives in Manchester with his family.